Runway Dreams

A Pricey Affair

T.K. Ambers

StarSpirit

Books by T.K. Ambers

<u>The Runway Dreams Series:</u>
Runway Dreams: A Pricey Affair
Runway Dreams: A Fox in the Fold
Runway Dreams: Prideful Vengeance

In memory of my cousin Kyle, and for his best friend Greg.
Two people who could make any activity an adventure.

"What Greg didn't think of, Kyle did,
and what Kyle didn't think of, Greg did."

– Suzette (Helm) Wysocky

A WITTY & STYLISH MURDER MYSTERY

Runway Dreams

A Pricey Affair

T.K. AMBERS

Chapter One

B ernadette knew she was in trouble, but despite her current predicament, she didn't give a hoot about anyone else on the road. She wanted to get as far away from her mistakes as possible. Still, she couldn't help but stifle a small laugh as she recalled the ridiculous scene that had played out only moments earlier.

She was flying, down the main road leading out of town at ninety-seven miles per hour, in her blue Mustang convertible with nothing but her birthday suit on. She debated putting on her sunglasses to stop her long red curls from lashing her in the eyes as she navigated the road, but even with the moon's brightness, sunglasses would merely add to the recklessness of her situation.

As she approached the edge of town, a sense of freedom washed over her. Nothing could stop her now— well, nothing except maybe the flashing lights that had appeared three-hundred feet behind her.

How had she gotten to this point? It hadn't been easy, that's for sure. The story began nearly a year-and-a-half earlier when she met Martin Day via an online dating site. She recalled every moment as if it had happened just yesterday.

"Hurry up, Bernie, you're going to be late!" Bell Price, Bernie's slightly older sister, was standing in the doorway to Bernie's bedroom, biting her nails anxiously as she watched her sister try on the ninth dress of the evening. She seemed more nervous than usual about Bernie going on a date. Bernie had met the guy on a local dating site called CountryClassy.com, and while Bernie continued to assure Bell that online dating was a completely acceptable way to find a partner, Bell still didn't seem comfortable with the concept.

Flipping her hair over her shoulder, she glanced at her sister and mentally noted the atrocity taking place between Bell's nails and her teeth. She was a beautiful young woman with a sparkling personality, but in moments like this, an outsider would have thought Bell had been born in a barn. She had her strawberry blonde hair piled atop her head in a messy bun, and she wore a pair of ripped grey sweatpants and a baggy old black t-shirt that had belonged to their father.

Bernie had tried many times to throw this exact outfit away, but each time, try as she might, the ensemble found its way back into

Bell's dresser drawer. She would never leave the house in such an overly comfortable look, but she couldn't seem to part with the old rags. She said it made her feel safe and warm and reminded her of happier times.

She didn't know what Bell meant by happier times other than their parents still being together. Honestly, she was glad their parents had split, because even though they weren't yelling all of the time, Bernie knew something was off. Her mother didn't always come home at night. Later she found out it was because she was busy drinking with other gentlemen from the club.

"You looked fine in the first eight dresses, ya fruit bat!" Fruit bat was one of the phrases Bell chose to use in place of cussing. Aside from her work as a runway model, it was the one lady-like trait she had going for her. Bernadette, on the other hand, was strong and serious when she needed to be, and every now and then, a four-letter word would slide out if she was feeling genuinely angered. She often spoke with certainty and composure, whereas Bell tended to sound less sophisticated due to her heavier southern accent. Bell was silly, clumsy, and absent-minded, whereas Bernie was poised, precise, and well-mannered. No matter how they sounded or acted, the Price sisters had one thing in common; they always looked flawless when they left the house.

Coming back to the present moment, she realized Bell was getting her knickers in a twist over this semi-blind date. Of course, she knew she looked good in all the outfits, but she needed to look amazing. She would only have one chance to make a first impression. Not just any ensemble could do that.

Bernie had exceptional taste when it came to clothing. Her closet was always stocked with the latest fashions, including handbags, shoes, and jewelry. She loved her Louis Vuitton bags, Jimmy Choo shoes, and Prada sunglasses. No one could ever say she wasn't stylish. Most people would think she spent money like crazy, but being one of the top models in the agency and in the United States had certain perks. She received a lot of freebies from photo shoots and companies who wanted her to be seen using their creations.

She looked over at Bell again, who was still gnawing on her fingers. "Relax, Belinda, it'll be fine. It's not like I'm running off with him. We're meeting at the club, under the staff's watchful eyes." Grinning at Bell, she said, "Who knows, he might be the one." Turning away, she scooted over to the mirror. "Stop chewing on your nails. You'll have to have them redone again before your next shoot. You know Daddy won't be happy if he has to buy you a fourth set this week. Bad enough, you ruined two others. We should send you to refinishing school with the damage you've been doing lately."

Bell and Bernie were part of a very prestigious family. Their father and mother had started the Price & Fitz department store and modeling agency, and they worked very hard to become number one in the business. Their models were requested all over the world. They had some of the brightest stars in swimsuit modeling, as well as designer clothing. Several of their models had even been in movies.

The sisters were born into the modeling industry. They began as babies and had been doing it ever since. Bernie took time out for school, but she quickly returned to what she knew and loved because it was one of her life's most satisfying and successful pursuits.

Aside from the agency, their family also owned a beautiful jazz club. The club had been a huge success from day one. Everyone wanted to be at the 365th Street Jazz Club because they knew who owned it and wanted to be near the beautiful people who frequented the prestigious establishment.

"Why do you do that?" snapped Bell. "You know I hate being called Belinda. I'm trying to help you. I can't help the nails. It's been a stressful week. I'm concerned for you and this blind date, and on top of it all, I broke an obscenely expensive pair of shoes and twisted my ankle. I can barely walk, and I'm worried I won't make it through the photo shoot tomorrow. On top of that, I'm still upset about the atrocious things that awful Emmy Lou Baker said about me in yesterday's paper. Hasn't she got anything better to do than to pick on me and my modeling career?"

Bernie glanced at Bell again. She was pouting as usual. That fake pout always made her laugh. She knew Bell's ankle was fine, but she would play along. A little. The only thing hurt was her ego from the silly mistake she had made. She laughed as she realized Bell had quit biting her nails and was now staring intensely at Bernie's dresses while petting a faux mink muff. It reminded her of her favorite *Austin Powers* movie.

"Stop it, Bell, you're making me laugh, and I'm trying to put this mascara on. You know I'll be fine, and you'll be fine, for that matter. You barely twisted your ankle. It doesn't even look swollen. Why don't you go sit down and watch a movie? Put that foot up with some ice if you think it needs it. Stop worrying about what Emmy Lou Baker said. Everyone knows she's an ice-cold snake. Anyone could have broken a shoe and fallen off the stage during runway week."

Bernie was trying hard to conceal her true feelings. Most people really wouldn't break a shoe and fall off the catwalk during runway week. She was genuinely embarrassed for her sister. She had warned her beforehand that those shoes were not meant to hold any real pressure on the heel. Bell didn't listen. Bell believed that her outfit required a confident, assertive walk. She thought she was invincible most of the time, but this happened to be one of the times she should have listened to her little sister. She had taken off down the runway with a thunderous clack, and halfway through her walk, the heel succumbed to the pressure.

"Whatever, Bern. You and I both know I made a mistake, and now I'm being called out for it. Anyway, enough of that. Are you sure this date is a good idea? I know you've been talking to him for six months online and via the phone, but you never know how honest people are when they know they're not being seen directly. Why can't you date one of the guys from the club, or another model? Any man would be crazy to turn you down." Reaching out, Bernie soothed Bell's concern with a gentle touch to her shoulder. Bell had always been protective of her, even though she was barely a year older.

Bernie looked at herself in the mirror. She had beautiful, piercing green eyes and long fiery red hair, which contained the optimal number of golden highlights. Petite, with sexy curves, her feisty yet charming personality contained the perfect mix of humor and sincerity. She knew people liked her, but she didn't want another model. She hoped to find someone different who wasn't originally from her hometown. She wanted to start a family with a nice guy who would love her for her personality and not her job.

"What about Bradley? I know you like him," said Bell.

"You know I can't date Bradley."

"No, I don't know that," said Bell. "Why not?"

"I'm not discussing this with you right now. Besides, Bell, I feel like Martin's the real thing. In all of our conversations, I think I'd know by now if something were off."

"Be careful. Okay? You know what Mama always says." Bell chuckled. "Make sure he's a white horse and not a zebra in disguise."

"I know, I know. I'll never forget that. She wants us both to marry Mr. Perfect. What if there's only one Mr. Perfect in the world, though? Whatever will we do?" Bernie's eyes went wide in mock horror.

"Nice," said Bell. "I guess we'll have to duel it out!" She smiled at Bernie. "What do you like about this Martin?"

"Well, he seems like a gentleman, and there are few of those left in the world. He makes me laugh no matter what my day has been like. He always has a compliment for me. He's well educated. He went to Notre Dame. His parents are wealthy and have taught him how to manage money, so he became a financial advisor. I suspect he's good at planning for the future. He'll be a reliable companion and should be able to take care of us once I'm finished modeling. At least until the trust fund kicks in."

"Does he have any siblings?"

"He had a sister. Neith, I believe. I guess she died a few years back. He doesn't like to talk about her."

"What are his plans for the future?" asked Bell.

Bernie glanced over her shoulder at Bell. "He wants to break into politics, then a few years down the road, he wants to start a family."

Bell's eyes narrowed as she stared Bernie down. "Okay. And where does he live?"

"When we started talking, he was living in Arkansas, but even before things became serious, he told me he already had plans to move here in a couple of months. He only lives five miles away in Hampton Grove. It's that new housing division on the south side of town. He has to be well-established to afford one of those homes, right?"

"Yeah, you'd think so," said Bell. Still, she didn't look too sure. She was hesitant about any man she couldn't see in person, even more so of the ones right in front of her. She had been hurt before.

Bernie finished applying her lipstick and blotted her lips with a facial tissue. She slid on her favorite diamond tennis bracelet and matching ring. Her earrings were one-carat diamond studs. She felt as though she had found the perfect outfit for a first date with her possible destiny.

"Okay, now how do I look?" She spun in a circle, and her short, shimmery, black dress softly floated around her as she moved. Bell gave her a grin and an approving nod. She loved it when she dazzled her beautiful older sister. She hated it, however, when she knew Bell was worried about her and whether or not she was making the right decisions.

"Come on now, you need to get moving," She brushed a few fly-away hairs off Bernie's dress. "He's probably already at the club waiting for you," she said, putting on a happy face.

Mom hadn't been in the house for a while now, but it still felt like she had a mother present when her sister was feeling concerned. Bell took on the role for several reasons, but the primary reason was that the one and only time Bernadette had been in love, she went completely off the rails when it ended.

Bernie was eighteen and still in high school. The couple had met at a mutual friend's birthday party. She had invested her heart one hundred percent, and in return, Eric, the boy she loved, had given her the world for six whole months.

The relationship had taken over Bernie's life. She stopped spending time with her family and friends. She talked about running off and marrying Eric once they graduated. Unexpectedly, fate stepped in and put a wrench in her plans.

Bernadette was supposed to be at a study group for her upcoming final with several classmates. Eric had asked her to come over because his parents would be gone that evening. She apologized and told him she couldn't skip the study group.

That evening, as she was walking to meet her peers, she suddenly decided to do something very uncharacteristic. She knew the material and was already prepared for the upcoming test. Why shouldn't she go relax and spend the evening with her boyfriend?

Arriving at Eric's house, she noted that his car was outside. She rang the bell, but no one answered. Turning the handle to the door, she found it unlocked, so she let herself in and headed toward Eric's room.

As she approached, she could tell he wasn't alone. Throwing open the door, she saw a sight that would haunt her for years to come. Eric and one of their classmates, Sarah, were doing unmentionable things. She turned and ran from the house, tears streaming down her face.

After the incident, she went to her final class, then hid away in her room for two months. She didn't even attend her graduation ceremony. She swore off dating for two years. Her parents never even noticed that something was wrong with their daughter. They were too wrapped up in their own issues, and the girls were already living alone in the bungalow off the side of their father's property. Bell took it upon herself to push Bernie into therapy since her parents were no help.

Their mother had never been present the way other mothers were for their children. Bell realized early on that something was missing, and she took it upon herself to ensure that Bernie and their adopted brother, Alex, were looked after, loved, and on track for whatever venture was next.

She watched as Bell looked her over one more time and then pushed her out the door toward her car. "Remember, don't give away the milk, or whatever, on the first date. He has to buy the cow first!" Bell chuckled as Bernie contorted her face into a scowl. She knew Bell was making light of the situation to hide her concern. She didn't think she had anything to worry about.

"Whatever, lady! I don't think likening me to a cow is going to get me out the door any faster. I might have to change clothes again," she threatened, giving her sister a devious smile.

"Don't you dare, Bernadette Price! You cannot possibly change one more time tonight. You've already tried on all the clothing in the state, I reckon."

Despite the number of dresses Bernadette had gone through that evening, every single one had been carefully rehung and put away in her closet. Had it been Bell in this position, the room would have looked like a tornado had passed through it, with dresses, shoes, and handbags scattered over every surface. While Bell was motherly in many ways, tidiness was not one of them.

"Fine. Then I'm off to dance till I drop with my charming prince. Don't wait up!" She skipped down the driveway and carefully climbed into her Mustang. Bell frowned as she waved her away.

As Bernie navigated the roads toward the 365th Street Jazz Club, she thought about how lucky she was. The club belonged to her father and would one day belong to her and her siblings. It was her father's most prized possession, and she felt the same, next to her beautiful blue Mustang convertible, of course. The car had been a sixteenth birthday gift from her parents, and she had treasured it ever since.

Bernadette looked into the rearview mirror to check her make-up one last time. She couldn't wait to see Martin. She had been talking to him for months and dreaming about this moment for just as long. He was smart, handsome, charming, and had studied International Business on top of Finance, so he also had a great educational background. He was everything her parents could have wanted for her; well, everything her mother could have wanted for her anyway. Her father wanted nothing more than for his children to be happy. Her mother wanted them all, including Alex, to marry rich men who would take care of them.

Bell had stated previously that she could marry a rich man, but never allow him to simply take care of her. She was the one who liked to take care of people. Bernie didn't care if she married a rich man, and she didn't feel like she needed anyone to take care of her. She liked working. Mariska's dream was none of her children's. Alex was already financially taken care of and quite resilient, so Mariska never worried about his future.

At twenty-six, Bernie had almost everything she could want—looks, a great modeling career, an education, close siblings, and the family businesses. The only thing she was missing was a man to settle down and start a family with. Martin seemed to fit into that plan perfectly. He even had parents who were well-known in society, or so he said. Bernie had never heard of them, but then she didn't know every rich and famous person out there.

Martin told her he was looking for a beautiful, smart woman who could help him advance his career and give him a family. He would most likely get along with her father because Martin loved golf, and he would get along with her mother because he had plenty of money and charm. Bell and Alex would be harder to win over.

She had seven years of college under her belt, and after all that, she had finally gotten her law degree, only to end up a full-time model back at Price & Fitz. One of the agency's specialties was clothing for curvaceous women. At 5'10", she had more curves than most models, so she fit the exact image her mother had envisioned when she began dreaming about the agency thirty years earlier.

Bernie's mind snapped back to the task at hand. Martin. His deep, cool voice sent shivers through her. She never grew tired of listening to him talk. He'd told her about his different travels throughout the US and how he loved Alaska. He was a true outdoorsman, and promised to take her on vacations and show her places she'd only seen in her wildest dreams. He was well-rounded, and his life sounded like an adventure.

As she turned the corner, she could see the club all lit up. It was 7pm, and for an evening in May, it seemed awfully dark, like a storm might be brewing. She hoped that wasn't the case. She'd never worn these Gucci shoes before and didn't want this to be their final debut. They went so well with her sparkly red Gucci clutch and her little black Prada dress.

Bernie pulled into her personal parking spot right next to the entrance, and a gentleman promptly came out. He opened the door for her and helped her out of the car. She looked him over briefly. Bradley was the VIP host and one of their best bartenders, but he did a little of everything for the club. At 6'5", he was an impressive man. She loved how his long blonde hair was knotted at the back of his head. It looked good on him, as did most anything. He only wore the best suits, and he always wore them well. His favorite color was purple, and Bernie found that to be quite charming. He frequently found a way to incorporate purple into his attire.

Despite being one of the most eligible bachelors in town, Bernie never allowed herself more than a friendship with Bradley out of respect for her father and the business. Just once, though, she would have liked to do body shots off of his perfectly formed abs. She knew they were perfectly formed because she had seen them once. One year earlier, there had been a small kitchen fire, and Bradley had singed his shirt while coming to the rescue of the distraught kitchen staff. Bernadette had found him a new shirt, and Bradley held no qualms about changing right in front of her.

"Good evening, Ms. Bernadette. The usual table? Is your father going to be joining you?" He smiled at her with his pearly white, perfect teeth and gorgeous dimples. He always gave Bernadette's heart a little flutter. She had to remind herself that she was there to meet someone else; someone who had also been able to stir passion in her heart.

She peeled her gaze away from his piercing blue eyes. "No, Bradley, not tonight. I'll take the usual table, but Daddy has other affairs to attend to, and tonight I'm here to meet a gentleman caller," she said, winking at him.

"Ah, I see," said Bradley. His eyes widened a little. "Here I thought you'd come to see me." He grinned. He knew about Bernie's guy. She had used his opinion as a sounding board for advice regarding Martin and this possible budding relationship.

He always gave great insight, and so she used him as what she believed to be her unbiased advisor.

"You always make me laugh." She smiled back.

"I'll procure your gentleman, but first, allow me to escort you to the VIP room."

"Thanks, handsome. I do appreciate how well you take care of me." Their eyes connected and Bernie instantly looked away. She couldn't let him know there was anything real behind the playful banter they so frequently took part in.

As he escorted her to the VIP room, she saw many of her friends and some of her family, all waving and smiling in her direction. She was the shining star of the club. Everyone loved her presence and wanted to be near her. She had a sense of humor and a loving nature that people couldn't get enough of. She knew this about herself, but for the most part, she didn't let it go to her head.

Her sister, on the other hand, was another story. As a teenager, Bell let her modeling income get the best of her. She spent her money frivolously and wasn't afraid to let her peers know she believed she was better than them because she could buy whatever she wanted. Her inflated ego needed to be put into place. Their father took extreme measures.

At age sixteen, the girls were cut off from their income. The money would be put into a trust fund that they would not be allowed to touch until they were thirty-five. They were each given $50 per week and expected to use that money to pay for gas in their cars as well as anything else they may have wanted. They were forced to budget, and if they needed more money, they were pretty much out of luck.

Alan, their father, felt this would be a great way to teach them about managing money and being happy with what they were given. Once they graduated from high school, the amount of money they were allotted increased, but they still would not receive the full amount until they were thirty-five. He would make sure his girls learned a valuable lesson from Bell's earlier indiscretion.

When Bell was younger and had gone overboard on her spending, there were murmurs around town that she was just like her mother. Even though their mother came from old money, she had a bit of a spending problem. She loved to maintain a glamorous lifestyle, and she didn't care what she had to do to achieve it. While she hadn't bankrupted her businesses or depleted her wealth, she still bought plenty of things that even Liberace would have rolled his eyes at. Their father learned very early in their marriage to keep an extra bank account that Mariska didn't have access to so that he could take care of the bills and everyday necessities.

As soon as Bell heard about the whisperings around town, she began pushing herself harder toward becoming a responsible adult. She hated the comparison to their mother. She knew she had messed up, and she vowed never to allow such an error to occur again.

Bernie would never be anything like Mariska. She had way too much love for the people in her life, and even though she was a model, she loved charity functions as well. People knew her as a kind-hearted young woman who could be counted on to be present when the homeless needed a new shelter or children were in need of shoes. The previous week she had even taken part in a date auction to help raise money for the hurricane relief effort. She'd brought in the most money and was proud of it.

Bernie's only real possessions, aside from the furniture in her home, were her car and her attire which she needed due to the nature of her job. Beyond that, she was quite the minimalist when it came to things. She preferred experiences and the occasional photo to document the much-cherished moments spent with her family and friends.

Bernadette looked up at Bradley and smiled. "Thank you for being such a wonderful escort." She noticed a momentary look of sadness in his eyes and wrinkled her brow at him.

Without missing a beat, he smiled back at her. "Now, where do I locate this mystery man?" He clearly didn't want to discuss whatever was going through his head, so Bernie pushed her concern aside.

"He should be in the bar, wearing a yellow rose on his lapel."

"All right, girlfriend, I'm on it," he said as he bent down to kiss her hand. He used her brother's lingo every now and then, which sounded quite awkward, but she knew it was his way of trying to connect more with her family. Alex always got this disapproving look on his face when he realized Bradley was taking a page from his conversational book. Bernie, on the other hand, thought it was kind of cute.

"Oh my, Bradley, I do declare, if this doesn't go well tonight, I may very well snatch you up for myself," she said with a grin.

As he disappeared from her sight, she again reminded herself that she needed to keep things to a simple friendship with him. The business had to come first. It was better this way. He had been a family friend for many years, and there was no point rocking the boat now. She would never want to cause any waves in the club, so she would admire him from a safe distance. Besides, he probably didn't feel the same.

Chapter Two

B ernie placed herself strategically on the plush purple chaise lounge. She was glad her father had picked the beautiful chair since it was the color and feel of royalty. She thought it gave the club a little more class. Her Prada dress and Gucci shoes made the chair look priceless.

She wanted Martin to see her as relaxed, confident, and of course, sultry. She felt the proper pose was important for a first impression, but then the model part of her sometimes took things to an extra level.

She watched him approach, her mouth parted slightly, her eyes widening as she took him in. She couldn't help but stare. He looked as if he could be a professional football player. Photographs had not done him justice. He had a perfectly shaved face, strong jawline, and deep brown eyes. His attire was immaculate. Reaching a height of six-foot-three, she could see how this oak tree of a man could command the attention of any room he walked into.

Martin had chosen a black pin-striped suit with a matching hat. His bronzed skin was like a light creamy chocolate, and she guessed it might taste just as sweet. Bernie couldn't take her eyes off him. She wondered what his bare chest might look like under his pristine suit. She wanted to rip it off and find out, but she reminded herself of Bell's comment about the milk.

"Well, hello there, Ms. Bernadette. Aren't you as pretty as a diamond?" He looked her over and smiled, appearing to approve of what he was seeing. The first impression felt like a success.

"Hi, Martin," she said breathlessly.

"How are you doing this fine evening?" he asked as he sat down beside her on the chaise.

No use losing it this early in the game, thought Bernie. No man made her weak. She was a strong woman. What would her mama say if she saw her acting this way? She snapped herself back to composure.

"I can't really complain. I'm here meeting a man whom I've been dying to meet for months. And I have to say, so far, I like what I see," she said. Nervousness was not necessary in this situation. She realized she was safe and on her territory. Martin seemed just as wonderful in person as he had been on the phone. "How long have you been waiting?" She watched his expression to see if he seemed to be enjoying the club.

"A couple of hours, I decided to come down early and get a feel for the place. I played some pool with a few fellows in the bar. It's been a nice afternoon." His smile continued to soften Bernie's heart. He seemed to be at ease in the club, which made Bernie like him even more.

She couldn't understand how this man was still single. He'd told her he hadn't found the right person to tie him down. She was beginning to hope that person would be her. She looked him over again. Everything seemed so perfect, from his clothes to his skin and even his nails which looked manicured. Bernie surmised that this man might be a little higher maintenance than she had first thought, which wasn't necessarily a bad thing. They could perhaps enjoy a spa day together.

"And, do you like what you see here?" she asked as she motioned with her hands their surroundings. If he wanted to be a part of her life, he would have to be okay with spending a lot of time there. She had basically grown up in the club, eating meals with her family, making faces across the table with her sister and brother. Being told to sit up straight and eat like a lady, by her mother. They were always in the public eye, even in childhood. People recognized the Price family because they were the most prominent family in town.

"It's great. I think it's got class. Hopefully the food is as wonderful as the rest of the venue. If it is, this will indeed turn out to be the perfect spot for all of my favorite things." He gave her yet another

Chapter Five

It was ten o'clock Monday morning, and Bernie had overslept. Her weekend had been eventful. Martin had shown up at her photo shoot with a big bouquet of Gerber Daisies just to say he missed her. They had gone to lunch and spent the whole afternoon together, wandering around Tulsa. She took him to her favorite spot, the gardens at the Philbrook Museum of Art. She loved everything from the sculpture walk to the meditation area.

Saturday night, she shoed Martin away so that she could spend some much-needed quality time with her father and siblings. They went out for a nice Italian meal and then spent some time at the club listening to a new jazz band her father had found.

She and Bell went shopping together and saw a movie at the local theatre on Sunday. The day was pretty low-key, but Martin again showed up unexpectedly and took Bernie to a new winery for a tasting and appetizers.

The couple stayed until 8pm when the establishment was closing. Everything was progressing smoothly between them. Bernie felt as if they had been together for years. When she got home that night, Alex was at the house, and he and Bell were about to watch a movie, so she joined them, and before she knew it, it was one-thirty in the morning again. The weekend had been full of surprises, and Bernie had enjoyed every single one.

Monday morning began when she awoke from the sound of a loud thud, followed by an even louder thud coming from the room next door. She wanted to ignore it, and she was about to fall back asleep when yet another thud sounded directly above her head. She lazily pushed herself toward the edge of the bed. Reaching out from the covers, she pulled her silk robe from the bedside chair.

"Bell! What are you doing?" No response came from next door, which prompted Bernie to catapult herself out of bed, running. "Bell?" she popped her head into the room to find her sister on the floor in a pile of clothing and shoes. "What's going on in here?" she demanded.

"Spring cleaning."

"This doesn't sound like spring cleaning to me," said Bernie. "It sounds like a thunderstorm raging in here." The room was a disaster. She wasn't sure how her sister knew what she was keeping and what was going. Everything seemed to be mixed together.

She looked up from the floor. "Whatever, Bernie. Some of my friends said I needed to update my wardrobe, so I'm trying to get rid of last year's trends and add some fresh new looks. Obviously, I have to do something. I can't be known as last year's fashionista. What would people say if I showed up wearing the shoes I had on last April for the Coventry Ball? Oh, wait, Emmy Lou Baker already commented on that in this morning's paper!"

"She didn't?" Bernie knew this was yet another attack that would be on Bell's mind for the coming weeks. "Ignore her. My goodness, girl, you're a model by trade, but that doesn't mean you have to be perfect all of the time. Wear what you like and forget what others say."

"You know that isn't true. We get hired just by being out in public, going to Daddy's club, etcetera. People look to us as fashion experts. You could learn something from this. If we aren't in line with the current trend, then we aren't in. If we aren't in, then we don't get jobs. Daddy wants us to promote and look good. We own high-end department stores. There is no reason we shouldn't look amazing at all times. *We* are the biggest sellers out there. Emmy Lou's words could really hurt my reputation."

"Seriously, I know in some ways you're right, but honestly, people know who you really are, and they know you pride yourself on being in line with current style and trend. You're one of the top models in the industry right now, so if I were you, I wouldn't worry too much. Again, it's just a tasteless attack, and she's trying to ruffle your feathers. Don't let her."

"Still, I have to make some updates," Bell said with a frown.

"You wore those boots once, and now you're chucking them?" Bernie didn't like to get rid of her favorite things. She didn't care if they were from the year before. If she loved them, she found a way to wear them. She was much more relaxed about style. Bell, however, rarely wore the same thing for more than six months. She understood the reasoning but still struggled with it.

"Someone else, who is less scrutinized on a daily basis, will find these at a thrift store, fall in love, and wear them until they die. They won't be harassed because it's okay for common people to do that sort of thing."

"Common people, Bell? Did you really just say 'common people?'" Bernie scowled. Sometimes Bell made comments that sounded like she thought she was better than others, though Bernie knew that wasn't true. She and her sister were as humble as they came as models. Bell was nothing like the stuck-up brat she had been in her teen years, so Bernie knew that, in reality, she meant nothing by the awkward comment she'd made.

"All I'm saying is, people who aren't held to standards as high as we are. People who have the choice in what they wear and if they wear it over and over again because it's the most beautiful, comfortable boot they've ever owned. They can get away with showing that love to the world on a daily basis. I'd give almost anything for that. So, yes. Common. A person who can do whatever they want. We chose to be in the public eye, though, so we have to deal with it and thus be more restricted in what we can and cannot do, so the Emmy Lou Bakers of the world leave us alone."

"You know you don't have to live like this, right?"

"Yeah, Bernie, I do know that. It's a love-hate sort of thing. I love Daddy and my career, but I hate not being able to wear these cute suede boots every day."

"Oh, Bell, get over it. We made our choices, and until we're a little older and not a part of such business, we have to deal with it and do what helps promote our image. Maybe you can dye them another color and just keep doing so until you run out of colors. Would that solve your problem?"

Bell laughed. "Not a bad idea, but knowing Emmy Lou Baker, she'd catch on."

"Yeah." Bernie smiled. "Maybe that wouldn't work, but it's a thought."

Bell lifted an eyebrow at Bernie. "Aren't you supposed to be somewhere this morning?"

Bernie's eyes darted to the clock on Bell's bedside table. "Oh shoot! I'm supposed to be at Martin's by noon! Dang it all, where'd the morning go?"

"You ask like you have no idea," laughed Bell. "I'd say you slept the morning away, Bern. That's where it went. Go jump in the shower, and I'll find you something to wear. What will you be doing at Martin's?"

"First, lunch, and then we're working in his greenhouse, so maybe I should wear a cute sundress or something. It's supposed to be fairly warm today."

"Sounds good. I'll find the dress. You get moving."

Thirty minutes later, Bernadette was in her Mustang driving down the street that led to Martin's house. She'd only be fifteen minutes late to lunch. She called to let Martin know. He didn't seemed surprised, which made Bernie wonder if this was a trend she'd started or just a common expectation of men regarding women of her profession?

As she pulled into the drive, her breath was again taken away by the exterior beauty of Martin's home. The house was even more magnificent in the daylight. Several bushes were already adorned with beautiful white flowers. The yard smelled heavenly. She hadn't even noticed Martin's greenhouse the first time she'd visited.

She got out of her car and approached the front door hesitantly. Would the inside have the same effect on her? Would she get used to it? She was already beginning to work herself up about the horror she was about to see when Martin came out the door from the greenhouse.

"Hey, beautiful! I'm glad to see you made it." He leaned in and kissed her cheek.

She smiled at the warm welcome. Martin seemed like a white horse to her. She was definitely falling for him.

"Why don't we head inside," he said, nodding toward the door.

"Okay," said Bernie, sounding somewhat hesitant. She was afraid to go inside because she didn't want to add any negativity to the day. She was generally a pretty positive person. Martin must have noticed her hesitance.

"Don't worry. I think you'll find things have changed since you were here last. Perhaps it'll be more to your approval."

She decided to brace herself and began walking toward the door.

"Close your eyes, Bernadette." He looked back at her to ensure she wasn't peeking and then shoved the doors open. "Okay now, watch your step. I'm going to take you into the center of the room so you get the full effect. I hope you're excited. I love surprising people, which you may have already noticed considering my showing up unexpectedly at your house and photo shoot this past week."

"Yeah, I kind of noticed." She smiled at the thought and followed his lead into the room. She was worried she might run into a foosball table or something. With her eyes closed, she noticed the scent of roses and lavender filling the air. She felt slightly more at ease.

"Okay, now you can open your eyes," Martin said with teenage enthusiasm.

Bernie opened her eyes and was dumbstruck by the sheer beauty and unbelievable transformation of the space she was standing in. The once gaudy décor had been replaced by elegant furniture, flooring, and rugs. The living room was now this beautiful plush space that could be lounged in while having a glass of wine. There was a fireplace at one end and a dining room at the other. Two big beautiful chandeliers hung from the ceiling, spraying little sparkles all over the room.

She was reminded of the home she spent the first ten years of her life in with her parents and Bell. It was a similar feel with the openness and the plush cushy furniture. This space felt safe and secure to her. They had moved to the place her father now lived by himself shortly after Alex had joined the family. They needed more space, and money was good, so they could afford to upgrade. Despite how much she loved her father's house, she still held a special place in her heart for that first home.

"Wow," she said. "I don't know what to say."

"Sweetheart, I did this all for us. I wanted a place fit for a queen, and you are my queen."

"How on earth did you make so many changes so quickly?"

"I hired one of the best interior designers out there. She works miracles in limited time frames. She has done this for friends of mine in the past, and I felt that her touch was greatly needed here. I didn't want my poor indoor decorating to be what ruined our relationship. Most of what you saw previously came with the house when I bought it."

"It's stunning. I can't believe someone could complete this in one week. I'm awestruck by the transformation of this room. I love the wood floors and the beautiful fireplace. The leather sofas are gorgeous. I can't believe how much you did, and all because I didn't like it?"

"You mean the world to me, and I want you in my life. Sometimes a man has to be willing to make some changes. I want you to want to be here. I realized that there was a good deal of truth to what you said. While the house may have had some fun aspects, it wasn't practical for a man looking to move up in the political world. I couldn't bring clients to such an unkempt home."

"Well, Martin," she said while stretching upward to kiss him on the cheek, "you have certainly grown in my book. Thank you. As for comfort, you have definitely accomplished that. This room reminds me of my childhood living room."

He smiled back at her. "I'm glad you like it. Would you like to see the kitchen?"

"Please."

Martin ushered her into the kitchen adorned with granite countertops and beautiful oak cabinets.

"I love the wine and glass rack. It has a sophisticated feel. This is a beautiful kitchen. The island will definitely come in handy for prepping food. Great for entertaining." She grinned.

"Why don't we make something to eat in my fabulous new kitchen? Do you like frittata? I know you haven't eaten yet. We can look at the rest of the house after brunch."

"Sure, I'm game for that," she said. "Let's get started."

Bernie was still in shock from the transformation. She couldn't believe he had updated more than the living room and entryway. This woman of his must be some kind of interior design goddess. She couldn't fathom doing such an extreme makeover in so short a time.

The pair went to work preparing their frittata. Bernie didn't want Martin to see her impatience, but the wait was agonizing. She wanted brunch to be finished so she could see the rest of the house. She wasn't known for great patience. She was too easily excited about surprises.

Once finished eating, they hurried through the dishes and put everything away. She wondered if the horrendous circular rotating bed would still be upstairs. Surely the design goddess would not allow him to keep such a thing.

Martin gave her a sideways glance. Her impatience and curiosity were obvious. "No," said Martin, as if he'd read her mind. "The bed's gone. It was one of the first things Kia told me to get rid of. She hated it more than you, I think."

Bernie let out a sigh of relief. Thank goodness for that. "How'd you know that's what I was thinking about?"

"I recall seeing that look on your face when you first saw the bed. Hey, relax. She took great care with the updates. I'm about to show you something I'm sure you'll love," Martin said with a wink.

"Oh, really, sir? What might that be?"

"You, my dear, need to have patience. Come this way," he said, leading her upstairs.

As they approached the door to the master bath, Bernie was again awed. She never even looked at the bathroom during her first visit. It was the size of a bedroom. It had two entries. One from the hall and one from the master suite. In the center of the floor sat the most beautiful sunken whirlpool tub she'd ever seen. She imagined it could fit six people. It was huge!

"Holy cow, Martin, this is amazing. I'm blown away by the number of changes you made in such a short time. How many people did you have working on this?"

"Let's just say, a lot. I called in some serious favors to get things taken care of quickly."

She confidently walked up to him and licked her red lips. Reaching up, she wrapped her arms around his neck and pulled him in for the most passionate kiss she could muster. Martin was amazing, and he was exceeding her expectations.

"Wow, what was that for?" he asked, looking down at her.

"It's because you're wonderful, and you've made me feel like the queen of the world. I'm shocked that you would do all of this for me. It's rather unbelievable."

"You deserve to feel comfortable and wanted in my home. I hope you'll live here as well in the future, which alone is motivating."

Reaching out, she squeezed his hand. "Thank you. You really are the sweetest man I've ever had the pleasure of meeting." She pulled him in for another kiss.

"Mmm, I could get used to this. Maybe we should go look at the bedroom next." He raised an eyebrow at her.

"Don't get ahead of yourself, sir. While I know it seemed I was ready for that sort of thing the first night we went out, I assure you that I have my wits about me now, and I have no desire to do such things until after we have dated a while longer. My sister is right. You should purchase the cow."

"Why, Bernadette Price, I do believe you just referred to yourself as a cow," he said with a laugh. "Or you just informed me that I need to marry you."

"Martin Day!" She playfully slapped his shoulder, "I shouldn't hear such talk out of you. You know very well what I was saying," she said with mock horror, "though the second statement is closer to the truth."

Bernie ran toward the bedroom, and Martin chased after her. Once there, she grabbed the first throw pillow she saw and threw it toward him. The cushion hit him in the head, then fell to the floor.

"Oh, getting a bit violent, I see."

Bernie grinned as Martin lunged at her, knocking them both onto the bed. He proceeded to wrap her in a bear hug.

"I'm never letting you go," he whispered in her ear.

"Don't," she whispered back, peering into his deep brown eyes.

"So, what do you think of the master bedroom?"

"It's nice. The bed's comfortable. It has a decent amount of light. I love it. Especially the walk-in closet. A girl can never have enough closet space."

"Do you like the décor I chose?"

"I love the Caribbean Blue curtains and the beautiful matching bedspread. I think the white and blue look amazing together. This is a color scheme that I would have chosen for sure," she said. "The bathroom is a huge highlight too. I'm a sucker for whirlpool tubs." She could soak for hours in a whirlpool. She always looked for rooms with them on vacation, and now she would have one to use on a regular basis.

"I'm relieved that you like it. I was worried that I'd pick something that wasn't anything near your taste, but as usual, I was stressing prematurely, I guess. Give me another kiss," Martin requested.

"Yes, sir," she said playfully as she leaned forward and placed her lips on his. *I could get used to this, too,* she thought. This was the first guy she had really dated since becoming an adult. How could she have gone this long without feeling someone's kiss? The feeling was amazing.

"So, Ms. Price, I take it things are up to your standards now?"

"Indeed, they are. I would love to spend more time getting to know each other here. It's a little quieter than the ranch. You never know who's going to be hanging out in our little bungalow. Alex and Bell are there almost nonstop, and also other model friends who stop by. Not to mention, Daddy stops in a lot to check on us. He wants to make sure his girls are getting along okay, even though he knows Alex is often around. I think he's trying to make up for not being around as much due to work when everything went awry with him and Mom."

"Do you like living on the ranch?"

"Sure, it's been home for most of my life."

Bernie thought about their home. It wasn't huge, but it was perfect for her and Bell. The living room was small but had a couch, and each girl had their own comfy chair that they had picked out. Bernie picked out a carousel chair with a bunch of pillows on it, and Bell chose an oversized leather chair with an ottoman. Alex often sprawled out on the couch when he was over with the girls.

Their house didn't have a great tub, but it had a wonderful oversized waterfall shower that made up for it to some degree. They had their own laundry room and a kitchen plenty big enough for the two of them. No dining room, just a breakfast bar with three stools. It wasn't much, but it was theirs, and for being only eighteen when she and her sister moved in, they were doing okay.

Martin's voice broke into Bernie's thoughts. "What kind of issues?"

"The kind that most marriages cannot bounce back from. Mom was a bit promiscuous, to put it bluntly. She constantly had a younger man on her arm. She didn't care if Daddy found out. One day he did, and while he still loved our mom, he couldn't find a way to forgive her. He thought she was out drinking, but when he found out it was other men, he had us move to the bungalow. He didn't want us to be a part of whatever was coming regarding them hashing out their differences. They stayed together for three more years, but it wasn't possible to repair the damage that had been done."

"Wow, how long was the cheating going on?" asked Martin.

"Years. Twenty or so, I'd say. Mom just didn't know the meaning of fidelity from the sounds of it. I hate what she did to our father, but I still love her. She's a different breed of woman. She can be pretty heartless. She's definitely the type that doesn't need anyone else." Bernie looked at Martin to see how he was reacting to this news.

"Hey, no judgment. My parents are wealthy, and they have been together forever, but my dad also has a problem with not coming home. And while my mom has her suspicions, she ignores it. Nothing like sweeping things under the rug. I hate it. They hate each other but won't do anything about it. To me, that's worse than showing your true colors."

"Yeah, I guess. Our parents never fought; they just didn't talk about anything, really. They had passion, I think, but not enough of everything else. We were the main reason Mom stuck around as long as she did. She loves us. We're her biggest accomplishment, she says. I don't think she means because we are her daughters, though. I think it's because we're successful models."

"That's at least one good thing, even if it isn't quite what you wanted from her," said Martin with a smile.

"Enough about my crazy mother. Why don't we head out to the greenhouse and you can teach me something new about plants," she said as she hopped up off the bed. She turned and held her hand out to him.

They walked out of the room hand in hand and said nothing else. It was nice to be with someone and feel happy and okay with the quiet moments.

As they entered the greenhouse, it was like walking into a tropical garden. Martin may be a man, but this greenhouse was not manly. It was tropical and exuded a certain femininity. Bernie didn't recognize any of the flowers, but she wanted to touch and smell every one of them.

"This is insane. It's as if I've stepped through a door that led directly to Hawaii. I didn't know such flowers could exist around here," she said as she bent to smell a large yellow one.

"Yeah, as long as you have a warm enough room with the right light and water, you can grow almost anything."

"That makes sense." A thoughtful expression crossed her face as she recalled information she'd meant to share with Martin upon her arrival earlier. "Hey, before I forget again, Daddy is having us over for a barbecue in one week, which should be Tuesday the twentieth. I've been told by my siblings that I'm to invite you to join us. Alex and Bell enjoyed your company so much the other night. They think you'd be a great addition to the gathering. What do you say?"

"I'd say it sounds like it's time to meet your father." Martin smiled. "And I think I love you."

Bernie's cheeks flushed. *Did he really just say he loves me? No, he thinks he loves me.* "I think I love you too," she replied.

Chapter Six

A n entire week had disappeared. Bernie and Martin had seen each other every day except Sunday. Martin had been busy that day with some political golf outing, but he informed her that he was missing her greatly and that he loved her. He'd sent flowers in lieu of his ability to be present.

Finally, it was the day of her father's barbecue. She couldn't wait to introduce Martin to him. The entire morning was a blur to Bernie. It started at five, with Alex leaning over her bed, whispering. She growled at him in return.

"Aren't we sunny this morning? Wake up. It's time for some pampering, little sister."

"Alex, what?" She opened one eye and peeked at her alarm clock. "Why are you waking me at this hour?" Wrinkling her face at him, she proceeded to roll toward the opposite side of the bed, disappearing under the covers. "I'm sleeping. Go away." Then rethinking her statement, she popped her head back out of the blankets and asked, "Did I forget something that I'm supposed to be doing today?" She doubted she'd forgotten anything. She usually was the one to remind her siblings.

"No, lady. Bell and I planned this last night while you were out. It's a spa day!" Alex clapped. "Just us girls."

She groaned and pulled the covers back over her head. "You're waking me at five for a spa day? What is wrong with you? Go without me. I'm tired," she whined.

"Sweetheart, I'm waking you at five because I need you to wake Bell. You know how long that can take. Besides, this is a special spa day." He paused, then sang, "We're going to La Crème!"

"*You* got us into La Crème!" squealed Bernie.

La Crème was only the best spa in all of Oklahoma and most of the US, and she had never been there. Her model friends spoke of weekend getaways and how wonderful they felt after. The spa treated you like royalty and offered only the best of the best when it came to food, drinks, treatments, and hospitality.

"Who's the best big brother in the world?" asked Alex.

"Oh, my goodness. I'm in shock. This is the best surprise a girl could ask for." Cocking her head to the side, she asked, "How much is this going to cost us?"

"This one's on me. A treat for my little sisters. I feel like I haven't spoiled you two, or myself for that matter, in a while, so why not,

I say? Let me take you both out for some fun. Now get up, get moving. We need to get Bell up and be on the road in half an hour."

"Aye, aye, captain," shouted Bernie as she catapulted herself out of bed. "I've got this." She ran from her room into the bedroom next door. She could hardly contain her excitement. With brute force, she leapt onto Bell's bed and started jumping up and down in a frenzied dance. "*We're going to La Crème! We're going to La Crème!* Get up, Bell, we have to go!"

"Bernie, stop it. You're going to step on me with all that flailing about. Knock it off! Bell grabbed Bernie's ankle and yanked her down onto the bed. She could be a little rough around the edges in the morning. Of the two sisters, she was by far the most brutal when awoken. "Ugh. Wait, did you say La Crème?" Bell began to perk up. She opened one eye. "We're going to La Crème?"

"I thought you knew? Alex said you knew." Bernie realized her sister had no idea which spa they were going to, which explained why she hadn't been the one jumping all over her this morning. The only person who wanted to go to La Crème more than Alex, was Bell.

"Alex! Get in here!"

"What's wrong? Aren't you excited?" he asked. A look of puzzlement crossed his face.

"You didn't tell her where we're going. I thought this was planned by both of you," said Bernie.

"Well, I also wanted it to be a surprise for Bell. We talked about a spa day, but she thought it was going to be local. Not two hours away."

Bell looked to Bernie. "Can we afford this right now?" Bernie took care of their joint finances. She was the more mathematically inclined of the two.

"Since our hero here is paying for it, I would say yes." She smiled.

"What? You're paying for this, Alex?"

"Sweetie, when was the last time I did something over the top for us? This is nothing, you know that baby, I'm set for life, and we don't need to keep having this money conversation where my money is concerned."

"Must be nice, money bags," said Bernie.

"Ha, you joke, but really it is nice," said Alex. "Not like you two aren't going to be in the same boat one day. Dad has definitely put away some pretty pennies for you two. Now come on, we need to get going. Put on your best comfort clothes, and let's skedaddle. I've got mimosas waiting in the limo with some wonderful mini quiche."

"Oh, score, let's do this!" said Bell. "I just need to brush my teeth, throw on a hat, and my black sweat suit. Done!" she yelled.

"Um, Bell, swishing water and toothpaste in your mouth doesn't actually count as brushing your teeth. That's gross. I'm not taking you like that," said Alex with a 'momma doesn't approve' look on his face. "Do I need to come over there and brush your teeth for you?"

"No," she said, grabbing her toothbrush.

Bernie laughed as she grabbed her toothbrush, "Kids these days."

Five minutes later, both ladies dressed, and the three climbed into the limo. It was five-thirty on the dot. Bernie was tired, but she knew the day would be spectacular. She could sleep in the limo on the way to the spa and on the way back home, if necessary.

Alex handed each of them a mimosa and then, holding up his own glass, said, "May this day be memorable and filled with fun, laughs, and relaxation."

"Amen to that," said Bell as she took a sip of her drink. "Mmm, this is good. Next time, however, we should hold the toothpaste," she said with her tongue hanging out.

"Nice bubbly choice, Alex," commented Bernie.

"You know I only get the best for my family," he replied, ignoring Bell.

Bernie held up her glass, "To Alex, the best big brother I could ever ask for."

"Aw, thanks, girl." He smiled at his siblings. He knew they weren't blood, but they may as well have been for how close they'd become over the years. "Bernie, how are you feeling about Martin these days?"

"I feel happy." She blushed. "I think I love him. We spoke for months by phone and internet, and it felt good then. Now that we've been seeing each other in person, it's as if I've known him forever. I can see getting married, starting a family, traveling, and experiencing all kinds of new things together. He's sweet, kind, and funny. It feels like he fits in with our family."

"Yeah, he does seem pretty great," said Bell. She was happy for Bernadette, but Bernie knew she was also scared. She didn't want her sister to move out. They were so close to one another. She hated change.

She reached out and put her hand on Bell's shoulder. "Whatever happens, I'm always here for you."

"I know, Bern. I just don't know what I'll do when you move out. It'll be so lonely without you."

"You can move in with me!" said Alex. He was clapping his hands, and Bernie could almost see the wheels spinning in his head. Alex was always four steps ahead of other people. She bet he had the entire plan worked out already. Though Bell was an independent woman, she knew Alex would always step in and care for her if necessary. Bell would be fine.

"Let's not get ahead of ourselves, Alex." She was also excited about the idea but would still miss Bernie. "I think once Bernie moves out, I'll probably stay alone in the house for a while and see what it's like living on my own for a change. It would probably be good for me."

"I think you're right," said Bernie. "You know Alex and I will visit a ton anyway."

Alex looked a little hurt. "Okay then, if you aren't moving in, let's move on and discuss our schedule for the day and what type of treatments we want.." He was paging through the La Crème booklet. "I say we get seaweed wraps, massages, facials, scalp treatments, and color, haircut, and style, as well as mani-pedis. Are we in agreement? Oh, by the way, I rented out the party room so we can enjoy each other's company during our treatments."

"Whoa, Alex, that seems like a lot. Maybe we should cut something out. When are we going to eat lunch?" asked Bell. Even though she was a model, Bell never missed out on food. She grabbed the booklet from him and turned to the food section.

"Oh fine, if you must eat." He laughed. "They'll let us know our food options and times once we get our treatment schedule in order."

"I'm down with everything Alex suggested," chimed Bernie. "Well, except the seaweed wrap. I don't know that I need a detox right now. They also cause you to lose weight, and the only area I could really lose weight is my chest, and I'm not down with that. I happen to like my girls as they are. How about a hot tub soak, then the salt scrub with the Vichy shower instead?"

"That sounds great. Let's do that. Get a salt scrub after our massages, a soak in the hot tub, and then a Vichy," said Alex.

"I think that sounds better, too," said Bell. "I'm not a fan of seaweed anyway. Also, I don't really need a scalp treatment."

"I agree," said Bernie. "We can cut that out too."

"Okay, it's settled. Then after we're done at the spa, we'll go to Ten and buy a new fun outfit for tonight's barbecue. How about that?" He was clearly amped up about the plans he had put into action and looked pleased with himself.

Bernie grinned back at Alex. "It's a plan, supa man."

The ride to La Crème was full of laughs and silliness. The group had a blast taking 'before' photos with Bell's camera. Alex had a sad pouty face in almost all of the pictures. Bell had a huge grin in all of them, and Bernie looked perfectly content, as always.

She couldn't help but wonder how much this spa day would cost Alex. She worried about money, even though it wasn't necessary most of the time. She knew Alex was well off, but she didn't really like taking things from others. Her parents didn't believe in coddling their children. Every now and then, a fun surprise would come up, but other than that, Bernie and Bell were expected to work for a living just like anyone else.

Thirty-five was the magic number for receiving their trust funds because Alan felt that by then, they wouldn't be modeling as much, they would be done with school, and they most likely would have started families of their own. He wanted his kids to know what it was like to work for a living and figure out the meaning of life before he handed them a free pass.

Alan had always worried about what would happen to Alex once he received his inheritance, but Alex continued to work and contribute to society, so Alan was perfectly content with how he'd turned out. Even though Alex was already a wealthy young man, Alan also put a trust-fund together for him. Alex was treated as an equal part of the family, at all times.

Bernie turned to look at her brother and sister. The ride was nearly over, and both Alex and Bell had passed out after the early rising. They were curled up together in the backseat. Looking at them together, she wished Bell would find someone with a personality like Alex, but then she wondered what would happen with her and Alex. Would they still be this close, or would that friendship end? Bernie wanted them all to remain close for the rest of their lives.

As the limo pulled up to La Crème, she finished her mimosa and gently shook Alex awake. "Okay, Alex, your turn to wake the sleeping monster." She grinned mischievously.

"Oh, thanks for the opportunity." He laughed through a yawn. "Bell," he said as he gently nudged her, "time to wake up. We've arrived."

"Nooo," said Bell. "More sleep, Alex. More sleep."

"There's no time for this. We're about ten minutes early but need to check in and stay on schedule. I'll let you sleep the whole way home if you like."

"Oh fine," she said. "I'm getting up. Man, twice in one day you people wake me prematurely. This is bad for business, I tell you. I'm going to have bags under my eyes and look scary as heck."

"Well then, it's a good thing we're at a spa," replied Alex.

He stepped out of the limo and grabbed Bernie's hand to help her up. Bell propped herself up and wiped her eyes. As slowly as possible, she climbed out of the car. Alex was tapping his foot impatiently.

"All right, ladies," he held out an arm to each of his sisters. "Let's do this. Look out La Crème, here come Alex and crew," he said with zeal.

The building in front of them was full of vibrant colors.

"Ooh, it's so pretty," said Bernie. The outside looked like a Chihuly museum. Chihuly was her favorite artist because of his beautifully colored work. His glass was pristine, and she loved that you could find his art all over the place. There were lots of beautiful blown glass flowers. She could get used to things like this. It was definitely a special day. She could feel it.

One small detail was nagging at the back of Bernie's mind. She was concerned about leaving her father to prepare the barbecue on his own. She didn't want him to be alone on this. "Do you think Dad will be okay finishing the plans for the dinner this evening?"

"Bern, don't worry about dad. He's got this. You know he'll call some of the alternate cooks from the club and, of course, Bradley."

"She's right, you know. I have faith in the old man. He'll get it done. He doesn't need you to constantly plan things for him," said Alex. "Besides, this is his barbecue. You watch over him like a hawk sometimes, and he is perfectly capable. He did fine when Mom was home, and we all know she wasn't much help."

Bernie knew they were right, but she still worried about her father. Ever since he found out about their mom and her antics, he had been off. She really hoped he was finally pulling it together. Eventually, she and Bell wouldn't live on the property anymore, and he would need to fend for himself. Bell frequently checked in on him, so usually Bernie wasn't overly worried, but today for some reason, she felt as if they had abandoned him.

"Earth to Bernie, are we going to do this or what?" asked Bell. Bernie had stopped walking and was dazing out at one of the glass sculptures as she thought about the barbecue.

Alex took a step forward, pulling the girls along through the doors to La Crème. The trio's jaws dropped open as they took in the inside of the spa. It felt like pure silky chocolate. It was covered in beautifully draped silks in shades of brown and cream. The couches and lounges in the waiting area were smooth, soft, dark chocolate leather with red and purple suede throw pillows. Many beautiful plants decorated the walls, and a fountain in the middle of the room sent out soothing sounds for nearby relaxing guests.

"Oh man, I want to take a nap on that chaise lounge over there." Bell pointed. "This is going to put me to sleep. Look how comfy and relaxing it is."

Bernie nodded and ran her fingers over the soft leather of a nearby chair.

"Why don't you two have a seat. I'll check us in," said Alex.

The girls walked over to the waiting area. Bernie plopped down on an overstuffed pillow back chair and threw her legs over the side. "This is so cushy." She knew she was not acting very ladylike, but she wasn't at home, and the other patrons in the waiting room had been ushered away before she sat down. It was okay to let her guard down for a little while.

She spent much of her time worrying about who was around and what others thought because she, Alex, and Bell, were under constant scrutiny. This brought her mind back to the earlier conversation she'd been a part of when Bell was cleaning out her closet. Despite how much they wanted to be normal, they really couldn't afford to be when in public.

"I know, it's ridiculous," said Bell. She, too, was splayed out across the chaise lounge in the most unladylike manner. Only Bell could take letting her guard down to a whole other level. "I couldn't get more comfortable if I tried."

"I noticed," said Bernie. "Let's nap," she said deviously, "Alex will love us."

A few minutes passed, and Alex returned, trailed by a young, willowy woman. Both girls jumped up and repositioned themselves on the chairs. No use creating any headlines for the local tabloids.

"Hi there, my name is Trista. Welcome to La Crème. Would the three of you like something to drink while you wait? We have several teas, champagne, mimosas, wine, spring water, and hot cocoa. Anything sound good?

"Oh, I'll take a hot cocoa," said Bell, "and so will my sister."

Bernie grinned at her. "You know me too well." Bernie was a hot cocoa fiend. It didn't matter what time of year it was.

"I will go with a glass of champagne," said Alex.

"Perfect. I'll be back shortly with your beverages, then Alexa, Cara, and Tori should be about ready to get started on your spa activities."

As she walked away, Bernie couldn't help but think how perky this girl seemed for seven-thirty in the morning. Way too perky for someone who does this every day. She didn't like early morning modeling jobs because she felt like she never looked like herself. This, however, was different because nothing about this had to look perfect. She need only let go of her stress and think about the relaxing, soothing environment she was in.

In what seemed like only a moment, Trista returned with the drink orders and carefully handed them to each sibling. "I hope you enjoy your beverages. I'll be back to check on you a little later, as I'm your personal hostess for the day. We'll have some treats in an hour, then again two hours after that. I hope you're ready for some fun and relaxation! If you have any questions at any time, don't hesitate to ask," she said as she turned to walk away.

"Does she know what time it is?" asked Bell.

"I find myself wondering the same," said Alex. He appeared to be losing some of his early morning energy.

Bernie laughed. This whole thing was slightly comical to her. They had gotten up early for this beautiful relaxing day, and all three of them were so tired that they only wanted to nap. *Heaven help us get some energy,* she thought.

Bernie was nearly asleep when their trio of wellness artists showed up.

"Hi there," said a short, stout young lady. "My name is Cara; I will be working with Bell today. This is Alexa," she said as she gestured to the tall thin blonde on her right, "she'll be working with Bernie, and Tori here," she motioned to the handsome, sturdy man to her left, "he'll be working with Alex."

Alex grinned. Tori had beautiful olive skin, and he was Alex's type. From the way he was dressed, he appeared to be batting for the same team. Alex looked at Bell and gave her a wide-eyed look. Bell discreetly gave him an approving nod.

"All right, friends, shall we start out our day with a lovely sixty-minute hot stone massage?" asked Tori.

"Oh, yes please," said Alex, as he scooted closer to Tori.

Tori smiled back. "Wonderful. Then we'll move on to our hot tub soak, salt scrub, and Vichy shower. After which, you'll enjoy a facial, then a cut and color, and lastly, mani-pedis. How does that sound?"

"I'm ready. It all sounds lovely," said Bernie. She hadn't been to a spa in ages.

"Great, this way, please," said Cara, walking toward a violet-curtained doorway.

Three hours after their arrival, the siblings were still tired but also ragdoll relaxed. Bernie enjoyed her massage the most. Somehow Alex behaved himself and didn't ask Tori out on a date at the most inappropriate time possible. He waited until after his Vichy shower, which was uncharacteristic of him, thought Bernie. Tori coyly gave Alex a maybe, but Bernie knew that answer usually meant yes in Alex's world. He was riding on his high horse, and it would take him all day to come down, but Bernie didn't care. She was relaxed and happy to enjoy quality time with her siblings.

At one-thirty that afternoon, all of the pampering had come to an end. The three walked out of La Crème feeling renewed. Alex's limo was waiting to take them to Ten.

"I feel amazing," said Bernie. "That was a great experience. I loved the facial. My skin feels so smooth."

"You look great," said Bell. "I feel pretty good myself. I'm glad I let you talk me into adding a few blonde foils to my hair. I feel it has more depth now." She beamed with satisfaction.

"Yeah, that color is great. Alex, how do you feel? Do you like your foils?"

"You're funny. You know I don't have any need for foils. My hair is already golden blonde. No need to change what's already perfect."

"Full of yourself much, King Alex?" asked Bell.

"I'm amazing," said Alex with a big grin.

"You're a dork. You and I both know you never act this confident around anyone else," said Bell. "Tori is bringing out the worst in you!"

"Whatever, Tori adores me. He gave me his digits and told me to give him a call tonight. He might drive in for the barbecue."

"Oh, my goodness, you invited him to Daddy's barbecue? He's going to have a cat, Alex. He hates it when we bring extra people without telling him. He needs his prep time."

"I'm joking, Bern. I didn't invite him over to the house. I invited him to the club after the barbecue, if he feels like meeting. If he doesn't, no loss. I still had a great day. The massage was worth every penny."

"I bet," retorted Bell. "Okay, guys, we're here. Let's go find our outfits so we can get back on the road."

"Want to make a competition of this?" asked Alex.

Bernie looked at Bell and shrugged in agreement. "Sure, what did you have in mind?"

"Well, we all know Ten is a pricey store. So, let's wager $100 each on who finds the least expensive but most attractive outfit for tonight. We won't tell each other what we spent, and we'll have the barbecue guests judge who they think got the best bargain. Whoever wins gets $300."

"It's a deal," said Bell. "If we win, we can split it," she said as she looked at Bernie.

"Sold, let's go bargain shop!" Bernie jumped out of the car and ran for the door. She wasn't wasting any time. She loved a good competition.

The inside of the store was huge, and it would take some serious effort for each of them to find the nicest, best-priced outfit because this place was by no means lacking in cost. Bell was tearing through dresses like they were paper sacks. She rejected them one after another with a flick of her wrist. Bernie was a little more precise. She grabbed things that she thought would look good, but only if they were below a certain cost. Alex had taken a totally different approach.

"Hi there, gorgeous," he said to the cashier, "could you show me what items you have in the store that are least expensive but still look amazing?"

Bernie and Bell's jaws dropped. Why hadn't they thought of that? *Tricky bastard*, thought Bernie. He knew exactly what he was doing.

"Bell, has he done this before?" asked Bernie.

"Oh yeah, he had this thought out. I bet someone else pulled this on him previously."

They watched as Alex walked over to the dressing room. The attendant followed him with a large armful of clothing. *He might just win this*, thought Bernie. She would never let him win. She was the queen of style at Price & Fitz and won the best-dressed award year in and year out.

"Move over, Bell. I don't have time for this." She hailed down the next available store clerk.

She ushered Bernie to a changing room and then disappeared briefly. Upon her return, the soft-spoken, tiny brunette said, "Okay, miss, I've picked out a few gorgeous clearance items for you. I think you'll be quite happy. I even found a few in back that weren't on the floor yet but are due to replace others that have sold out."

"Thank you," said Bernie as she grabbed the pile of clothes and walked into the changing room. There was no way Alex would win. The clerk had brought back several red items, and Bernie always looked stunning in red. She began throwing clothing on and off. After the third outfit, she thought she had found a winner.

An hour later, they were back on the road. All three were passed out in the back of the limo. Alex was snoring lightly from the awkward angle he had fallen asleep in. Everything was going great until all three were jolted awake by a loud popping sound. The limo began to wobble. A look of panic showed on Alex's face. He launched himself forward and pressed the call button.

"Andre, what's going on?" he demanded.

"Sorry, Alex, we appear to have hit something. I'm pulling over. It looks like there's a scenic overlook roughly 75 yards ahead. You all can get out for a stretch. I'll check out the tires. Hopefully, we'll be back on the road shortly."

"Keep me posted," said Alex. "All right, gang, sorry about that. I guess we're making a short pit stop. Anyone want to walk over to the scenic overlook?"

"I love scenic overlooks," gushed Bell. "Let's go!"

The group climbed out of the limo. They were only forty-five minutes from home, but luckily this happened at one of the most beautiful overlooks on the road. Bell walked over to the edge and gasped as she peered out over the most luscious valley she'd ever seen. Bernie walked up beside her to see what had provoked such a breathtaking response from her sister.

"Wow, I second that reaction. Where's your camera?" asked Bernie.

"Oh, it's right here," she said as she pulled it out of her purse. The girls turned around and took a photo of themselves overlooking the valley. Bernie was happy that Bell had lived up to her reputation of always carrying a camera. Some of their best photo memories had been unexpected happenings.

"I can get a photo of all three of you if you like," offered Andre as he approached the group. "We may as well get something good out of this moment, right?"

"Thanks. That's a great idea," said Alex.

Bell handed the camera to Andre, and Alex joined them on the edge of the cliff.

"Alright now, smile. Alex, my man, you can do better than that." Andre chuckled.

"Alex, come on, give us a real smile. You look constipated," chided Bernie.

"Okay, are you ready? Here comes the Alex prize smile," said Andre. "One, two, three—" The camera clicked, and like clockwork, Alex put on his prize face, the one that made him one of the most sought-after male models in the lower half of the US. The photo was like a painting. It looked too perfect, and it would have a front-and-center spot on Alex's fridge for many years to come.

"Okay, gang, now let's take a silly one," said Bell.

"Whoop!" chimed Bernie, "Let's."

The funny photo would find its home on Bernie and Bell's fridge.

After the photos were finished, Andre informed them that they had blown a tire but everything else seemed fine. It would be about twenty minutes, but he would get another tire on the limo, and they would be on their way. On the upside, the limo was equipped with a full-size spare, so the ride home wouldn't be changed in any way.

While they waited, the siblings sat on the ground at the cliff's edge and looked out over the valley as some deer walked through and grazed in the field. Bernie mused at the beauty. She felt at peace and happy to share the moment with her family.

She'd learned to enjoy the simple things in life and how to turn something negative into a positive. For instance, there had to be at least thirty different flowers in the valley. There were many different colors, and the breeze blew the most beautiful scents their way. If it weren't for the breakdown, she never would have gotten to experience this moment. The moment was Zen-like. Little did she know how much that feeling could change in such a small amount of time.

The flat tire was remedied, and they were back on the road. An hour later, they arrived at their father's house. The three had managed to change and get themselves put together in their new looks while riding in the limo. They stepped out like they were walking the red carpet. Each had chosen to go with an outdoorsy party look. They all looked fantastic.

Bernie was wearing a red, flowing cotton, knee-length dress with white flowers, a brown belt, cowboy boots, and a cowboy hat with her hair pulled into loose flowing pigtails. Bell had on a blue cotton maxi dress, also with cowboy boots, but her hair was pulled up into a messy bun on top of her head. Alex wore some high-end-looking distressed blue jeans with a black cotton button-down shirt, gray loafers, and a gray golf hat.

The second the limo had pulled up, Alan came flying out of the house. He was always excited to see his family together. "Aren't you all a sight for sore eyes! You look wonderful. Clearly, the day at the spa benefited all of you, especially my Bell. You look much more relaxed now."

"Thanks, Daddy, it was a fun day."

"The fun isn't over. Now you get the pleasure of my company." He grinned. Alan Price had a naturally relaxed and upbeat attitude. It was hard to believe anyone could ever dislike him with how contagious his personality could be.

He had a brilliant mind that knew how to create lucrative business concepts. Beyond his conceptualization, however, he needed help keeping business growth on track and managing his finances. He hired only top-notch people to run his affairs. Above business, his pride and joy was his family. He created the thriving businesses he had because he wanted to give something back to his girls and Alex. He wanted them to be as successful as he was.

Bernie walked up to her father and gave him a big hug. "Oh, Daddy, we always love your company."

"Pops, you have to help us out," said Alex. "We need a judge to decide who bought the best outfit for the best price."

Alex had barely finished his sentence when a black Camaro pulled into the drive. Bernie's heart flip-flopped as she watched Martin step out of the car and walk her way. He wore black slacks with a red button-down shirt, tie, sunglasses, and leather boots. He looked like money. Bell's jaw dropped, and Alex nonchalantly reached over and closed it for her. If Martin had been a part of the contest, the whole group would have given him the win.

"Don't do that to your sister's man," he whispered to Bell. "Find your own." He laughed.

"Martin!" yelled Bernie as she ran into his arms. "I declare I couldn't miss anyone more than I have, you, today."

"So, I guess that makes me chopped liver," Alan said to Alex and Bell. He smiled as he watched Bernie and Martin.

"Nah, she's just in love. You'll always be our Daddy. Nothing can change that," said Bell.

"I know, sweetie, but I've never seen her act this way before. I have to admit. He does know how to dress."

"Yes, he does," said Alex. Alan watched the couple for a moment and then said, "Hey, you two, stop making out and get your butts over here. I believe I'm due an introduction."

"Oh, sorry, Daddy," said Bernie as she pulled Martin over toward the rest of the group. "This is Martin Day. Martin, this is my father, Alan Price."

Alan held out his hand to Martin, and Martin looked him in the eye and shook it firmly in return. "Nice to meet you, sir. I'm quite fond of your daughter."

"I can see that, Martin. I appreciate your feelings for my daughter. I'm quite fond of her myself," he replied. "As long as you treat her well, I'm sure I'll be a fan of yours, too. Now what do you say to helping me judge some runway models?"

"I'd say I don't know anything about judging models. What are we judging them on?" asked Martin.

"It looks as though my family has made a bit of a wager. Alex, you want to explain this?"

"I thought you'd never ask," he said with a mischievous smile. "We went to Ten, and each picked out new outfits. You'll be judging on looks, as well as best price, to decide which outfit makes up the smartest buy."

"Huh, okay," mused Martin. "I'll give it a try if you want."

A look crossed Alex's face as he turned toward Alan. "Is this going to be fair, considering we're family and Bernie is dating one of the judges?"

"Oh, Alex, that's the risk you take, I guess. Besides, did you tell them where you got this idea from?" asked Alan.

"No," said Alex sheepishly.

"Well, ladies, your brother here got this idea from me when he first started in the industry. I whooped his butt on this little game which at the time wasn't at all surprising. No offense, Alex, but your taste wasn't what it is today."

"None taken. I learned from the best," said Alex.

Bell looked at Bernie and then at her father. "You came up with this, Daddy? No wonder Alex was so eager to make this wager."

"Well, my dear, as he said, he did learn from the best," replied her father. "It looks like we need at least one more judge, or do we want three more to try to make it fair?"

"I say we get three," said Alex.

"I knew you would, son," laughed Alan. "Okay, let's see here, we'll call in Avril to be a judge and Mika. Alex, who do you want?"

"I feel good with Avril and Mika since they judge us normally on clothing before shows. How about Valerie? She'd be an excellent judge."

"Valerie from makeup?" asked Alan.

"The one and only," said Alex.

"You really think she knows what's what?"

"Daddy, Valerie is multi-talented," said Bell. "She's helped fix our outfits on many occasions. She's amazing. I think she should be more than a makeup artist. She's way too smart and talented to do makeup alone."

"Hmm, that's interesting. I didn't know that about her, and I've worked with her for the past two years. She may have a promotion coming." Alan was very good about giving credit where credit was due. He was fair to all of his employees, and in return, he earned great loyalty and respect.

"You learn something new every day," said Bernie, "and I think a promotion would help her out a lot."

"Good, I like promoting hard work," said Alan. "Okay. All three of them should arrive shortly for the barbecue. Alex, perhaps call them to let them know we have another little event we want them involved in."

"I'm on it," said Alex, pulling out his phone.

While Alex was on the phone, the girls ran inside the house to check on dinner preparations. The first person Bernie saw when she walked into the kitchen was Bradley. Noting that he was holding a bottle of champagne, though she didn't know why, she eyed him suspiciously.

"Well, hello there, Miss Bernadette. How are you this lovely May evening?" he asked.

"I'm quite well. I spent the day at a spa and bought this new outfit. What do you think?" she said as she spun in a circle for him.

"I think you look like a beautiful spring flower," he whispered as he kissed her on the cheek.

Bernadette lightly touched his shoulder as he pulled back. "You smell great. What is that?"

"My favorite cologne. Moves."

"Yum," she said, smiling.

"Don't play with me. You know I have a certain love for you," he whispered back.

"Now who's playing?" she asked quietly. She never knew if either of them was serious. "Why are you holding a bottle of champagne? Are we celebrating something?"

"Oh, this? Nah, your father wanted me to restock a few things at the house, and this is one of the bottles he requested. I was putting them away and forgot that one had been loose in my car, so I ran back out to get it."

Bernie looked over her shoulder. She had completely forgotten that Bell had come in with her.

Bell gave her a curious look. "Hey, Bern, doesn't this corn salsa look delicious?" She held out a big bowl she had pulled from the fridge.

"Oh, yeah, you should try it. That's Lou's specialty. He makes it for the Cinco de Mayo party we hold each year at the club. It's hard to pass up," said Bradley.

"Bradley, my dear, may I have a word with you?" asked Bell as she handed her sister the salsa bowl.

"Oh, sure," he replied. Bell grabbed him by the arm and pulled him into the next room.

Bernie set the salsa on the table. She grabbed a bag of chips from the cupboard and was about to dip a chip into the bowl when the kitchen door swung back open.

"Bernadette, it's been a pleasure. Have a lovely evening. I must be going," said Bradley. Bernie noted that he seemed a little red in the face. "I have some things to deal with back at the club yet. We'll catch up again soon." He bolted from the kitchen before she had a chance to respond.

Bell walked back into the room as if nothing had happened.

"What was that all about? He seemed to leave awfully fast," said Bernie.

"I'm not actually sure. I asked him if he wanted to get a drink sometime, and apparently it freaked him out," responded Bell.

"Dang, girl, if that's the effect you have on men, no wonder you're single."

Bell scowled back at her. "Wonderful, Bernie, that's so sweet," she said sarcastically.

"Sorry, just saying."

"Oh, I hear what you're saying," she snapped.

"No, Bell, I don't think you do because you keep sabotaging yourself. You know I love you, but you might be a little too abrupt at times." She turned toward her sister and wrapped her in a big hug. "I love you, even if you are a cold-hearted b—" said Bernie.

"Gee, thanks. I love you, too. Now let's go back outside. I saw potato salad and a pile of meat in the fridge. Maybe the boys are ready to start grilling."

As they arrived back out on the patio, it was clear something had been going on. The guys instantly stopped talking and turned to greet them. Alan had a discontented look on his face, and Alex seemed concerned. However, Martin appeared completely oblivious and was grinning.

"What's going on out here?" asked Bernie. "You all have some secrets you want to share?"

"Yes indeed. We have something to share," said Martin as he walked toward her.

"Your father and I have just been agreeing upon how beautiful you are," he said as he took her hands and began to get down on one knee, "I l—"

"Stop!" she screeched as she pulled him upward. Bernie knew what was coming but didn't know how she should feel about it. "What are you doing? Isn't this a bit soon? We've only been seeing each other for two weeks."

Martin lightly pulled Bernie's arms downward and continued to get down on one knee. "As I was saying, my dear, I love you so very much. And while this may be fast, I don't think I could be surer of my decision. The past six-and-a-half months have been amazing."

He pulled out a small blue box. He opened the box and presented it to Bernie. The ring was a stunning flower-shaped, two-carat, white diamond on a platinum bezel set diamond band. "Will you, Bernadette Price, do me the honor of making me the luckiest man alive by saying yes to becoming my wife?" He slid the ring onto her finger and grinned as he looked into her eyes.

"Oh, Martin, it's exquisite. Yes, I will! I will!" She pulled him into a hug and kissed him passionately. She had no idea what she was doing or if it was the right decision, but she knew that she loved him and couldn't picture life without him.

"Well now," said Alan. "This is an interesting turn of events." He didn't seem overly happy about this news but was the type to swallow his concern until the appropriate moment presented itself. He would never want to ruin someone's excitement. "Congratulations, kids. I declare this picnic an engagement celebration. Forget the runway competition and the barbecue. Let's go to the club, have a nice dinner, and open some Champagne. Barbecues aren't good enough for my little girl's engagement celebration." He gave Bernadette a hug. It was all he really could do at that moment.

"Wait a minute, what about the food inside?" asked Bernie.

"Sweetheart, the food will keep. It's in the fridge. Besides, most of the food in there will be great for snacks later tonight when we get back," said Martin.

"What? This was planned ahead of time?" asked Bernie.

"Oh, honey, that's why I planned this fun spa day because Martin was planning to propose tonight. I wanted you to feel your best so that this day would be happy and memorable for you," Alex said as he grinned back at her.

Bernie noted that her father was awfully quiet. It seemed that he had not been informed of Martin's plan. He stood by with a solemn look on his face. She was certain that he was not happy about his barbecue being hijacked.

"Wow, you all fooled me," said Bernie. She was too excited to worry about her father any further at this time. She knew if her engagement was an issue, he would approach her later. Right now, she wanted to enjoy the moment.

"I know, little sister; it's obvious that you had no clue. Oh, and by the way, since we're going to the club, we all brought different clothing to change into. I brought you something special," said Bell. Her eyes sparkled. "I know you're going to love this, Bern. I'll be right back."

Bell ran off toward the house, and Alex disappeared into his limo to change into pants and a vest. Martin and Alan sat down at the picnic table to wait. Martin whipped out two celebratory cigars and handed one to Alan. Alan eyed the cigar as if it were a snake ready to bite him.

While everyone else was doing their own thing, Bernie was left standing there in awe of what had just passed. She was shocked that Martin had proposed but completely delighted at the same time. Bernie knew she wanted nothing more than to throw a big wedding and marry a man as wonderful as her daddy. Finally, she found someone who lived up to her expectations.

"Bernie," said Bell, "are you okay? You look a bit dazed."

She hadn't noticed her sister's return. "I was musing over the proposal and my beautiful new ring, but then I noticed that Daddy looks upset."

"He'll be fine. I'm sure he's just sad that his youngest is getting married. You should muse over this," said Bell as she handed Bernie the most beautiful, shimmery, white gown she'd ever seen.

"Wow, that's gorgeous! Where'd you get it from?"

"This is one of the newest dresses in Hector Perago's summer line. He's giving it to you as an engagement gift and wants you to model it in his show at the end of the month."

Bernie's mouth dropped open, "Seriously? Hector Perago is one of the most up-and-coming designers around. How did you pull this off?" She was blown away. She would have given anything to be a part of Hector's show, and now not only would she be part of the show, but she owned one of his dresses.

"Hector may have a little soft spot for our boy, Alex. He said that he would give me whatever I wanted if I could arrange a date between them. So, I used it to our benefit and asked him to give us a dress for your engagement party and a spot for both of us in his show."

"Dang, girl, you know how to work a deal." Bernadette was thoroughly impressed with her sister's negotiating skills.

"Indeed, I do," she said. "I also got him to agree to design your wedding dress and the bridesmaid dresses. If Alex takes a second date with him, the wedding dress will be free!"

Things just kept getting better. "Wow, I'm speechless. You're amazing. So, why did we go shopping for our competition clothes if you two knew this was going to happen?"

"We knew you'd have fun buying a new outfit. We haven't been out shopping in quite a while, and I wanted the day to be perfect. I thought you deserved an amazing memory of the wonderful day he proposed." Bell smiled warmly at Bernie.

"Thanks, Bell. You're the best." Once again, Bell's thoughtfulness exceeded Bernie's expectations by miles.

Alex emerged from his limo. He had traded his jeans for charcoal pants and a charcoal vest. He looked quite suave. *Anyone could see why Hector would be into him*, thought Bernie. Her brother had great taste.

"You know, my little ducklings, I don't recall agreeing to this date." Apparently, Alex had heard everything going on outside the limo.

"Come on, Alex. Hector is ridiculously good-looking and well-manicured. He's a smooth talker and an amazing designer. You actually have a ton in common. He's also worldly. Why wouldn't you want to go on a date with him?" asked Bell. The sisters both knew Alex was being difficult on purpose. There was almost no plausible reason for Alex to not be attracted to Hector. He was exactly Alex's type.

"Oh, all right, you got me! I could barely contain myself when you told me he was interested. I could just die. Hector Perago wants to date lil' ol' me? I'm sold. You don't have to ask me twice."

"Thank you, Alex," said the girls in unison.

"We'll be back shortly," said Bell. "We need to change."

"Okay. Hurry," he said.

The sisters turned and ran toward the house like two little kids, laughing and squealing with delight as they went.

It had only been five minutes when both Bell and Bernie re-emerged from the house.

"Okay, that really was fast," said Alex. "Are we ready? You both look wonderful."

"Let's do this, kids," said Alan. "I'm starving, as I'm sure you all are." His spirits seemed lifted. Perhaps it had been the cigar he finally tried. Alan loved a good cigar.

The group piled into Alex's limo and set off down the street toward the club. Excitement was in the air, and even Alan had a smile on his face. The day had been like a dream. Bernie was happy she could share such an important moment with her family.

The next morning, Bernie was feeling like a princess. She couldn't believe Martin had proposed so soon. She never thought her dreams could move so quickly. She was already imagining her dress and what the reception would look like. She knew it would be at her father's place. His land was beautiful with all of the flowers and green foliage.

As she lay in bed thinking about her future, her phone rang.

"Hello?" asked Bernie.

"Hi, Sweetie, it's your father."

Bernie had to laugh to herself. Even though they were on cell phones and she could see who was calling, Alan always announced himself like it was some mystery. She loved that about him.

"What's up, Daddy?"

"Sweetheart, I wanted to talk to you about this engagement." His voice was full of concern.

"What's wrong? Do you not approve of Martin?" Bernie felt a little defensive. She hated the thought of her father not liking Martin.

"Baby, it's not that I don't approve of Martin, it's just that I don't know him all that well, and I want to make sure you are confident in your decision. Marriage is a huge commitment and shouldn't be taken lightly."

"I'm not taking this lightly. I'm quite certain of my feelings for Martin. I know he loves me as well. He has been nothing but polite, honest, and respectful from day one."

"Your mother and I don't want to see you go through what we've gone through. Divorce is messy and painful. All I'm asking is that you bring Martin around more often so that I can get to know him better and keep your mind open and vigilant to be sure you are making the right decision."

"I will, Daddy. I want you to get to know Martin too. I'm sure you'll like him as much as I do once you spend a little more time with him."

"Sure, Sweetie, I'm sure I will. Anyway, that's all I wanted to say. I love you, and I hope you have a nice day."

"Love you too, Daddy." The conversation wasn't exactly what she'd been expecting, but at the same time, Bernie understood her father's concern, and she felt better after the phone call.

Chapter Seven

Six weeks had passed since the engagement. Bernie and Bell were busy shopping and making plans for the big day. They'd already decided it would be an outdoor tent wedding at their father's section of the ranch. They had booked the tent and bought tons of decorations for it. Today they were out choosing linens and flowers and finalizing the last little touches. Everything was set.

Martin hadn't been much help. He was a very busy man. He spent a lot of time working and had established a regular routine of playing golf with some local businessmen on Thursdays and their father on Saturdays. Bernie and Bell would shop and make wedding arrangements while he was golfing.

It was Saturday afternoon, and the girls had arrived back at Martin's house to relax for a while before preparing dinner for that evening. They would be celebrating Father's Day that night because their father had been away on business when the actual date had come and gone.

Bernie walked into the house and tossed her purse on the table. "I need to visit the powder room, be right back," she told Bell.

As she awaited Bernie's return, the phone began to ring. Bell, unable to tolerate a ringing phone, decided to answer it. She was both curious and impatient, which never seemed to work to her advantage.

"Hello?"

"Hi, is this Bernadette?" asked a somewhat hesitant male voice.

"No, this is her sister, Bell. Who's this?"

"My name is Matthew. I've been trying to contact your sister for two weeks now. I think she believes I'm a telemarketer. She keeps hanging up on me before I'm able to fully explain why I'm calling."

"Okay. So why are you trying to contact her?"

"I'm a private investigator, and I'm tracking someone with whom I believe your sister is fairly well acquainted. I'm not trying to harass anyone. I would like to verify a few details," he said. Bell heard a sense of urgency in the man's voice, so she continued to listen. "Your family may be in danger, and I want to help protect you."

"How so?" asked Bell.

"Any number of things could happen, but I believe your sister is involved with a man named Martin Day, who has several aliases, and is suspected of murder and fraud. There's also the possibility that he may have defected from one of the intelligence agencies, but I don't have enough proof of that situation."

"How did you come to know Martin?"

"We have a colorful history. We were in college together and were friends for quite a while. He seemed like a normal guy when I first met him, but then he started doing things uncharacteristic of a friend. It didn't take long to find out that he's a con artist who preys on the daughters of wealthy families."

Bell took a moment to consider his accusations. "That's a lot to swallow. I'm going to need more information and some evidence before I pass any sort of judgment. I don't even know you.".

"I can tell you this much, you're a lot safer around me than you are around him. I was hired by the aunt of one of Martin's victims to prove that Martin had a hand in her family's deaths. Martin is smart, and he's managed to elude me on multiple occasions. No one has been able to gather enough evidence to link him to these crimes, which is one reason I suspect he may have been a member of one of the intelligence agencies."

"This whole thing sounds completely insane," said Bell. "You're telling me my sister is engaged to a spy who cons people out of money? That seems farfetched."

"Why don't we meet someplace and grab coffee or a drink, and I'll answer all your questions. I'll also show you my credentials and the file I've created on Martin," he replied.

"What about Bernie? She isn't going to buy any of this."

"How about I meet you first? Then, if you're on board, we can approach Bernie together."

"Okay. I guess I'm fine with that, as long as we meet in a public place," said Bell. "Why don't we meet at my family's business. The 365th Street Jazz Club. It's a great place with many wonderful food options, and I'll feel safe."

"Okay. I'll meet you there in one hour. Sound good?"

"Six o'clock is perfect. Wear a lime green tie so I know who you are, please." She smiled, as she knew it might be hard to find on short notice.

"That's an odd request."

"Well, how many other men do you think will walk in sporting a lime green tie?"

"Yeah, I suppose." He laughed. "See you soon."

Bell had no more than re-stowed Bernie's phone to the counter when she walked back into the kitchen.

"Were you on my phone?" asked Bernie.

"Yeah, that guy you keep ignoring called again."

"The telemarketer? Why would you answer that call? They're so annoying."

"I thought I'd see if he was selling anything useful."

"Whatever makes you happy. I'm going to pick out some wine and start prepping for dinner. I want to get everything ready so I can easily toss it in the oven when the time comes. What's your plan?"

"I'm actually meeting a blind date for drinks before dinner, so I'm heading out. I'll see you later tonight."

"My sister has a blind date? Very good," she said approvingly. "Don't forget, seven o'clock, and feel free to bring your date. Martin's friend will be here as well." She turned away and headed for the cellar, leaving Bell alone.

Bell couldn't believe how frustrating Bernie could be at times. She couldn't even take the time to speak to Matthew. She assumed he was a telemarketer. Her sister was impatient, and that impatience frequently had a negative impact. She decided to go for a quick run and think about things before meeting him. Maybe the cool air on this cloudy day would help her relax and process things better.

After her run, Bell was feeling more at ease. She knew she could handle this. Why get Bernie involved if it weren't a legitimate situation? She climbed into the shower, washed herself up, and hopped out. She decided to throw on something comfortable, which meant a skirt and shimmery top in Bell's land.

At a quarter to six, she was ready to go out the door. She would meet this Matthew, but she'd have backup. She informed Alex of her plan, and he was going to stay near enough to sound an alarm if anything went awry. She knew, however, that meeting on her own turf had been Matthew's choice, so her fear was mild at most.

"Good evening, Bell. How's my other favorite sister?"

"Bradley, I have my eye on you," she warned. "You upset Bernie when you bolted out of the house the other night."

"Whoa, girl, you know I only have the best intentions. Besides, you didn't leave me much choice. By the way, I also have your back tonight. Alex told me to keep an eye out for any foul play, so I'm ready in case either of you needs me," he said and then smiled at her.

"You're the best. And who knows, perhaps you'll get that wish regarding my sister one day."

"Don't say that. You just build my hopes up, and then you kick me out of the barbecue. Everyone here knows how I feel, and she hasn't a clue, has she?"

"I think she knows, but she chooses to ignore it for other obvious reasons. Sorry for kicking you out. I knew you wouldn't want to be present for that."

"Yeah, well, you were right. I didn't want to witness their engagement. I would do anything for that girl, but she just sees me as the helper who works at her father's club."

"Now that's not fair, Bradley Cordine. You know she feels more strongly.. She appreciates you and respects the great business you do. You're one of the draws for the women in town to get dolled up and come out here for an evening. Everyone loves you. You make every woman in here feel special. Without you, this club would just be a big old man cave of sorts."

Bradley blushed at the compliment. "Come on, Bell, I have your table waiting, and your lime green tie is already there."

"Oh good, at least he's punctual. How bad can he be?"

"I hear some murderers are the most punctual people around."

"Yikes," she said. "That reminds me of a bit by one of my favorite comedians.

"I love that you and your sister both have a great sense of humor. Don't ever lose that, my friend.

"Oh, I won't. It's what keeps me going." She reached up and brushed his face. "You're a good man. Thank you for watching out for Bernie and me both. You're part of this family in my book."

As Bell walked up to her table, she took in the sight of the man sitting at it. It was safe to say that even if he hadn't worn the lime green tie, which actually looked great on him, she would have still been able to pick him out. He was a well-built black man with clear skin and short, well-kept hair. His grin could light up a room, and nothing about his appearance made her uncomfortable. His eyes were dark but seemed to sparkle. He waved at her, flexing his bicep. She was pleased with the view and wished she could see a little bit more.

"Hi," she said.

He looked up at her, his teeth glistening as he smiled. "Matthew McKinney," he said and held out his hand. She gave it a gingerly shake. "It's a wonderful day, don't you agree, my dear?"

"That depends on what you have to tell me about my sister's situation, I guess."

"Now, don't you worry. We have some things to discuss, but rest assured, we'll figure this out." Matthew held out his identification so she could see he was who he claimed to be. "Satisfactory?" he asked.

"That'll do," she replied. "You really made that tie work for you."

"What's not to love? I look good in black, and black and lime go well together. Just so happens I already had this tie with me."

"You didn't?" Bell giggled and blushed like a schoolgirl.

"I did. It's my favorite color." Matthew smiled at her. "Anyway, let's get down to business. We only have an hour before we need to be at Martin's house."

"You're the dinner guest?"

"Indeed, I am," he said. "Martin believes that we just bumped into each other. He doesn't know that I know anything about his history. He expects me to come to dinner and give my congratulations on his engagement. However, I'm here to gather evidence against him and to bring him in when the time is right."

"Okay. So, tell me what you've got. I want to know what sort of situation we're dealing with.

He pulled a file out of his briefcase and laid some articles, documents, and pictures on the table in front of them. "These are his alleged victims. There were eleven different photos. Bell began looking them over and committing them to memory as she listened to him speak.

"Oh, hold on. I think I have his picture here too. I should show you that first. His legal name, by the way, is Falkner Halstrom, but he was born Falkner Gamal. He's originally from Hurghada, Egypt. His family were simple fishermen. His mother rejected her arranged marriage against her father, Faramond's wishes, in order to marry for love. Faramond rejected his ungrateful daughter, but once he realized that he had a grandson, he took custody of him and brought him to America. Upon arrival, he had his last name legally changed from Gamal to Halstrom to better fit in. Faramond passed away unexpectedly when Falkner was nineteen. He left him a large sum of money, but Falkner was used to an extravagant lifestyle and blew through it like it was nothing, so he turned to his manipulative ways." He pulled out another photo.

"Dang, there are a lot of people in these articles." Bell looked at the photo Matthew placed before her. It didn't look like Martin. This man had long, messy hair, and his face didn't seem to have quite the same features. "Is that really him?"

"It is. He's been known to change his appearance with plastic surgery in the past. That photograph is from college, when I first met him." He slid some news clippings toward Bell. Each contained pictures of Martin, but he looked slightly different in every single one.

"Wow, he has definitely changed over the years. How did you know Martin was your friend from college if he doesn't look the same or have the same name?"

"Good question. I've been tracking him for eight years via tips regarding his whereabouts, and I've made extensive documentation regarding his habits. Certain things just added up. I had lost his trail for quite a while, but a good buddy of mine was in this area, and he overheard Martin's conversation at the golf course. He couldn't help but think that he reminded him of the man I'd been looking for. It was a complete long shot, but it made sense considering his past patterns of movement and the type of people he has been known to go after."

"That's unbelievable. What did Martin tell you regarding his changed name?"

"He told me he had to change his name and appearance because he was put into witness protection for a reason he could not discuss. He was clearly shocked that I recognized him."

"Geez, he has an answer for everything, doesn't he?"

"Yeah, well again, that's Falkner, or Martin, for you. He was always a smooth talker, which is how he so easily charms his way into other's lives."

"Tell me about these photographs. Who are these people, and what did he do to them?" A shiver ran down her spine. Who was Martin? How did they allow someone so crazy to get this close?

Matthew looked at Bell. "Some of them are of the same family. I included the photos for clarity. These first two are sisters. His first victims. They had some pretty hefty funds left to them as an inheritance. Martin wooed them both. Each, in turn, put him on their bank account. Neither knew the other was seeing him. One day he drained their accounts and skipped town. This was straight out of college. He concocted this whole scheme while still in school." He looked at Bell to make sure she was following how serious this situation was and how long it had been going on.

"So, what do you have on them besides a picture of the girls?"

"Here's the newspaper article about the heiresses and their betrayal. Neither sister will speak to the other since this happened. They rarely go out in public after the humiliation. They'll be fine, though. No one was killed, and they come from a very wealthy lineage. Their money has basically replenished itself. Their egos, however, will take some time."

"What else?"

"Okay, now these four were a family in North Carolina who took him in. The Corlani family. They were wealthy and had just moved here from Italy. They needed a handyman to help get their home in order, and he passed himself off as one. He, again, got the daughter to fall for him. He married her and became a part of the family. One day the family left town on vacation and was never seen again. It's believed that their personal plane crashed. Of course, Martin was not on the plane, and he acted as though he was devastated when the police confronted him. We have no real proof that he was the culprit, but knowing Martin, his hands were all over this so-called accident. The father's sister hired me to track Martin and find proof that he killed her family."

"That's crazy. You think he tampered with the plane?" asked Bell.

"Yes. I believe he did, but there's no plane to inspect, which makes this all the more frustrating. I can't really bring this to a jury since there's no evidence at this time."

"How does he get away with this stuff?"

"He's been lucky. Until now. We're going to stop him." He pushed another photo toward Bell. "This is Evangeline Simmons. She was a very wealthy widow who lived in San Diego, California. He heard about her and passed himself off as an electrician who was there to check some faulty wiring. My guess is that he tapped her phone, so he knew how to pull her into his game. Evangeline is very passionate and does things on a whim. She made her money as a porn star in her earlier years. He found a way to make one of those movies a reality for her by showing up in his work gear and taking an interest, if you know what I mean."

"Okay, I'm struggling on this one. She was a porn star, and he basically walked in like, 'I'm here to check your wires,' and she jumped up on that?"

"Yeah, she did. Sometimes all people want is the fantasy, you know?"

"Well, she got it, I guess."

"Yeah, up until the part where she put him on her bank accounts, and he ran off with her money like he did to the first victims."

"Well, at least she's still alive."

"Unfortunately, she's not. She hung herself. She was heartbroken and broke. I guess she couldn't see a way out of the situation. She fell for him, and all she was looking for was love in return."

"That's so tragic." Bell frowned at the photo.

"This last family is the Valens family, which consists of the parents, three sons, and one daughter. They were old money. He again found a way into the daughter Rita's heart. He married into the family under the name Dexter Hillard. Like his prior victims, Rita fell deeply in love with him."

"When I first heard about this family, I thought maybe he had changed, maybe he truly loved her. He stayed with them the longest. One day he and Rita got into a pretty bad fight. She came out of it with badly bruised wrists and a black and blue face. She swears this had never happened before. Martin disappeared that night."

"So, wait, he didn't take all their money, but he beat her up?"

"No. He didn't take the family money, but he did take off with some very expensive and precious heirlooms that had been in the family for many generations. Rita was heartbroken that he left. Of course, she says she hit him, too, and that the whole thing was provoked by her. She swore they'd never been in a physical fight before and she wanted to go after him. Her parents and brothers were completely appalled by what had happened. They felt it was better for everyone to cut ties."

"What are these other papers?"

"These are all articles on what happened in each situation. They all include a photo of Martin."

"Seriously, why hasn't anyone caught him yet?"

"He's careful, and as previously noted, he frequently changes his appearance and whereabouts. Once he makes a decision, he covers his tracks and follows through. He never leaves evidence of where he's gone."

"I can't believe this. He seems so convincing, but he's actually a sociopath?"

"Yeah. That's the most efficient way to describe him. He doesn't care about who he hurts. He wants his lavish lifestyle and to be the center of attention."

Bell's brow wrinkled as she stared back at Matthew. "What do you propose we do?"

Matt tapped his hand on the table. "First, I want to see him again and try to catch him at his own game. We need to go to dinner and act like nothing's happening until we can get your sister alone. We need her on board. He has to stand trial for the crimes he's committed, and to do that, we need him to either admit to what he's done or catch him in the act."

"What if she doesn't believe any of this? She can be a bit oblivious at times. She generally believes that everyone is good."

"Well then, she's in for a rude awakening, and we'll need to take extra precautions to keep you and your family safe. Obviously, he hasn't been proven guilty on the plane incident, but I truly believe he did it. And if he could do something like that once, who knows what else he could be capable of. After all, he did beat Ms. Valens up. We need to get a confession somehow. That won't be easy. I want to take him in on something that will keep him locked up for good, not just money theft."

Bell could see where he was coming from. If there was no evidence that he killed that family in the plane crash, Martin might not stay locked up long at all.

"Oh, crud, we have to go. It's ten to seven!" Bell hopped up from her seat.

"Okay, just remember what I said, act like nothing happened. Try to act normal until we can get her alone."

"You got it," she gave him a half-smile.

Matthew reached out and took Bell's hand. Smiling back at her, he placed a light kiss on it. "It's been a pleasure, despite the circumstances. I'm looking forward to spending more time with you this evening."

Bell smiled at him and then, turning toward the bar, gave a nod to Bradley, who nodded to Alex in return to signal the end of the meeting.

At seven o'clock, the doorbell rang, and Bernie bounded excitedly out of the kitchen to answer it. She looked through the peephole and saw that Bell was standing outside with a man she'd never seen before. She threw open the door.

"Hi, you must be Matthew," said Bernie. "Hello, Bell. Both of you come on in."

"And you must be the ever-lovely Bernadette," he responded. "I am indeed Matthew McKinney, but you may call me Matt."

"Bern, something smells great. What are you fixing?" asked Bell as she sniffed the air.

Bernie was a sucker for compliments on the meals she cooked. She loved cooking when there was a hungry group to be fed. "I went for comfort food tonight. I made meatloaf with sweet potatoes, asparagus, and fruit salad, along with a chocolate cake for dessert." She knew these items would be crowd-pleasers. Her father especially would be excited. It was his favorite meal.

"Ooh, sounds perfect," Bell was beaming at Bernie. She hadn't had a decent home-cooked meal in quite a while.

"I'm with you," said Matt as he nudged Bell lightly in the shoulder and grinned.

"Seems you two are instant friends," commented Bernie as she gave Bell a suspicious look. "Why don't we go into the living room and make ourselves more at home. I'll crack open a bottle of Chardonnay, and we can have a drink while the meatloaf finishes cooking."

"That sounds nice. By the way, where is that old man of yours?" asked Matt.

"Oh, he's out in the greenhouse, but he should be in momentarily. He just loves his plants." Bernie rushed back toward the kitchen to grab the wine.

"She seems like a sweet young lady," said Matt.

"She's amazing. She'll do almost anything to make the people she cares about happy. I can't even imagine what she would do for Martin, which is kind of scary."

"That makes her all the more vulnerable to his antics."

"Yeah, you're not wrong about that. I don't want to see her hurt. I love my sister. She's my best friend. One of my only friends. And she's one of my biggest allies in life."

"Come now, you must have more than just a couple of friends. You're a beautiful young woman and a model to boot. You've got those bright green eyes and that warm smile, not to mention your angelic laugh. Surely most people love you and want to be near you?"

"Most people love to hate models or are intimidated by them. I've been one of the top models in the area for the past few years; when that happens, people treat you differently. It's as if they think I'm too good to be around them. Other models often look out for themselves and have no problem trying to push someone else down to be number one. I'm especially vulnerable because I'm considered the second most sought-after model in this area. Bernie is first. I think despite being models, my sister and I are pretty normal people."

"You definitely don't seem normal from an outsider's standpoint. You seem so exotic because of your profession."

"I hear that, but again, it isn't all it's cracked up to be. I have men and women who hate me simply because I can eat what I want and don't gain weight. I don't have to stick my finger down my throat, take pills, or starve myself. That can really get people going. They think you're hiding some big old secret. No secret. I'm just lucky, I guess."

"That's interesting. I'm sorry they treat you so differently. I hear the word *model,* and I think loved, lots of friends, money, and the good life. It isn't right to be so judgmental."

"What about you? What's your story? Who is Matthew McKinney?" She reached out and gently touched his arm. She wanted to take this time to be more candid with him. He was interesting, and she didn't really want to admit it, but she found him quite attractive. She watched as his face lit up with what appeared to be determined passion.

"Matthew McKinney is an old college buddy of Martin's who wants to see that he is made to pay for the horrible things he's done to so many people over the past several years. I grew up in a family where integrity is very important, and Martin let go of that some time ago. I was in love with one of his first victims. He stole her away from me, but one woman wasn't enough. He chose to play her sister too. It hurt to see what he could do to someone I cared so much for and what he could do to me. I was his best friend."

"That explains a lot. This is a very personal situation for you."

"It's the reason I became a private investigator. I couldn't stand to see him get away with such horrible acts of cruelty. As I said before, I intend to bring him in. I'm not playing any more games. This has to end."

"With all this information, I feel much more at ease," joked Bell. Matthew was quickly becoming even more attractive. She looked at his face. He had a strong jawline, and his eyes were bright and sincere. He was freakin' hot. "What were you going to be, before you became a PI?"

"If you ask my parents, I was supposed to be a lawyer. Instead, I was a police officer for two years, but then I became obsessed with bringing Martin to justice, so I made a change. Anyway, I'm going to ask you to keep my business a secret. I don't want Martin to find out and run. That will make this much more difficult if he catches wind of my intentions."

"Roger that," said Bell. She was a level-headed woman who could keep a secret most of the time. She did, however, struggle if the secret was exciting news and supposed to be kept from her family. She told her sister and brother nearly everything.

"All right you two, I'm back," said Bernie. "Here's that wine. Sorry it took so long. I had to go down to the cellar. I thought I'd grabbed the Chardonnay, but I was wrong. We're all out. Hopefully Pinot Grigio is okay." She smiled. "Are you sure you haven't met before? You look awfully comfortable with one another."

Bell looked at Matthew and realized their hands were resting on the coffee table and nearly touching. She slowly moved hers away and reached for one of the glasses Bernie was holding. "I'll take that from you. You know me. I'm equal opportunity when it comes to wine."

"My favorite," said Matthew. He, too, reached out and grabbed a glass from Bernie. "And in response to your question, today is the first we've met." Bell gave Matthew a kind look and swore she saw his eyes darken for the briefest moment.

"Hey, guys, what's happening? This looks like a fun little group," said Martin as he casually walked into the room. "How is everyone this fine evening?"

"Great," said Bell, "we're getting to know your buddy Matt here," she said, patting Matthew on the shoulder.

"So, Matt, where've you been all these years?" asked Martin. "I haven't seen you in— how many has it been now?"

"Four, I believe. I haven't seen you since you were in California. What a crazy happenstance that was."

"Yeah, who would have expected to run into their college roommate in a totally different state?" he said. "So very odd, but we did have a good time that night, didn't we?"

"Oh yes, indeed we did. I don't think I had drunk that much wine in years. Let's not repeat that tonight," laughed Matt.

"I am going to check on dinner one last time. I think things should be about ready. I hope Dad and Alex arrive soon," said Bernie, hustling out of the room.

"Do you need any help, Bern?" Bell asked as she began to follow her.

"No, Bell, it should be fine," she called back. "The table is already set with most of the items, just need to bring out the meat."

Bell worried that Bernie suspected something was going on between herself and Matt. Bell wasn't the type to allow any man to get close to her without more than a couple of dates. There were plenty of guys in town who thought Bell was just plain cold, but in reality, she was afraid.

When Bell was a teenager, she'd been the victim of a very mature and pushy boyfriend who had tried to force himself on her. Luckily, Alex had come home early and chased the jerk away. After that, she was never quite the same when it came to men. It was highly unusual that she felt so drawn to Matthew. For the sake of his work, she would have to distance herself some.

Despite Bernie's protesting, Bell decided to head into the kitchen to help anyway. In the kitchen things were as expected. All of the food was finished.

"I'll take these out," she told her sister. She grabbed the two loaves of meat and carried them off toward the dining room. Everything smelled great. Bernie was an awesome cook. As she arrived at the table, she heard the doorbell sound and a familiar "hello." Alex had arrived, along with their father. *Good*, thought Bell, *the gang's all here*. She heard Bernie wish their father a happy Father's Day. She was glad they were lucky enough to celebrate together, even if it weren't on the actual day. Last year Bell and Alex had been away on shoots in other states, and they couldn't be present. Bernie had told Bell that Daddy looked sad and she didn't want to repeat that situation.

"Okay, family and friends, this meal is ready," said Bernie as she waved everyone toward the dining room.

Alan gave Bernie a big hug. "Hey, kid. My how you've grown up. Look at this food! It looks like all of my favorite things. A father couldn't ask for more," he said, beaming at her.

"Thanks, Daddy. I'm glad you approve. Hopefully it all tastes good," said Bernie.

"I'm sure it will, Pumpkin. It always does." He turned and grabbed a seat at the opposite end of the table.

"Alex, where are you? Get in here and give me a hug," said Bernie.

"Yes ma'am," he said as he appeared around the corner. "Smells tasty, Bern."

The group followed him into the dining room, everyone chattering as they walked. "This is nice, isn't it?" Bell asked her sister.

"Yeah. It's nice to have everyone together in the home that will one day be mine and Martin's. It feels like a real family gathering, even if we aren't married yet. This is the first I've felt this way since Mom left."

Bell reached out and squeezed her sister's arm. "Well, if it's any consolation, you did a great job. The food smells wonderful, and everyone is smiling."

Martin walked up to Bernie and wrapped his arms around her. "She's right, the food smells divine, and the pumpkin-scented candles are also a nice touch." He gave Bernie a peck on the cheek and proceeded to sit at the head of the table. "Alan and Alex, this is my old college roommate, Matthew," he said, motioning to his left.

"He was in the area and wanted to drop by and congratulate us on our engagement."

"Very nice to meet you," said Alan as he leaned over and shook Matt's hand.

He smiled warmly at Alan and said, "The pleasure is all mine. My father is no longer around, so spending Father's Day with you and your family reminds me of fond memories from growing up."

The rest of the group arranged themselves around the table. As everyone sat, they looked at Bernie, still standing to Martin's right.

"I would like to say something. Thank you for being here. I'm glad our family could be together this year to honor our father. Alex, glad you could get here so promptly." She grinned. "This is the first holiday we will celebrate together in this house. Daddy, happy Father's Day. We love you very much." Alex raised his glass, and the rest of the group followed. "To you, the best father we could have asked for. Cheers." The room rang out with the sound of clanking wine glasses.

"Anyone want to say grace?" asked Bell.

"I will," said Matt, "though it may not be the traditional grace you are used to."

"Let's hear it," said Martin.

"Great Spirit, please bless those at this table with honest and loving hearts, and let this food nourish us and keep us full, happy, and healthy. Amen."

"You are right, that was not what we traditionally say, but it was nice just the same," said Alex. "I appreciate your words."

"Thank you," said Matt.

"Okay everyone, let's eat. This food is going to get cold," added Bernie.

After dinner, they all adjourned to the family room, where they decided to play some poker. Everyone was getting along swimmingly.

Bell wrinkled up her face in disgust. "I cannot believe how poorly I'm doing tonight. This is usually my game," she said.

"Well, we're out of wine," said Martin, "Maybe that's the problem." He laughed. "Shall I grab a couple more bottles from the cellar? How about a nice Chianti?"

"That sounds perfect," said Alan and Alex in unison. They loved their red wines, and Chianti was at the top of the list.

"Okay, I'll be back, don't go anywhere," he said, shaking his finger at them.

"Oh, don't worry, you are bringing more wine; we'll stay right here," said Alex.

"Actually, I'll come with you," said Alan. "I'm a bit of a wine connoisseur, and I may know some good wines to stock your cellar with as part of your wedding gift." He raised an eyebrow and grinned. The only thing Alan loved more than good wine was giving good wine as a gift. The club was always stocked with the best vintages.

After they left the room, the awkwardness crept in. Bernie fidgeted nervously with a cocktail napkin. Bell realized she was staring at her.

"Is there something going on?" asked Bernie. "It feels like you're all watching me as if I'm going to spontaneously combust."

Alex looked at each of them in turn. "Is there something going on? I didn't notice at first, but the air in here does feel quite thick."

Bell looked at Matthew and nodded.

"We would like to discuss something with you, but we don't have much time," he said.

"So, you do know each other? said Bernie.

"No. We really did meet today," said Matt. "I approached her and asked her to meet me before dinner. Anyway, this isn't easy. Let me just put it out there. I believe your fiancé is a con artist. He finds wealthy women and families, works his way into their good graces, and then leaves with their money."

Bernie gaped at Matthew and slowly shook her head. "What are you talking about? You sound crazy." Her eyes narrowed and her cheeks flushed as she stared him down.

"I know this is shocking," said Matthew. "You need to hear me out. He's stolen money and valuables from several wealthy families, and in one case, he's suspected of murder. He could be very dangerous. We believe he tampered with one of the family's airplanes and caused the crash that killed them all. I've been following him for several years, but I haven't been able to obtain enough concrete evidence.

"If he's done all of these things, how could you not have proper evidence?" asked Bernie.

Matt gave her a grave look. "He's thorough at covering his tracks. I told your sister I suspect he may have links to one of the intelligence agencies, which is why he's so good at what he does. He also changes his appearance and name after each incident. He's no stranger to the knife. When I ran into him, he was shocked that I recognized him from back in California. His real name is Falkner Halstrom."

Bernadette rolled her eyes and looked up at the ceiling. Shaking her head again, she turned her attention back to Matthew. "I don't know you. I've never met you before. I'm not listening to this! You come into his home and tell me my husband-to-be is a con artist and doesn't care about me. I spoke to Martin online for six months before meeting him in person. This can't be a lie. I need you to leave."

"But Bernie, I've seen the case files," said Bell. "They look pretty legit. There are even articles about the families."

"No!" yelled Bernie. "This is a lie!"

"What's going on?" boomed Martin as he walked into the room. "I leave for ten minutes, and I come back to find people yelling?"

Alan surveyed the group. "Yeah, what's happening?" he asked cautiously.

Bernie turned and looked at Martin. "I'll tell you what's going on. Your college friend over there is trying to turn my sister against us, and he's telling me that you're some kind of con artist or something."

"Sweetheart, why don't you have a seat. We'll set things straight," replied Martin. "Matthew, is this true? Are you trying to turn my future wife and sister-in-law against me? Why would you do such a thing? We were so close in school. You were my best friend."

"Best friend? If this is how you treat your best friend, then I'm glad we weren't enemies. One woman wasn't enough for you. You had to have her sister too. You took her away from me, then you took everything from her family. You leave nothing but heartbreak and wreckage in your wake. You deserve to be behind bars." "Get out! I'm not listening to another minute of this," said Bernadette hysterically.

"You heard her. Leave, or I'll have you formally removed, which won't end well. As for the rest of you, if you want to buy into these stories, you can leave too. I don't know who this person is that he's referring to, but it's not me. He must have suffered some kind of psychotic break. He's nothing but a sore loser who can't handle that his female friend chose me over him. That was years ago, and it was a boy's game. Those days are long gone."

Matthew took a step toward Martin. "You know I'm right, Falkner, or whatever your name is. This isn't going to end well for you. It's only a matter of time."

Martin reached for his phone with one hand and pointed to the door with the other.Matthew gave one abrupt nod and said, "Consider me gone. Bernie, take care of yourself," as he walked out of the room. He gave Bell the smallest of smiles as he passed by her. A moment later, they heard a car pull out of the drive.

Alan had a look of sheer confusion on his face. "What was that about?"

Martin ignored Alan's question. "Now that the trash has been taken out, let's get back to our game," he said without missing a beat.

Alex and Bell exchanged concerned looks in front of their sister, then moved on with their evening. Bell knew this wasn't the end of that particular conversation, and now Bernie knew too.

Chapter Eight

The next morning, Bernie awoke to breakfast in bed at the ranch.

"Morning, sweetheart," said Martin.

"When did you get here?" Bernie gave a big sleepy stretch.

"I came over about an hour ago to make breakfast."

"That's sweet of you," she said.

"I also think we need to have a conversation regarding what happened last night."

"Oh?" Bernie figured this might come up. She'd lain awake for hours thinking about what Matthew had said. The thing that really got to her was the look she saw Alex and Bell exchange. Any time she was wrong, they gave each other 'the look.' The look that says, *we know better. You're going to find out the hard way. How can you be so blind?* She hated that look. How could they be right in this situation? Martin had shown nothing but kindness to her, and he hadn't mentioned money once. This time, they were the ones who were wrong.

Martin reached out and took Bernadette's hand in his. "Matt and I go way back. We had a bit of bad blood between us. Which I thought had been forgiven after California. But now I realize that couldn't be further from the truth. You see, he and I were roommates in college, and we were hanging out with a couple of sisters who lived in the townhouse a few doors down. Matt failed to tell me that he was into one of them, and this particular sister actually liked me instead. I started dating her, and he was extremely hurt. He accused me of knowing he had feelings for her, but I had no idea."

"So, what happened? He said you took her money."

"I continued dating her, and Matt took off. We became quite serious, and we took a risky gamble with some stocks. She and her sister both wanted to invest. The stocks tanked, and we lost everything. I had no idea at the time that they'd given me all of their savings. Their family wasn't wealthy like Matt made them out to be. The loss was huge, and they suffered major depression because of it. She broke up with me, and I packed up my things and moved on. Her family blamed me, but it wasn't my fault that they were not honest with me about the money they brought to the table.

"Matthew didn't speak to me for years. When I ran into him in San Diego, he said all was forgiven. I took his word on it. I guess I shouldn't have. I had no idea he would take things so far as to spread rumors. Even in college, Matthew faced some of his own challenges with mental health. If I remember correctly, he was diagnosed with bipolar disorder. Maybe he's off his meds again?"

Bernadette studied Martin's face. He looked and sounded like he was being honest. She knew mental illness could really mess with people, especially if they didn't stick to their medication.

"I want you to stay away from him," said Martin. The look he gave her was stern. "If your sister says anything else about Matt contacting her about this situation, I want you to let me know immediately. If he is off his meds, there's no telling what he might do. I just want you and your family to be safe. Okay?"

"Okay," said Bernie. "I'll let you know, but I doubt anything else is going to come of this. You made it pretty clear that Matt isn't welcome around here."

"That may be true, but you never know what will happen when mental illness is involved. Let's move on from this. We have much more exciting things to think about. We're getting married in less than a week." He squeezed her hand.

"I know. I'm so excited!" said Bernie.

Martin leaned over and kissed her on the forehead. "Eat up, kid. We have things to do today. I brought you this dress to wear," he said as he pulled a hanger from her closet.

Wrinkling her brow, she said, "I didn't realize we had plans."

"Oh, didn't I mention the benefit? I could have sworn I told you. I have to make an appearance to gain new clients. I need my beautiful fiancée there with me. How would I look if I were to show up alone, especially when I hope to become the town treasurer eventually."

"Yeah, I guess, but I had been planning to put in our reception numbers today, and I also need to find a dress for our rehearsal dinner."

"That can wait. This cannot, sweetie. Now finish eating and get dressed. We need to leave here in half an hour." He smiled fondly at her and walked out of the room.

Bell walked in as soon as Martin was gone. "What in the freak is going on?" she hissed.

"I guess I'm going to a benefit with Martin today."

"You guess? Really? Since when do you guess?"

"Since Martin came in here and asked me to go with him, that's when," said Bernie, feeling defensive.

"Well, Bern, we had plans, important wedding plans. Some things need to be done on a schedule. This wedding is next week. Besides, he didn't ask you. He told you that you were going. He even told you what you were wearing. Pardon me for eavesdropping, but this is crazy." Bell's nostrils flared as she spoke. "When one person in a relationship dictates what the other person does, it's no longer a genuine relationship. Relationships are supposed to be two-sided, or people would just marry themselves. And another thing. Do you really buy that story he told you about Matthew?"

"Yes," she replied firmly. "I do believe him. And it's fine. We can deal with food and dresses tomorrow, all right?"

Bell shook her head. "I feel like you're missing the big picture," she replied. "Don't you think this is cause enough to put a pause on things?"

"Everything's fine," said Bernie as she slammed her plate on the bedside table and began getting dressed. "He's never made a request like this before. Maybe he's just worried about making the right impression on everyone at the benefit."

"Fine, whatever. Have fun," said Bell as she marched out and slammed the door behind her.

An hour later, Bernie stepped out of Martin's car at a lavish-looking estate. As a financial advisor, Martin had been asked to make an appearance at the fund-raising event, which was being held to raise money for building a new community center and playground. Bernie thought it was a good cause. If anyone else in the community had asked her to get involved, she would have been there in a heartbeat.

"Okay, Bernadette, I need you to always stand by my side and look gorgeous. I'll do all of the talking. If everything goes well, I'll hopefully gain some ground with reaching my goal of becoming town treasurer, which would be an excellent achievement for us."

"Okay," said Bernie. She didn't realize so little would be expected of her.

"Hi, Martin," said an older, distinguished-looking gentleman. He reached out and shook Martin's hand. "Lovely to see you here watching over things. Who might this be?" he asked as he looked at Bernie.

"I'm Martin's fiancée, Bernadette," she said with a smile.

"Lovely to meet you, my dear. You certainly are the better half." He winked.

"Why thank you, sir," said Bernie.

"Yes, she's a gem. I'm a lucky man," said Martin. "Tom, help yourself to some champagne and hors d'oeuvres. We can catch up more later."

"Sounds good, bud. I look forward to it," said Tom as he walked away.

"Who was he?" asked Bernie after Tom was out of earshot.

"More importantly, what happened to standing there and looking gorgeous?" asked Martin.

"I was introducing myself," said Bernie. "I didn't realize that would be a problem."

"Bernadette, I will introduce you. You just do as I say," he replied curtly.

Bernie was shocked by Martin's reaction. What had gotten into him? How could he speak to her like that? She stepped back so that she stood slightly behind him. "Sorry. It won't happen again," she said. Perhaps he was still upset about the Matthew situation. Bell would have a cat if she found out. She made a silent vow not to tell Bell about this situation.

For the rest of the afternoon, Bernadette stood quietly beside Martin. After the fund-raiser had ended, Bernie had Martin drop her off at home. He wanted to take her to dinner, but she protested and told him she was tired and wanted to sleep. He let her be. She was thankful for the time away. She decided to forget about his weird reaction. Most likely, it had to do with the prior evenings' events.

She found Bell pulling apart some pizza in the kitchen.

"Want a slice?" asked Bell. "You can have some, but you'll have to apologize for abandoning our girls' day first."

Bernie knew Bell meant what she said. Bell had refused to give her a bottle of water one time when she was coughing uncontrollably because she didn't say sorry for showing up late to one of her sister's shows. "I'm sorry. I don't really know what happened today. The whole day was just odd. All I want to do is forget about it." Turning away from Bell, she felt a tear roll down her cheek.

"Are you crying?" asked Bell. "Don't do that. Here," she said. "Have a glass of wine and some pizza. Let's watch a movie and enjoy some girl time. I got a hold of Alex's copy of *Runaway Bride*, if you're interested."

"I'm not crying. I've had a long day. Can we watch *Rock of Ages* *after that*? I've been craving some good music. I love that movie."

"Sure, we can do that." Bell smiled at Bernie. "Tell me why you're upset." she said quietly.

In the end, Bernie resolved to tell Bell what had happened. "I just don't get it. Martin was so weird today. It was so unlike him."

"Did something else happen?" She looked at her expectantly. "He didn't hurt you, did he?" Bell was in parent mode again. "I swear if he hurt you—"

"No, Bell, he didn't hurt me. Just my ego. I can't imagine him doing anything to physically harm me. He was very blunt about his expectations of how I should act. He didn't want me to speak. He wanted me to stand there and look pretty, I guess. Anyway, I don't really want to talk about it anymore. I'm tired, and I want to relax." She looked at her sister and smiled apologetically.

"I don't want to drop this conversation, but I guess we can discuss it more later. Let's enjoy the rest of the evening," said Bell.

The girls grabbed their food and beverages and adjourned to the living room. Bernie flopped down onto the oversized leather chair and admitted defeat to having any more expectations about the day. She'd sit there, relax, and veg out with her sister. If she didn't hear from Martin Day that evening, everything would be fine.

"Let's get this party started!" said Bell as she queued up the movie.

The rest of the night was exactly what they both needed. Fun, relaxing, and just plain normal.

"I'm glad we got to hang out alone tonight," said Bernie.

"Me too. Sometimes it makes the most sense for a weird day. Night, Bern, let's do this again soon," said Bell as she yawned and headed for her bed.

Chapter Nine

The rest of the week passed by without incident. Bernie's family threw a huge 4th of July party at the club, and she'd been a part of two ridiculously long photo shoots on Wednesday and Thursday. It was finally Friday night, and she was ready to have some fun. Her sister had wanted to throw her a bachelorette party, but Bernie wasn't really into getting crazy with a big group of ladies. Bell talked her into a family night with bachelorette fun instead.

The siblings were heading to their mother's house in Alex's limo. She wanted them to come over for a nice dinner before they moved on to silly bachelorette games and hitting the bar scene. Alex was super excited to be a part of the festivities. It wasn't very often he got to enjoy the silly games that women played, but he loved them.

The group stepped out of the limo and walked up the drive to their mother's beautiful brick mansion. Bernie felt it was more house than one woman could need, but it made her mother happy, so she didn't say anything. She reached out and rang the doorbell.

Mariska threw open the door and greeted them with a rare smile.

"My babies, how are you all doing this evening?" she asked.

"I'm great!" said Alex.

"I think we're all looking forward to some fun," said Bell.

"Yes, a night out with you kids does sound refreshing," said Mariska. "Come on in, let's have some dinner, then I have a gift for the bride-to-be." Bernie noted that her mother seemed genuinely excited, which was not an emotion she often showed.

Dinner was perfect. Mariska made lasagna because she knew it was one of Bernie's favorite foods. She served a chocolate cheesecake for dessert, which everyone approved of. Most people would never know this, but Mariska loved to cook and was very good at it. Bernie admired that about her mother. It was one of her best qualities. Most of her body had been altered in some way, and her personality wasn't always appealing, but her food always looked and tasted great.

After everyone had finished their dessert, they moved into the sitting room.

"Sweetheart, here is your gift." She presented Bernie with a beautiful blue and gold wrapped package. Bernie carefully removed the matching ribbon and slipped the box out of its perfect paper. Inside was a stunning antique locket. "Open it," said her mother.

There were three photos inside. One of her parents, one of her grandparents, and one of her, Bell, and Alex. "Mom, it's beautiful," she said as a tear rolled down her face. "Was this Grandma's?"

"Yes, it was your grandmother's. She passed it on to me, and I'm passing it on to you. You'll always have your family with you when you wear this locket." Mariska glowed with adoration for her daughter. It was a rare family moment. Bell and Alex were shocked that their mother was being so sentimental, but they were just as excited about Bernie's family heirloom as she was.

"That's really neat, Ma," said Alex.

"Yeah," said Bell. "I didn't know you had anything like that from Grandma."

"Come on now, kids, your mother isn't all callous and cold," she said, smiling.

"Thank you, Mom. It means a lot to me." Bernie got up and gave her mother a big hug, and Mariska tightly hugged her back.

"I can't believe my baby is getting married," she said as tears ran down her face.

"Ma," said Alex, "knock that off. You never cry. Now you're going to make me cry." He joined in on the hug.

"Well shoot," said Bell, "Now I feel left out." She came over and joined the embrace as well.

"Okay now," said Mariska, "Who's ready to go out and party?!"

Alex jumped up. "Oh, me! Me, me, me!" He ran out of the room and then back again. "I got this for you," he said as he held up one of those bride shirts that had the checklist of crazy things to do on it.

"Oh, this will be fun," said Bell. She grabbed her mother's and sister's hands and pulled them up. "Let's go. Sentimental time is over."

The group piled out of the house and into Alex's limo to start their bachelorette night of fun.

Chapter Ten

After the bachelorette party, time seemed to move at ultra speed until the wedding day arrived. It was Saturday, July twenty-ninth, and an uncharacteristically rainy morning put Bell in a mood. Bernie looked at her sister and shook her head. Bell was pouting, complaining about her hair, and worrying about ruining her heels. She was acting more like a bridezilla than Bernie.

"Suck it up, Belinda. The rain may not even last all that long. Look, the sun's trying to come out. Why am I the one consoling you? This is my day. If anyone is going to be upset about the weather, it should be me." Bernie was irritated, to say the least. She looked out the window toward her father's house. Tents were popping up everywhere, and several people ran around in the rain. At least Bell wasn't outside setting up. Then she would have had something to complain about.

Bernie remembered a time when she was a little girl watching white tents just like the ones in her father's yard being set up for her aunt's wedding. She was amazed by the beauty. It was like a fairytale, and from that day forward, Bernie knew she wanted white tents with fairy lights too.

Bell cut into Bernie's thoughts. "You never get upset about the weather. You seem to think that weather is some great magical thing that brightens and cleanses the world."

"It is magical and exciting. I love thunder and lightning. I love the sound of the raindrops on the roof. It's soothing. You know it won't last long. The wedding's at one, and it's only nine in the morning. Now, let's go get our hair and makeup done. They invented umbrellas for a reason, Bell."

"Fine, but I'm grabbing the biggest umbrella I can find," she said.

"Be my guest. I'll have Alex grab Daddy's golf umbrella."

Bernie grabbed her cell phone and texted Alex. She wondered if Alex was fretting about the weather as much as Bell? Probably not. He was more like her. He loved a good thunderstorm. The roof of his house was tin, so whenever the girls visited him during a storm, he would muse over his roof and the amazing sounds it made.

"Okay, Bell. Alex will be here in five minutes with the umbrella, and then we're going. He said he'd give us a lift up to the main house. Valerie, Mitto, and Mitzi are already there and waiting for us."

"Oh sweet, you got Mitto and Mitzi? This should start the day off with a bang." Bell chuckled. "Those two loved us oh so much the first time we met them. I bet they're thrilled to be here." She rolled her eyes.

"Bell, seriously. I know they're a bit eccentric, but they do an amazing job. Evie sent them over as a gift because she knows they're some of the best in the industry for styling hair for any event." Bernie hoped that this truly was the case. She hated the idea of someone touching her hair for the wedding without knowing what they planned to do.

"Okay, but I hope they aren't sewing any giant headpieces on us, and heaven forbid they put us in our dresses. That was a night-mare."

"Honestly, what is your problem today?" asked Bernie con-temptuously. "Everything seems to be a battle with you." Truth be told, Bernie was secretly thinking the same thing—no giant headdress.

"My problem is that I think you're making a mistake, and I have done everything I can to try to get you to see it without pushing you." Bell stepped closer to Bernie and put her hands on her shoulders. Looking Bernie in the eyes, she said, "Are you sure you know what you're doing? Just say the word. Tell me you truly believe that this is right and that he is trustworthy, and I won't say another thing. I'll lead you down that aisle and stand by your side. I will be happy for you. But I can't help but be freaked out, considering all the things Matthew said and the fact that he acted all weird at that event earlier this week. I think you need more time to explore things and to know for certain what his intentions are."

Bernie looked back at her sister. She could see now that Bell was trying to protect her. Anyone else could be offended or angry at this outburst, but Bernie knew that Bell had always had her best interest at heart and would not say this if she didn't mean it protectively.

"Yes, Bell, this is what I want. I love him. I don't believe he did the things that Matthew says he did. We don't know anything about Matthew. He could be lying about everything just to get back at Martin." Bernie hoped this was convincing enough for Bell. Part of her wasn't sure she was being convincing enough for herself. "Anyway, he's been perfectly normal since the benefit. Loving and thoughtful. He's brought me breakfast in bed twice since that day, and we have been feeling quite close."

"Great, let's get this day started!" said Bell in an exaggerated tone.

A knock sounded on the front door.

"Hello?! It's Alex! I've come to take you lovely ladies to get your beautification on!"

"Good morning, Alex!" called Bernie. "I hope you brought coffee and one of those chocolate muffins. Someone needs a little more energy and a shot of happiness!"

"Hey, whatever," said Bell. "I was up before you this morning." She shoved Bernie out of the way and ran to the door.

"You're such a freak sometimes!" yelled Bernie after her.

"You mean freaky," snickered Alex.

"That too," laughed Bernie as she squeezed under the big umbrella with Alex and Bell. The rain had turned into a torrential downpour.

"All right, on the count of three, everyone shuffle toward the limo," said Alex. "One, two— hey!"

On two, both girls gave Alex a friendly little shove and tore off down the walk with the umbrella, leaving him soaking in the rain.

"That is so unfair. I brought you that umbrella!" he yelled after them.

They both laughed as they climbed into the limo. Alex piled in behind them. Despite the short time that had passed, he was dripping like a waterfall. The silly prank had helped Bell's mood. She sat and grinned triumphantly as she watched her drenched brother climb into the backseat.

"Well, thank goodness I'm not in my tux yet," he growled.

Bell tossed him a beach towel from the emergency bag they kept in the limo. It had everything from extra clothes to first aid items.

"Thanks."

"Oh, come on, Alex, it's just a little rainwater," said Bell.

"A little?" Alex shook his head in disagreement, and large droplets flew toward the girls.

"Hey," screeched Bernie.

"A very small taste of your own medicine," said Alex. "Very small. I'll owe you more later."

"We were just trying to lighten the mood," said Bernie.

"Well, I hope it worked. Now, let's go get serious about making you a knockout bride," said Alex.

The car had pulled up to the house. Everyone was careful not to get wet this time, though the rain seemed to be slowing. Inside the house, Mitto and Mitzi were waiting impatiently.

"What took you so long?" asked Mitto.

"Yeah, why are you so slow?" asked Mitzi. "This is a big day for you."

"Sorry, we had a few loose ends to tie up this morning," said Bell trying to calm the two down.

"Come. Sit," said Mitto. He stopped to look at Bell's hair. "What's happening here?" he asked irritatedly. "This is a great big mess. What am I supposed to do with this? Your hair is awful. No life. May as well cut it all off and start over. I don't know how I'm supposed to work with this. Terrible."

"Oh, hell no! Hellllll no!" shrieked Alex. "Now you've done it. No one is going to talk to my girls like that! You can consider yourselves fired, and I'll be having words with Evie. Leave, both of you. The door is the one that will smack you in the behind on the way out." He waved the two hairdressers toward the door and turned back to Bell and Bernie.

Bernie watched Mitzi give Mitto a death glare as she grabbed him by the arm and pulled him toward the door. Clearly, she was not happy with her brother.

Once they were gone, Alex said, "That should never have happened. I'm so sorry, Bern."

"It's not your fault. Bell's right. I never should have gone with them."

Bell turned toward Alex. "Go get me the intern, please. She's amazing, and I know she'll do an exceptional job with Bernie's hair."

Alex followed Bell's directive and left the room. Five minutes later, he returned with Georgette and Marietas.

"I had them on backup in case something like this happened." Alex shrugged. "I knew those two were trouble."

"You are indeed the most thoughtful brother and best friend, I could ever ask for," said Bell.

"Marietas, you do Bernie's hair since you have the most experience with wedding hair. No offense to you, Georgette. I know you're amazing, but as a full-time stylist that already works for us, Marietas has a little better feel for her hair."

"No problem," said Georgette. "I'm happy to help in any way I can."

"Okay, let's get started," said Marietas. "We have a lot to do and little time to do it in."

"Here," said Bernie, "This is the hairstyle Bell and I thought would look best with my dress."

"Oh, I like it," exclaimed Marietas. "Let's make a bride!"

Bernie sat and thought about the wedding while Marietas did her thing. She had chosen to have only one bridesmaid, and Martin had decided to have Alex stand up with him. His parents were not coming to the wedding because they were overseas and unable to get back on such short notice. Martin didn't seem to mind.

The wedding would be simple but elegant. Bernie wondered how the yard was coming. Several people were busily decorating the tents, building a dance floor and stage for the entertainment, and setting up tables and chairs.

The actual ceremony would take place in the courtyard of her father's home, where they had set up chairs and an arch for the couple to say their vows under. After the ceremony, they would parade to the back of the house where the tents were. The entertainment would be a string quartet during dinner and a band after dinner around seven. There would be tons of lights and flowers hanging from the ceiling.

Bernie had spent a lot of time planning the decorations. Hundreds of red roses would be in miniature mason jars hanging from the ceiling of the tent. There would be thousands of lights with tulle spread throughout. The guests would be blown away by the beauty of the wedding tents. She couldn't wait to see them.

After an hour, Bernie and Bell were ready to get their makeup and nails done. They both looked beautiful. Bell had a fancy updo with a few ringlets hanging down, and Bernie's hair cascaded in curls down one side of her neck. She wore a sparkling band of roses in her hair. They matched her glistening dangling earrings.

The rest of their beauty regimen was quick, and before she knew it, Bernie was pulling on a breathtaking champagne-colored wedding gown. She looked amazing. Bell and Alex couldn't stop staring at her. The dress hugged her curves beautifully on top and flowed out in soft, full layers at the bottom. The whole thing sparkled and shimmered when she moved. She chose the champagne color because she thought it was elegant and wanted it to be a little different from the traditional white dress.

"You look like a princess, sweetie," said Alex. "I can't believe how gorgeous you are."

"Awe, thanks, Alex," said Bernie.

"I'm proud to call you my baby sister," said Bell.

"Yeah, this might be the only time I look better than you," winked Bernie.

"Ha, I still look great, but you should look like the 'Bell' of the ball," she chuckled at herself. Alex and Bernie rolled their eyes as they usually did when Bell made silly jokes.

A knock sounded at the dressing room door.

"Bernie, baby, it's Mom, your father and I wanted to see how things are coming. Are you ready? It's nearly time for photos."

Bernie found it weird having both of her parents together in the same place, but so far, they were acting like nothing was wrong and being respectful of one another. As long as they continued with this front, things would go smoothly. She knew neither of her parents would risk ruining her day.

"You can come in," said Bell. "We're finishing up the last touches."

Alex opened the door for Mariska and Alan. "We need to put Bernie into her strappy little Choo shoes, and we'll be headed to the green to have our photos taken."

Bernie looked at her father. He looked amazing, as always. Alan Price was aging gracefully, and he could easily pull off any suit or tux. He always looked relaxed. Even today. He was acting as if they were still one big happy family.

"Bernadette, you look stunning," said Alan as he wrapped his daughter in a warm embrace.

"Thanks, Daddy. You look great as well." She smiled at her parents. "Mom, you look beautiful as always. I love that red dress on you." Mariska was wearing a long, flowing red dress and black stilettos. She could still pull off some pretty impressive heels with her long, lean legs.

"Sweetheart, I have to ask before you go forward with this. Is Martin your white horse?"

"Mom, really? On my wedding day? Why didn't you ask me this sooner? Maybe at the bachelorette party?"

"Oh, honey, you know, life is busy. It's never too late to ask when it has to do with your daughter's future." Her mother smiled at her.

"Yes, Mom, I know the decision I'm making. I love Martin, and he treats me well. He's always looking out for my best interest."

"Oh good. I'm glad to hear that. Men can surprise you sometimes. You never know when they'll turn into a zebra. Zebra can be tricky. I've known many in my life, and they can do some serious damage."

"Mom, he isn't a zebra. He makes me breakfast in bed, and he tells me how beautiful I am all the time. He opens doors for me." Bernie felt good thinking about the nice things Martin was capable of. How could he be a zebra if he did those things?

"How charming. Okay, honey, that's all I wanted to say. I'll see you out there." With a flourish of her hand, she cut off the conversation in true Mariska style. There were murmurs from the women in town. They believed that Mariska was the devil in disguise. While she was no zebra, she did her fair share of breaking hearts with her fiery touch and mysterious, dark eyes.

"Well, that was a lovely discussion," chimed Alan. Bernie knew he wanted to add something else, but for her sake, he did not.

"You know Mom. She has so much finesse when it comes to talking to her daughters, or any woman for that matter. Honestly, I don't think I've met a colder conversationalist."

"Very true. Which makes me question my past decisions," trailed Alan.

Bernie decided to chime in before the conversation took a turn for the worse. "Daddy, how's Martin doing?"

"He's doing wonderfully. Why don't you go see for yourself? He's waiting for you in the courtyard. You can meet him there for a quick five minutes, and then we'll go get the photos out of the way. How does that sound?"

"That sounds great," she said. "I'll be back shortly,"

"Go get 'em, tiger," said Alex with a silly high-pitched roar.

"Ha! I will." Bernie headed out the door toward the courtyard. She hoped that Martin would be as happy as her family was to see her. She was a little bit nervous and didn't know what to expect.

When Bernie reached the courtyard, she paused to take things in. Martin stood there looking incredibly suave in a black and grey tux. He smiled at her and held out his hand. She proceeded toward him.

"Hi there," he said, grabbing her hand and pulling her to him. His arms felt strong and warm as he leaned in and kissed her forehead.

Looking up at him, she said, "Hi, yourself. You make that tux look good."

"Thank you," he replied. Stepping back, he looked her over. "You don't look so bad either." His brow wrinkled as he continued to look at her.

"Am I sensing a *but*?" she asked.

"I'm wondering if you'd be happier if your hair was up on top of your head? It looks so pretty when you wear it up."

"Oh," said Bernie, "you don't like it?" She was hurt and shocked by his response. She had expected him to say how gorgeous she was. Was she misinterpreting his reaction?

"Darling. It's not that I don't like it, but with the weather and all, I think you'd feel less warm if you wore it up. It's just a thought. Do what makes you happy. Other than that, you look ravishing." He grinned.

"Thanks," said Bernie. She couldn't help but feel as if she'd done something wrong. This wasn't at all what she'd pictured for their first viewing. "I can have Marietas put my hair up. You're probably right."

Martin leaned in and kissed her on the cheek. "Let's go get your hair fixed, and then we can do our wedding photos."

"Okay," said Bernie, confused about how she should feel at that moment. She thought her hair looked amazing. She thought this was supposed to be a special moment, but it all seemed so businesslike. Martin wasn't looking at her all dreamy and dazed like she was the most beautiful woman he'd ever seen.

As they walked back to the dressing room, they passed Marietas. She smiled at Bernie but wiped the smile away when she saw the distressed look coming from her favorite model.

"Marietas," said Bernie, "I'm going to need you for a bit longer."

"Is something wrong, Bernadette?" Her eyes were bugging.

"I think I've changed my mind. I apologize, but with this heat, I think it would be better if I wore my hair up tonight to avoid getting too warm while we're dancing. Can you fix it?"

"Oh, that's easy enough. All I really need to do is pin it up, maybe add some more curls and hairspray, and you'll be set."

"Sounds good," said Bernie.

"Bern, I'll be outside waiting for you with the guys. Hurry up," said Martin. He blew her a kiss before he left.

Bernadette felt as if she'd been slapped. What was happening?

Bell came around the corner as soon as Martin was gone. "What are you doing?" She eyed her crookedly. "I thought you loved your hair?"

"I've decided to have Marietas put my hair up. I think the weather is too warm, and I don't want to be uncomfortable," said Bernie.

"I lm, I never knew Miss Bernadette to care about that sort of thing," said Bell. "You endure hours of modeling gigs under hot lights and put up with it, but it's too much for your wedding?"

"I guess I care today," said Bernie. She gave Bell a stern look but knew her sister could see right through her. She had to keep her cool and be tough. She couldn't break down and let her see her cry. This wedding had to happen. They were too far into it to call things off. She refused to give Emmy Lou Baker a story.

"Fine, have it your way." Bell turned and walked back out. She had a look of pure disgust on her face. Bernie hoped she would keep her mouth shut and not go after Martin.

"Bernadette Kelly Price, you did not make this decision!" shouted Alex, who had been sitting quietly off to the side drinking in the scene.

"Why would you say that?" Bernie asked calmly.

"I saw the look on your face when he walked out the door. It was a look of frustration and confusion. Things didn't go as you'd hoped in the courtyard. He asked you to redo your hair?"

"No, things are fine. This is my decision," said Bernie.

"Uh huh, sure it is, sweetie, and I eat kibble for breakfast." Alex hopped up from the easy chair he'd been relaxing in and walked out the door, his face mimicking Bell's.

Bernadette felt as if she'd been slapped by three people. Was this a nightmare? Was she asleep? Would the rest of the night be like this as well? She took a deep breath and let it out slowly. "This day is not off to a good start," she mumbled.

Marietas was quick about fixing her hair. It only took ten minutes to pin it up and shellack it with hairspray. "There you go, honey, that gorgeous mop of yours isn't going anywhere tonight." She turned Bernie so that she was facing her. "Listen, sweetie, I know this is none of my business, but you just ignore all the bull tonight. You go out there and dance and have fun. No one can ruin this night for you if you don't allow it."

"Thanks, Marietas. I needed to hear something kind. You're always so sweet."

"You deserve it, kid. Now you go out there and wow them."

Bernie turned and walked out the door with a smile on her face. Marietas was right. No one could allow this night to be ruined unless she allowed it. She was not about to let anyone get the better of her. Just because Martin suggested she wear her hair up, doesn't mean he loves her any less.

"There she is! Beautiful as always," said Martin as he ran to meet her. He swatted her on the behind and ushered her toward the rest of the family. Martin seemed happy, and that made Bernie feel better.

Alex and Bell exchanged looks, and Bernie pretended not to notice.

"Are we ready to go get the photos done now?" asked Alan.

"Yes, Daddy, I think we're as ready as we'll ever be," said a smiling Bernie.

"All right, gang, let's get up into these golf carts and head out," Alan said with some rather animated hand motions. He'd been a big fan of hand motions since the girls were little. He was always dramatically pointing and motioning to emphasize what he wanted them to do in photo shoots.

The entourage took off for the ninth green, where the photographer patiently awaited. He smiled as he saw them crossing the hill in the golf carts. Bernie was happy to see someone was still in a pleasant mood.

"Hi, Huey, how are you doing?" asked Bell.

"Doing wonderfully, girly, just wonderfully. How are ye all gettin' along? Weather wasn't so great an hour ago but looks to be cooperating now," he said.

Bernie loved his Scottish accent. He was her favorite photographer and was always in a cheery mood.

Alex looked over at Bernie, and she smiled at him. "I think the bride is anxious to get this photo session started. What do you say, Hue? Impress us like you always do."

"I say I'm ready to make this camera's day." He laughed. "I couldn't ask for a better group of subjects or a more fun occasion."

"Oh, heck no," agreed Alan. "You really couldn't," he turned to Bernie and motioned her forward. "Why don't we start with the lovely couple?"

"Okay, kids, come on up here. I want Bernie to stand in front of Martin. I want you to look over yer shoulder up into Martin's big handsome eyes, and with yer left hand, lightly touch his cheek. Martin, you'll put yer hands on Bernadette's waist. Good, that looks great."

Huey began clipping off photos and calling out poses. He shot several family photos that included Alan, Mariska, Bell, Alex, and of course, Bernie and Martin. The photo session went fast and before long, they were shuttling back to the house and lining up for their big entrance. As the music commenced, Alan looked down at his daughter, and his eyes began to water.

"Daddy, don't you dare," said Bernie. "If you start crying, then I'll start crying, and I'm not about to cry on my wedding day."

He looked at the smile on Bernie's face and let out a little laugh as he pulled himself back together.

Before she knew it, she was walking down the aisle with her father, and all of their friends and family were standing up watching her. She couldn't help but look at her dashing husband-to-be. He looked so handsome, and he seemed genuinely impressed with her. Things felt like they were falling into place.

Once they reached the altar, Alan shook Martin's hand, and Bernie stepped up to join Martin.

"You are stunning," he said. "I truly am blessed to have found you."

Bernadette felt as if she weren't really there. The whole thing seemed surreal. She held her bouquet out to the side. It was dripping, and she didn't want to get water on her dress. *Look at all the people*, she thought as she sat at the altar next to Martin. The Priest was telling a story. She hadn't even heard what he was saying.

Before long, they had exchanged vows and were sealing their nuptials with a kiss. Bernie hoped they looked decent in front of everyone. Martin pulled back and looked into her eyes.

"I'm such a lucky man to have a woman as beautiful as you by my side." Dipping her back, he kissed her again and then said, "I love you, Mrs. Day. Let's go celebrate us." He gave her a wink, then pulled her to her feet.

They turned and walked down the aisle and out the door toward the tents. Bernadette, for once, was speechless. All she wanted was a glass of champagne and to dance with her new husband. She was happy that she decided to brush away her earlier fear. She was going to go enjoy the night to its fullest.

"Sweetie, do you want to go up to the big house and have a drink with the rest of the wedding party while we wait for everyone to get settled into the dining tents?" asked Martin.

"That sounds delightful," she said. She reached down and grabbed his hand. He helped her into the golf cart. Alex, Bell, Mariska, and Alan had already piled into the first golf cart and were raring to go. Bell punched the gas, and they jolted forward. Mariska almost fell off the back end, but Alan belted her back with his long arms. Bernie and Martin followed the group in their own cart. Martin didn't like being in the back, so he punched the gas and began to pass the others. Bernie held on for dear life since the grass was so wet and slippery.

"It's good that you're holding on tight. It's too early to be cashing in those insurance policies," Martin said with a grin.

Bernie laughed and wondered to herself what that was supposed to mean?

As the carts reached the back entrance to their father's home, Bell hastily jumped out, pulling Alex with her. Once they were safely out of earshot, she looked at him and said, "What the hell was that? Did you hear that? Did he really say that to my sister? I should take him out back and teach him some manners."

"I heard him too, love, and I don't know what to say. We know he wanted her to see it as a joke, but that was pretty ballsy considering he knows everything Matthew told us."

"What do we do?" she asked.

"Nothing. There's not much we can do at this time. We can keep an eye on her and try to keep her safe. Try to let her know if something is wrong. That's all we can do."

"I love her so much. I don't want anything to happen to her. I'm scared," said Bell.

"I know, honey, me too."

Alex and Bell headed for the house. The others were still chattering by Bernie and Martin's cart but turned to follow when they realized the party was moving inside. Alex walked around to the back of the bar and hastily grabbed some champagne out of the fridge as Martin walked in.

"Here, Martin, will you do the honors?" he asked, tossing the bottle toward him.

"Whoa, easy, buddy. We don't want to break this expensive bottle now, do we?" asked Martin.

They each enjoyed a glass of champagne and reminisced about the ceremony, and then it was time to head back to the tents. The moment came and went so quickly. Bernie was in a bit of a daze.

Was this all really happening? She'd gone through many different feelings. It was like a rollercoaster. Next thing she knew, they were being introduced at the main dining tent.

"I now present to you Mr. and Mrs. Day!" said the announcer as Bernie and Martin entered the twinkling room. Martin pranced her around the dancefloor, spinning her and causing her dress to flair. Friends and family clanked their glasses in anticipation. Martin dipped her back and kissed her passionately. The room exploded into cheers. He even took a moment to ask their guests to applaud the hard work his beautiful new wife had put into planning such a spectacular wedding. She pulled his face to hers and kissed him in return.

Hand in hand, Martin and Bernie walked over to their table and took their seats. The rest of the room followed suit, and the caterers began serving the head table. Halfway through dinner, Alan stood up and called for the guests' attention.

"It is my pleasure to host this lovely gathering for such a wonderful couple. As you know, Bernadette is my youngest daughter, and with that title comes a little extra protectiveness. As of today, I can worry a little less. I am beyond elated that my daughter found such a wonderful young man. He's smart, talented, and successful, and I'm proud to call him son. Here's to the both of you. May you have a long, happy, and loving marriage." Everyone raised their glasses and toasted them. Bernie felt blessed to have so many wonderful people surrounding her and Martin.

Martin leaned over and kissed her. "I love you," he whispered.

"I love you back," said Bernie.

"Now," said Alan, "if I can get the lovely couple out on the floor for their first dance."

"Mrs. Day," said Martin as he held out his hand. "Would you like to dance?"

"Why yes, I think I would, Mr. Day," said Bernie with a laugh.

He led her out onto the dance floor, where they danced to the song *Open Arms*. Bernie felt herself relax into Martin's embrace. She felt safe. Everything before this had to have been normal pre-wedding jitters.

They danced to several songs, but they also mingled with a lot of guests. It was hard to spend much time enjoying themselves when there were so many people. At times, Martin would disappear, and she would find him sitting at the bar drinking scotch. *Men,* thought Bernie. *They leave all the important stuff to the women even when they should be a part of it.*

Even though Bernie could tell Bell and Alex were concerned, the siblings still partook in several dances together and had fun. Bernie even agreed to let Alex be involved in the bouquet toss, which he managed to catch. Several of the ladies gave him dirty looks, but Alex was never one to care about such things.

"It's mine, all mine!" he yelled excitedly. Bernie had never seen such a huge grin on his face. It was like Alex had won some trophy. He gloated around the room and waved the bouquet at all the single women. Bernie thought it was actually kind of perfect that Alex caught it. She knew he'd probably settle down long before Bell would.

Bell grabbed the bouquet from Alex's hands and whacked him lightly in the back of the head with it.

"Hey!" yelped Alex.

"This wasn't for you!" said Bell.

"Just because you weren't fast enough," he teased.

"Ugh, seriously, Alex, you're such a freak."

He looked at her and laughed. "I prefer freaky!"

"Yeah, right now you're a freaky queen." Bell chuckled.

"You know it, girlfriend." Alex grinned at her, and all was forgiven in the bouquet battle.

"Geez, you two are like children," said Alan as he walked up to the group. "How's your night going, sweetheart?" he asked Bernie.

"It's great, Daddy. Thank you for everything." she smiled up at him. She felt happy and relaxed. The champagne had helped. She was a little bummed that Martin wasn't with her at that moment.

"Where's the groom?" asked Alan, as though he had read Bernie's mind.

"Oh, he's at the bar drinking scotch with some guests," replied Alex.

Bell looked over at the bar. "Yeah, some of the female guests."

"Now, Bell," said Alan. "Leave it be. He's not doing anything wrong. If Bernie's okay with it, then it shouldn't matter."

"I'm fine with it. I trust him," said Bernie.

"That's what we're worried about," said Bell under her breath. Bernie, once again, pretended not to hear. Alan gave Bell a stern look.

"Let's go get a glass of champagne and see how the groom's night is fairing," suggested Alan.

"Good idea," said Alex. "I think it's time to hang out together instead of with everyone else. We've done enough mingling for one night."

"Yeah," agreed Bell. "I'm all mingled out. Let's blow this popsicle stand." She laughed, exaggeratedly tossed her hair over one shoulder, and stepped off toward the bar. The group followed her example to the tee. If anyone were watching, they would have either thought they were the snobbiest group of socialites or the dorkiest. And they probably would have been right, but hopefully, they would have laughed.

Alex pushed past Bell and approached Martin. "Groom, how is your night going?" he awkwardly blurted.

"Groomsman, it's going quite well," said Martin in a mirrored response. "How's your night going?" he asked Alex.

"Oh, it's just peachy. I'm having a blast on the dance floor, which I think you should join us on shortly."

"Hm, you do, do you? What says my lovely bride of this? I wouldn't want her to think you are trying to steal me away from her." He chuckled.

"Oh, no, friend, I want the whole group to get out there to shake their behinds. This could be one of our last dances together. You never know. Obviously, Bell's too old to get married at this point."

Bell elbowed him in the side. "Thanks a lot, Alex."

"Now, children," laughed Alan. "Bell, we all know you'll make a lovely bride someday. There has never been a question about that, and there is no hurry either."

"Thanks, Daddy."

"No problem, sweetie. I will probably be entirely broke on that day.".

"Oh great, now you're helping him pick on me?"

"Bell, darling, he's one of my kids, too. Of course, I have to play along with him every once in a while." He grinned back at her. "Besides, you know we're joking. Tonight is about fun. Lighten up, girlfriend."

"I know," she smiled. "For the record, that sounded awkward coming from you, Dad."

"Alan, she's right. That was awkward. Bell, they wouldn't tease you if they didn't love you," said Martin.

"How true," chimed Bernie. "I get my fair share, too."

"Okay, kids," Alex handed them each a glass of champagne. "Let's take this party to the dance floor."

Bernie, Bell, and Alex barely left the dance floor for the rest of the evening. Alan left to tend to paying the caterer and a few other business details, and Martin went back and forth between the dance floor and the bar grabbing drinks for himself or others. Bernie noted that her mother had disappeared early in the evening. Probably ran off with one of the waiters.

Alan had a surprise for the wedding couple at the end of the night.

"Okay, lovebirds. I just want to say congratulations again, and as part of your wedding gift, I've reserved you a room at the East Tropic Bed and Breakfast. A limo is waiting outside to take you there. I hope you have a wonderful evening." He leaned in, kissed Bernie on the cheek, and then shook Martin's hand. "Take care of my little girl, Martin."

Martin flashed him a smile. "I will, sir."

Bernie and Martin said goodnight and went on their way. They would spend the night at the East Tropic B&B and then fly out for their honeymoon in Ixtapa, Mexico, the following afternoon. Bernie couldn't wait to hit the beach. She was looking forward to some much-needed downtime with her new husband. She was tired of wedding planning and thinking about all of Martin's business events.

"Sweetie, we're here," said Martin.

Bernie had nodded off in the car. The day had been so long and full of excitement that she had worn herself out. Part of her wanted to sleep, but the other part knew that wedding nights were supposed to include other ventures as well. She smiled, thinking about it. A nice soak in the whirlpool might be just what she needed to wake up a bit more.

"Sorry," said Bernie.

"No need to apologize. I know you're tired. Let's go relax in the whirlpool and then catch some sleep. The hot water should help us wind down from the excitement of the day."

"Sounds good," she agreed.

They opened the door to their room and were shocked by its exotic beauty. It was like they'd walked into a tropical cabana. The smell was even that of the sea. The sound of waves gently crashing was playing in the background. The whirlpool was huge and built into one corner of the large luxurious bathroom. The bed had a beautiful canopy and decorative netting around it.

"Wow," said Martin, "This is pretty sweet."

"Yeah, it is. Let's get that whirlpool going," said Bernie.

Bernie meandered over to the nightstand, where she found chocolates and a bottle of champagne chilling in a bucket. Her father had thought of everything. She set them down by the tub and opened the card tied to the bottle's neck.

The card read: *Congratulations, Love, Dad*. It was simple and sweet. Sitting down on the edge of the tub, Bernie dipped her feet in as the water slowly filled. Martin walked up and sat down beside her. He leaned over and kissed her shoulder.

"I think tonight went quite well. What do you think?" he asked sweetly.

"It was great," said Bernie. "This is a perfect end to a beautiful day."

"I agree. We can soak away our dancers' wounds and wake up nice and refreshed in the morning for our trip."

"Dancers wounds, huh?"

"Yep, dancers wounds. I have these long dancers' legs, but they aren't used to dancing this much." He chuckled. "Might I add that you look delightful sitting here on the edge of this whirlpool? What do you say I help you take some clothes off, and have our own little private dance right here?"

"Why sir, I do believe you must be a mind reader." Bernie stood up so Martin could help her out of her dress. She'd been looking forward to this part of the evening. The whirlpool was just an added bonus.

Chapter Eleven

The honeymoon started off like any typical honeymoon would. Martin and Bernie arrived in Ixtapa. After a brief rain shower, long enough for them to receive their beautiful suite and unpack, the sun was out, and they walked together on the beach.

Bernie reached out and grabbed Martin's hand. "Isn't this beautiful?" She'd never been to Ixtapa before, but she had friends who swore it was the best spot in Mexico. So far, she was quite happy with her short experience. Now that the rain had stopped, the weather was perfect.

Martin looked over at her. "Yes, it is by far one of the most beautiful places I've ever visited, and lucky me, I get to be here with someone just as beautiful as this place," he said.

"Want to grab a drink and relax under the umbrellas?"

"Sure, sweetie, that sounds nice. We could probably use some rest after the short amount of sleep we got last night." Martin grinned at her. They had definitely given one another a workout. Bernie had been worried they wouldn't make love on their wedding night due to how tired they were, but they both got a second wind.

The night had been full of passion. It was the first time they had ever slept together, and it had gone quite well. She'd been a little nervous, but her nerves had quickly subsided.

"I'm pretty tired," said Bernie. "That flight was too bumpy for me to comfortably fall asleep. I'll go grab us some seats over there," she said as she pointed to her right.

"Okay, I'll grab us a couple of what?" he asked.

"How about a couple of Paralyzers? That's kind of how I'm feeling right now, like I just don't want to move." She laughed.

"What's in a Paralyzer?"

"I think it's Kahlua, cream, and I don't really know, it has a mocha flavor. Tastes good."

"Alrighty, two of those coming right up," he said as he walked away.

Bernie lucked out and found two loungers nearby. She threw down a couple of towels and was getting comfortable when Martin returned.

"Here you are, my lovely," he said as he handed her the drink.

"Martin, this isn't a paralyzer," she said with a confused look.

"No, I decided to go with a Pina colada. I hope that's okay?"

"Sweetie, I'm allergic to these. I thought you knew that?" Bernie also recalled that Martin had told her he shared the same allergy.

"Oh, my goodness, I must have forgotten. I'm so sorry."

"No worries, I haven't drunk any of it." She was thoroughly confused. "Martin, didn't you tell me you have the same allergy? You know these have coconut in them, don't you?"

"Oh, holy cow! I totally forgot what was in them."

"You didn't drink any, did you?"

"No. Thank goodness." He set both drinks down on the table. "While we are on this subject, are you allergic to anything else?"

"Nope, just coconut."

"Wow, of course I picked the one neither of us can have."

"Oddly, I first learned about my allergy while drinking a Pina colada." Bernadette remembered it like it was yesterday. The incident was so traumatizing that Bell and Alex swore off coconut with her. They didn't want to chance her having another episode ever again.

"Where were you when that happened?"

"I was on vacation in Belize with my brother and sister. It was a crazy night. My throat started closing up. Thank goodness for Alex and the fast-acting staff at our resort. They called paramedics and were able to get me taken care of before the coconut was able to take care of me. It was scary. Bell was panicking. Alex was the calm one. He was able to relay what was going on and get the staff whipped into action. There was a whole write-up about it online. It was slightly embarrassing."

"Wow, well, don't drink any of those on our trip," he said. "I'll make sure no coconut gets near us."

"Thanks, sweetie, you are a gem. Anyway, I think it's better I don't have any drinks after all. I could really use a nap."

"Yeah, this is the perfect spot for it, that's for sure. Would you like me to put some sunscreen on you before your nap so you don't get burnt?"

"That sounds like a lovely idea." Bernie reached into her beach bag and grabbed a bottle of sunscreen. "Here, I love this stuff. It smells like a fruity cereal I used to eat as a kid."

"Sweet, my wife is going to smell like a breakfast cereal." He shook his head as he began to smooth the lotion over her back.

"That feels great."

"I bet it does after that long plane ride."

"Would you like me to put some on you?" asked Bernie.

"No thanks, baby, I don't burn all that easily. I prefer not to smell like breakfast cereal. Ya never know, it might attract the wrong sort of people."

"Ha ha," said Bernie. "I doubt you're going to be attacked by children." His comment was kind of cute. She could give him points for that. "This is an adult's only resort."

"All the reason more, some may not be able to resist the scent of a delicious fruity cereal. Who knows how far this scent may travel—" He was cut off by Bernie whacking him playfully with a beach towel.

"Enough of that. Give me a kiss and let me take my nap so I can be awake for other more interesting activities this evening." She intended to soak in the whirlpool later with a nice bottle of wine and her new hubby.

Martin leaned in, kissed her on the lips, and then took a comfortable seat on the lounger beside her. Bernie was in heaven. The weather was perfect, and the sun felt great. It couldn't get much better than this.

Two hours had passed, and Bernie was feeling much more awake. She'd fallen asleep almost immediately. Martin had left their Pina coladas sitting on a table a short distance away. They were still full, but they had turned into a sticky melted liquid. She looked at them with distaste. As she turned to look at Martin, she realized he wasn't there. *Hm*, she wondered, *where could he have gone off to?* She decided to investigate.

She walked up the path toward the main pool and bar. Sure enough, there he was, sitting at the bar with a couple of blonde model types. She laughed at her own observation as it rolled across her mind. Sitting on a nearby chair, she watched him for a moment. It didn't take long for her to realize she recognized both girls.

Audra and Linz. The two ladies had been at a photo shoot with Bernie and Bell a few months earlier.

She took off her wrap and left it on the chair. Then she let down her hair and pushed up her girls. She knew that, hands down, she would win this little silent battle. She daubed on some red lipstick and shoved it back into her clutch. Audra and Linz were known for stealing other women's men, but Bernie wasn't just any other woman.

"Hi there," she said to the ladies as she approached. "I see you're keeping my husband company." She gave them a prize-winning smile.

"It's the least we could do, seeing as you let him out of your sight," retorted Linz, the mousy looking blonde to Martin's right. Her friend turned to look at Bernie, and her jaw dropped. Her eyes nearly popped out of her head.

"Oh, uh, hi," she sputtered. "Linz and I were about to head back to the pool." She grabbed the other girl by the elbow and gave her a tug. "I'm so sorry."

"What's your problem?" asked Linz as she turned toward her friend. It was then that she caught a glimpse of Bernadette. "Oh, dang," she said. "We'll get out of your way, Bernadette. We didn't know he was here with you, and you know the rule." The girl looked like she wanted to crawl into a hole and die. "I feel like such a jerk."

"Forget about it, Linz. I know you'd never intentionally do me any harm." Bernie noted that Martin was not wearing his wedding band. "It's an honest mistake since my new husband seems to have forgotten his wedding band."

"Perhaps we can meet up tonight for a drink? We could do some catching up. It's been a while since the swimsuit shoot in Tallahassee," said Audra. Bernie smiled at the women. She knew that both of them liked to party like rock stars any chance they were given.

"Yeah, that might work. We'll see how the day goes," said Bernie. She had no intentions of meeting up with them later, but the least she could do was be nice in the moment.

Linz smiled at Bernie. "Well, we best be going. We haven't eaten anything yet, and it's about that time."

"Audra, Linz, nice to see you both. I'll see you at the shoot next week if we don't see you for that drink later."

As the girls turned to walk away, Linz looked back and mouthed the word "sorry," again followed by "my bad."

Bernie had modeled many swimsuits and been featured in several magazines. She and her sister were swimwear icons in the United States. Linz and Audra had recently been signed to Bernie's agency. There was no way either of them wanted to jeopardize their new careers. Besides, they knew Bernie was not one to be trifled with because her family always backed her, and her sister always spoke up if she didn't like a situation.

Bernie looked at Martin. "Well now, I wake up, and you're gone, Mr. Day. On top of that, you aren't wearing your wedding band. What have you to say for yourself?" she asked.

"Sorry, sweetheart, you looked so peaceful. I didn't want to wake you. I have only been here for about five minutes. I was grabbing us a couple of Paralyzers." This time he handed her the correct drink.

She grabbed the icy beverage from his hand and took a sip. It cooled her throat and relaxed her mind.

"Those two sure took off in a hurry," he said. "What, is there some secret model code that tells other models to get lost?"

"There's a nasty little code that most models I know seem to follow. Basically stated, any man, married or single, is free game. As models, we strive to not settle down until we can no longer work. Most of us do not want to get serious for fear of ending our careers prematurely. Those two, however, were just signed to my agency, and they know that I'm an exception to the code. They also know I could end them if they make me mad. We all try to play nice and stay out of each other's way, if possible."

"You don't have to worry. I think you're the hottest thing since fire."

"Thanks." She laughed. "You didn't answer my question about your ring."

"Oh, yeah, sorry about that. I took it off because my fingers were swelling in this heat. I might have to get a second ring for summer that's a bit bigger."

"Oh, okay, we can look into that." She was satisfied with his response. Her hands were a little swollen too.

"Come over here and give me a kiss," he said.

"I think I can do that."

He pulled her close and slowly kissed her lips. It felt heavenly to be kissed with such passion.

"Why don't you sit down here," he said as he patted the chair next to him. "I have something I want to discuss with you since we're on the topic of modeling careers."

"Are you sure you don't want to go back to the room instead?" she asked.

"Not right now, Bern. I'm really enjoying the sun. There will be plenty of time for play later," he said with a smile.

"Okay," she replied, feeling a little bummed. "What's on your mind?"

"Now that we're married, I want to put more focus on moving into politics. I think it's time for you to consider hanging up your modeling career so that you can be by my side throughout my political endeavors."

The color instantly drained from Bernie's face. "Wait, what? You want me to end my career? Modeling is who I am. It's part of my family and it's what I love." She could feel the heat rising up inside her. She was not okay with giving up her career for his. That was not part of the bargain when she married him. They had never discussed it.

"Yes, I know, darling, but you are more than just a model. You're also my wife, and we have each other. Is it really that much to give up? Think about it. You can let me know later what you decide. I'm sure you'll make the right decision for our future."

Once again, Bernie was shocked by the words coming out of her man's mouth. Why should she even have to make a decision like this when she was perfectly healthy and in the best shape of her life?

"Martin, I'm going to go back to the room to take a shower." She needed to remove herself from the situation before she said something regrettable.

"What's up? Are you upset?" he asked. "There's no reason to be upset. This is just part of being a couple. Part of life in general." He looked at her and raised a questioning eyebrow.

"Martin, that's a pretty tall request, and I'm not sure I'm even remotely okay with it. You get to do what you want, but I'm supposed to give up my passion in order to stand like a dog at your side?"

"Now wait a minute, Bernadette, that's not what I said at all. You're so much more than some dog. You're my beautiful, talented wife, but sometimes that means giving certain things up to support one another."

"What exactly do you think you're giving up for me?" she growled and stormed away. She would be damned if Mr. Martin Day would get away with such requests. *Ridiculous*, she thought.

Once she got to their room, she grabbed the first pillow she saw and screamed into it. Who did he think he was? What man of her dreams would ever say such a thing to her? Had she not made it known that she planned to model as long as possible? She was a huge part of the agency, for heaven's sake.

Even after she finished modeling, she was still planning to work either with the agency or the club. She wasn't some trophy wife who wanted to look good and stay home all of the time. As she sat pondering, tears ran down her face. Her phone began to ring. It was Bell. She took a deep breath and reigned in her emotions.

"Hello?" she said as she held the phone to her ear.

"Bernie? What's going on, girl? Did you make it to Ixtapa okay? How are things?"

"Yeah, we made it without any issues. Things are great. How are things with you? Did you get the tents taken down okay?"

"Oh yeah. No worries on that. We had some fun doing it. Alex played some music while we took care of business. We did some more dancing. You know how we are."

"Yeah, I know how you are," said Bernie. She was glad her siblings were able to enjoy themselves during a not-so-pleasant task.

"Well, hey, Bern, I'll let you get back to whatever you've been doing. I'm sure you're approaching dinner time over there."

"Yeah. I'm getting cleaned up from being on the beach. Would you believe that Linz and Audra are here, and they were hitting on Martin?"

"What? Shut up! Did you put those little trollops in their places?"

"It didn't take much. They realized who I was immediately, and they both felt like heels."

"No doubt." She laughed. "It's nice to be on top, isn't it? Not that I want to make people feel like they aren't as good, but when it comes to defending a relationship, I wouldn't blame anyone."

"Alright, sis. I'm gonna let you go. I love you. Nice to hear your voice," said Bernie.

"Love you, too. Have fun and be careful," said Bell. Bernie could hear the extra inflection in her voice. Her sister knew her better than anyone else. Alex knew her almost as well. Even though they were trying not to show it, she knew they were both on guard. She hoped they were wrong, but strange things were happening, and she couldn't find a positive way to explain them.

Was she overreacting? Was this normal for a man to ask his wife to quit her job and just be with him? She felt so out of place in her own life at that moment. She didn't really know what to do. She remembered a time when she was five. She'd been at the grocery store with her mother, and while her mother was talking to a clerk, she wandered off. She'd only been lost for ten minutes, but she panicked, and it had felt like an eternity. That was how she felt at that very moment.

Bernie peeled off her swimsuit and began filling the oversized whirlpool. Maybe a nice bubble bath would help her process these new feelings. The past few days had been highly stressful. Maybe she was just feeling emotional and blowing things out of proportion.

As she waited for the tub to fill, she walked over to the fridge to see what items were inside. "Fully stocked," she mused aloud. "Don't mind if I do." She reached in and grabbed a mini bottle of sparkling wine. "At the very least, I'm going to enjoy this bubble bath." She popped the bottle open and poured it into a glass.

Slipping into the tub, she realized that, ironically this seemed to be the highlight of her honeymoon thus far. She took a sip of wine. It refreshed and relaxed her as it slid down her throat. She needed to let go. Too many things were whirring about her mind.

Had she made a mistake marrying Martin? She didn't know what to do other than give it more time. She didn't believe in divorce. She believed in working through problems and growing stronger. Leaving was not an option for her at this point. Besides, they hadn't even been married for two full days. Marriage could take some adjustment time, couldn't it?

An hour and a half had passed when a knock came at the door. Bernie had been putting the final touches on her makeup for the evening. She was dressed in a sparkly light blue evening gown.

"Hello?" she asked the closed door.

"Hi, this is Rod from guest services. I have a delivery for you," he said.

"Is it Chinese food?" Bernie laughed. She had been thinking about Bell and how it was mostly Chinese or pizza when a delivery came to their house.

"Um, no, but you did just guess my other job." He laughed.

"Oh, just a second," said Bernie as she fumbled with the door lock.

The gentleman on the other side was tall and kind-looking. "Here you are, madam," said Rod as he put a vase of two dozen roses down on the table.

"Oh, wow, those are gorgeous."

"Here's the card that came with them."

Bernie dug into her purse and pulled out a five-dollar bill. She handed it to Rod. "Thank you," she said as he turned to leave. She shut the door behind him and tore open the card. It read:

Darling,

I'll be late to dinner. I'm playing volleyball with a couple of guys on the beach.

I love you,
Martin

"Wonderful," said Bernie. "Just wonderful." She wandered over to the window and looked out at the beach. There was no one at the volleyball court. Not one person. *Great,* she thought. Where on earth had that man gone? She continued to scan the beach. Why did he think it was okay to be late to dinner on the first night of their honeymoon?

As she was about to give up, she saw him emerge from a tent on the beach, a brunette in tow. Bernie watched as he stopped and turned toward her. He touched her shoulder and then walked away. Bernie was fuming. What in the hell was going on?

Fifteen minutes later, he entered the hotel room. Bernie was still fuming. The fuming had required another mini bottle of sparkling wine.

"Where have you been?" she demanded.

"I see you got the flowers. Did you read the card?" Martin asked.

"Yes, Martin. I read the card. The card was a lie," she seethed.

"Let me explain," he said with a fearful look.

"Yes, do explain. I saw you with the brunette on the beach, coming out of a tent. Please explain that."

"I was getting a massage, Bern. I didn't tell you because I didn't want you to be upset about missing out on that. Obviously, I made a mistake in saying I was playing volleyball. I should have just told you, but I was also embarrassed."

"Why on earth would you be embarrassed?"

"Well, I've never had a real massage before. It doesn't seem like something men should do," he replied sheepishly.

"Martin, lots of men get massages. It's not unusual at all." She thought about the situation for a moment. Apparently, she'd been wrong in surmising that he might be the type of man that would join her for a spa day. "It doesn't make you less of a man," she said. "It's the lying that makes you seem like less of a man. If you can't be honest with me, then we shouldn't have even bothered with this marriage," she began to tear up again. "I can't handle this!" She screamed. "This whole day has been horrible. We've only been married for a day and a half, and it feels like a great big mess!"

"Whoa, calm down, Bern," he said as he grabbed her and wrapped her in a bear hug. "Things are going to be okay. I didn't realize you were feeling so awful. What can I do to make this up to you? I want you to be happy." He grabbed her chin and tipped her head back so that he could look into her eyes. "You're my whole world now. We'll figure this out, okay?"

"Okay," she said with a whimper.

"What would you like to do right now? Do you want to get some food? Maybe a nice meal will help."

"Yes. Please." She turned away from him to wipe the tears from her face. "I want this to work."

"Baby, why wouldn't it work? We're great together," said Martin. "This is a new phase in our relationship, and the past couple of months have been very stressful for everyone, especially you. Let's just relax. No business until we get home. Things will get better. I promise. Now let's go to the Italian restaurant and get some tasty food," he said, reaching for her hand.

"That would be nice," she said, smiling back at him. Maybe he was right. Maybe this was just stress related. They did plan a lot of things in a very short amount of time. The wedding, the honeymoon, and moving. She picked up her purse and turned toward Martin. Linking her arm through his, they headed out the door.

Martin was right. The rest of the honeymoon was spectacular. They snorkeled, para-sailed, hiked, and of course, enjoyed lots of relaxation and love-making. They even made love on a private boat which was as close to being an exhibitionist as Bernie would probably ever get.

The trip overall was memorable. All was right in the world once again. The following day they would fly back home and into reality. Bernie didn't want to leave, but she knew the real world was calling.

Chapter Twelve

As they picked up their luggage, Bernie heard a shrill voice squealing her name. She had no idea that Bell and Alex were meeting her and Martin at the airport, but she was happy all the same. She had missed her crazy sister and couldn't wait to tell her about the rest of the trip.

"O.M.G.!" yelled Alex. "You're so tan, girl! I want to hear all about this trip. Don't spare a single detail! Hello, Martin," he said as an afterthought.

"Alex," acknowledged Martin. "You're awfully awake for this time of the morning."

"Oh, you have no idea. We just left the club. It was a blast. I'm wired!"

"That's an understatement," said Bell. "I think someone gave him something." She glared at him.

"Whatever. You know I'm just in a great mood," said Alex.

"Your great mood has a name," said Bell, "and it's Hector Perago."

"Oh, my goodness," said Bernie, "you finally followed through with it? I thought we were going to owe Hector forever on this one. On top of that, it's working? I'm not sure which has my mind blown more? Not that I didn't think you two would be perfect together, but you can be stubborn."

"Hey, kids," interjected Martin, "I would like to go home, please. It's four in the morning, and I didn't sleep at all on the plane."

"Neither did I," said Bernie, "but that doesn't change my excitement about seeing my siblings."

"Please, I beg of you. I need some sleep," he whined.

Bell rolled her eyes from behind Martin. "Come on, let's go."

The foursome each grabbed a piece of luggage and headed for the car. Bernie was so tired she decided to ignore Martin's childlike behavior. As a matter of fact, everyone seemed to be ignoring everyone. No one spoke the entire ride across town. Bernie fell asleep and did not wake up until they reached her and Martin's home.

The first morning she officially woke in her new home, Bernie felt pretty good. She gave a big yawn and stretched. Martin was no longer in bed. She got up and walked over to the edge of the balcony.

"Morning, babe," said Martin. He was completely dressed and ready to go somewhere.

"What are you up to?" asked Bernie.

"Your father left a message on my phone last night asking me to meet him this morning for a round of golf. He wanted to discuss a few things with me."

"How come you didn't tell me this yesterday?"

"It was late when I got the message. You had already crawled into bed and fallen asleep. Sorry, babe. Anyway, I have to get going. Tee time is in twenty-five minutes. I don't want to be late, you understand, right?"

"I thought we'd have a nice quiet day back home, but I suppose I can meet up with Bell. Have fun." She didn't really understand, but she didn't seem to have much say at this point.

Martin blew her a kiss and walked out the door. Bernie once again was left feeling slightly confused by the man's behavior. She picked up the phone and dialed Bell's number.

"Hey. What's up?" asked her sister from the other end of the line.

"Hi, Bell, what are you doing today?" asked Bernie.

"I don't really have any plans. Do you want to grab some brunch and go shopping? Maybe see a movie? I can pick you up."

"Actually, I'll meet you at the mall. I have no idea what Martin's plans are for this evening, so I'd rather drive myself.

"No problem," said Bell. "I'll see you there."

Bernie hung up the phone and skipped off toward the shower. She supposed she should be clean if she was going to go out to brunch and a movie or whatever. A shower would be welcome after the flight home. She'd been much too tired to do so earlier.

Bernie turned on the radio and stepped into the hot steamy water. It felt nice. Martin had picked up her favorite toiletries, so everything was already in place. Technically she hadn't moved all of her stuff in yet. That would happen later in the week. She hated moving, but this move was clearly different than others.

Martin was pulling up to the clubhouse on the other side of town, where Alan patiently awaited him. Alan had made it his business to get to know Martin better. He felt that if his youngest was certain that this was what she wanted, he should make an effort to know who was joining the family. He didn't like surprises, so he chose to keep Martin close. Thus far, Martin seemed like a decent guy. Most of what Alan did was for his daughter, even though it may have appeared that he was doing things to be nice to Martin.

"Good morning, Mr. Price. How are you fairing on this gorgeous day?"

"Wonderfully, Martin. I've been looking forward to this game of golf since we discussed it at the wedding reception." He grinned like a schoolboy. Any day he could play golf was a great day for Alan. The only thing better would be if he could get his children to take up the sport. Try as he might, he could not convince them to golf regularly. They just didn't care about the game as much as he did.

Martin took a moment to scan the course. "Me too, sir, me too. Why don't we get our cart and let this little competition commence?" He hadn't been to this particular course before, but it was considered more challenging than usual, and he thought it might be a lot of fun.

The first hole was pretty long but a straight shot down the fairway. Both men were able to knock in at one under par. The two made great competitors since both had been avid golfers since childhood. Martin knew that he would be greatly respected if he could beat Alan at this game.

Alan wanted to destroy Martin on the golf course to prove he could, but it was still all in good fun. If Martin won, he would have to play him again to take back the title of champ. Alan was always up for a nice competitive rematch.

"Martin, this second hole is going to be a little bit trickier. It's a par six. Ya think you can handle all those twists and turns?"

"Bring it, Mr. Price, just bring it," he replied with a grin.

"Oh, I will, kid, and please, call me Alan. After all, we are family now."

The rest of the afternoon was back and forth. Sometimes Alan was ahead, and other times Martin would squeak by. At the eighteenth hole, Alan had clearly become the winner. He sunk the ball in at two under par, beating Martin by four strokes. Alan smiled to himself. He rarely ever lost, and he hadn't really thought this time would be any different. He was still the big man on the course.

"Good game, kid. Let's go to my club, and you can buy me a drink" He laughed. "No, but really, let's go to the club. I have something to discuss with you. We can have the girls meet us there for dinner. I heard they were out shopping together."

"Okay, sounds good," said Martin. "Lead the way." He wasn't happy that he'd lost, but he knew there would be plenty of time to steal the title. Besides, he had put up a pretty good fight.

Alan stepped off across the lot and then turned toward Martin. "Why don't you ride with me? We can get your car later. It's silly to waste gas when we're going to the same place, and we both have to come back this way to go home."

Martin gladly hopped into Alan's Porsche. He hadn't ridden in this car yet, but he'd been dying to ever since he laid eyes on it at Alan's house. Alan had kept it tucked in the garage, and Martin had taken a peek at it on his and Bernie's wedding day. He instantly fell in love.

"Smooth ride, isn't she?"

"Oh, yes she is," said Martin.

"You think you could handle a car like this, son?"

"I would like to think so."

"Well, why don't you drive," said Alan as he pulled over to the side of the road. "I love this car, but I can also tell when a man is in the presence of something he finds spectacular. You have a look on your face that tells me this would mean a great deal to you."

"Wow, you can see all that on my face?" asked Martin.

"Ha, nah, Bernie told me she thought you may love my car more than her. She said she caught you staring at it on your wedding day."

"Oh great, my wife thinks I love this car more than her, and it's not even mine."

"Don't worry. I told her that the love a man feels for his car is on a totally different level than the love he feels for his wife. She seemed to understand. Also, I'm pretty sure this car now belongs to you, son." He handed the keys to Martin. Martin's jaw dropped open, and his eyes widened in disbelief.

"Wha—what?" Martin was rarely speechless. He would have never dreamt that Alan would give him such a gift. It made him feel like he had a real family for once.

"It's yours. I'm making a new tradition. When one of my children marries, I spend a fun day on the golf course with the new family addition, and then I give them a very expensive gift." He laughed, and then his face became serious again. "Seriously, Martin, I want you to have it. I've already found my next vehicle, and this one clearly makes you happy. Bernie also loves it, so I thought it would be nice for the both of you."

"Wow," said Martin. "I don't know what to say."

"A 'thank you' will suffice," said Alan.

"Thank you, sir." He reached out to shake Alan's hand.

"No, son. This is more of a father-son hugging moment," he said, pulling Martin into a hug. "You make my daughter happy, and that makes me happy. Not to mention you're a great competitor on the golf course, which makes me even more ecstatic to have you in my family, and call me Alan, please."

"Thank you, Alan. I'll take good care of her."

"I know you will. Now, let's get you into the driver's seat, and we'll continue on with our schedule," he said as he hopped out of the car. "We have much to discuss."

Martin trotted around the outside of the car and climbed into the driver's seat. He was still in shock at this sudden exchange, but he couldn't have been happier.

Over at the mall, Bell was making a scene.

"I cannot believe they don't have these shoes in my size. They always have my size. I'm so frustrated and disappointed. Why is this happening to me?"

"Bell, calm down. It doesn't matter anyway. You heard the sales associate. She said they could order them." Bernie rolled her eyes. She didn't know what was going on with her sister. She was acting like a child. Everyone in the store was staring at her, which meant negative press if anyone recognized them. She hated shopping at the mall, even if it was considered high-end. It felt too risky.

"I'm not waiting for them to come in. I need them for tonight, Bernadette!"

"Wow, it's not like you to become this upset over a pair of shoes that are out of stock. What's going on?"

"If you must know, I have a date, and it's an important one."

"With whom?" asked Bernie.

"Oh no, I'm not telling you. Not until it becomes more serious. Whenever I tell you about my dates you pick on me, and then I get psyched out, and everything goes to heck. I won't do that ever again. I've learned my lesson."

"Seriously? What are you talking about, Bell? When have I ever picked on you about a date? You sound crazy right now, and you're acting like a spoiled brat. Honestly, it's embarrassing. People are staring."

Bell looked at Bernie and burst into tears. "Everything's a mess," she howled.

Bernie gave the sales associate an apologetic look and ushered Bell into a dressing room to further deal with the situation. Luckily the dressing rooms were enclosed from floor to ceiling and padded so that people outside couldn't hear her sister's incessant wailing.

"You need to stop now and tell me what's really going on," said Bernie. She handed Bell a facial tissue. "Please, Bell. I'm listening," she begged.

Bell's tears began to slow. She wiped her face off and looked up at her sister from the bench she was sitting on. She looked like she was far away in deep thought. She barely blinked as she zoned out, staring past Bernie.

"Bell," Bernie snapped her fingers. "Hey! Bell! Can you hear me?"

Bell jolted back to the present moment. "Sorry."

"That's fine. I know it happens to the best of us sometimes, but seriously, please tell me what's going on?"

"I feel like I'm losing you."

Bernie took a step back, her brow wrinkling. "What do you mean you feel like you're losing me?"

"Bernadette, you got engaged to Martin, and you haven't acted yourself since. You've barely gone anywhere with me and Alex unless it was wedding business. You send my calls to voicemail more often than not. You cancel plans. You seem short when you do talk to me, and it's as if you now have a curfew when we do get together. Bernie, this isn't you."

"Bell, I just got back from my honeymoon. I haven't even seen you for a week. I think you're imagining this. You don't understand long-term relationships because you've never had one. Things can't be the same as they were. I cannot go gallivanting all over the countryside with you and Alex for the rest of my life. I have things I need to do. I have responsibilities and a husband to tend to."

"Can you hear yourself?" asked Bell. "It's like you contracted some disease rather than got married. You sound more like a slave than a wife to me."

"Whatever, Bell. If this is how it's going to be, then perhaps we shouldn't have these get-togethers at all. I love Martin, and I'm sticking by him. He's a good man, and he takes care of me."

"Does he, Bernie? He didn't even tell you about this golf outing with Dad, did he? He's known about it since the wedding night. I overheard them discussing it. He keeps you in the dark so he can control everything."

"Of course, he told me about it," Bernie lied. She couldn't let Bell know she was right. "I'm leaving." She stormed out of the dressing room.

"Bernadette!" yelled Bell.

Bernadette didn't stop. She walked right out of the mall and headed straight for her car. She shook her head as she thought about what Bell had said. She just got home from her honeymoon, there hadn't even been time to settle into her marriage, and her sister was already whining about change.

As Bernie approached her car, someone leaning up against the passenger side caught her off guard. It was Matthew. She hadn't thought she'd see him again, but then that wouldn't be the first time she'd been wrong that day. Her blood began to boil as she prepared herself for round two.

"Hey, Bernadette. I know I'm the last person you want to see."

"You're correct," she replied curtly. "If you know this, why are you here?"

"I'm here for two reasons, but only one really concerns you at this time. I'm sorry about how things went the other day when we first met. I should have known better than to bring up something so sensitive in the manner that I did. I need you to understand that if you ever need me for anything, if things do get bad, if you start to see any signs of what I informed you of, you have an ally in me. I will fight for you and your family."

"Thank you for the apology, but I don't trust you in the least. I won't be needing you as an ally, so please, move along." She heard every word he said and hoped she would never need to cash in on his offer. She couldn't stand the sight of him.

"That may be true now, Bernadette, but I still want you to know where you can go if you need help. I'll stand by what I said. Anyway, I'm leaving in a few days for Texas. I have an ongoing case out there."

"Please go." Bernie pointed him away from her car.

"You take care of yourself," he said as he turned and headed for the mall entrance.

"Bernadette got into her car and plopped down on the front seat. The day had been torture in so many ways. *What next?* she thought as her ringing phone broke into her thoughts. It was Martin.

"Hello?"

"Hey, baby," he purred from the other end.

"Hi, Martin. How are things going with Daddy?" She wasn't happy with him at the moment either. He'd pushed off this golf outing like it was a last-minute decision when, in reality, he'd known about it for over a week.

"Things are going swimmingly. Why don't you come over to the club and have dinner with us. There's a lot to tell you," he said.

"Okay, sweetie, I'm on my way. Love you." She didn't even wait for him to respond. She hung up the phone and began to pull out of her parking spot.

As she drove down the road, she couldn't help but wonder why Martin was so excited. Something great must have happened. There was a huge difference between the days they'd had. As she pulled up to the club, she noted that Daddy's car was in its usual spot, but Martin's was nowhere to be seen. Had he arrived yet?

Bernie opened her door and slid her long legs out. She stood up and stretched off the stress and anger. The night would be better. It had to be better than the day.

"Baby!" yelled Martin from the doorway. "Come on in." He grinned with his usual charm. He sure was handsome.

"Hold your horses. I'm not going to run," Bernie said with a laugh.

He met her halfway and picked her up, swinging her in a circle. "I've missed you."

"I missed you, too," said Bernie. "This day has been rough. I got into it with Bell. She's so frustrating."

"Oh, I'm sorry. It'll get better. I swear on it." He grabbed her hand and ushered her through the door toward her Daddy's favorite table. Bradley gave a small acknowledging wave. She smiled back.

"Who are you smiling at?" asked Martin.

"Bradley," she said without hesitation.

"I wish you wouldn't. You're my woman, after all." His face became stern as his eyes darkened.

"It's nothing, Martin. He's just an old friend. He's been with the club for a very long time."

"I don't care. Anyway, let's go eat."

"Hi, Daddy."

"Bernadette, you look lovely as always. How'd I get so lucky to have two of the most beautiful daughters in the world?"

"The world, Daddy? Try the universe," she joked.

"Ah yes, my mistake, the universe." Adoration shone in his eyes. "We have some exciting news for you, Bernadette. I've decided to give you and Martin my Porsche. She'll be in better hands with you, and as I told Martin, I've already picked out my next car."

"Wow, that is quite unexpected," said Bernie.

"I know how much you enjoy riding in the Porsche, so I figured why not give it to you and Martin as a gift. I was planning to get a different car, and it would be nice to keep her in the family in case I ever have the desire to see her again."

"We'll take great care of her," said Bernadette. "Thank you."

"I know you will. Now where is that sister of yours?" asked Alan.

"Bell's at the mall, and she has a date, so I don't think we'll be seeing her this evening."

Alan frowned. "That's unfortunate. I guess we'll have to try to enjoy dinner without her."

The evening was low-key. They ate and chatted about cars. Bernie was happy to spend time with family, but sad that she and Bell were not speaking. She knew that an argument like this could drag on for a while. They rarely fought, but when they did, there were times when the silence lasted for days.

Weeks went by. Bell didn't call Bernie, and Bernie didn't call Bell. Their father and Alex pleaded with them both, but neither wanted to be the first to contact the other. They were busy with their lives and were both okay with the distance.

Bernie was okay with the distance because she knew Bell didn't approve of her marriage. She was tired of the jabs and pointed comments her sister made at Martin's expense. She didn't want to give her a chance to add any more pain to her already frustrating life because she was definitely putting up a front regarding her happiness. She was not as happy as she'd been before she married Martin. She was still, however, hell-bent on making it work.

Bell was okay with the distance because she had a secret of her own. She was seeing someone that Bernie would disapprove of. She had hit it off with Matthew and didn't want Bernie to know about their meetings. Matt was a sweet, caring guy. He was genuine, and she believed in him. She believed now, more than ever, that Bernie had made a poor choice in marrying Martin.

Despite being in wartime, Alex was the connection between Bernadette and Bell. Each wanted to know what the other was doing. Alex had not told Bernie about Matt, but he was telling Bell and Matt anything questionable he saw going on between Martin and Bernie. He was their eyes to make sure Bernadette was safe. So far, Alex hadn't seen any issues, but he didn't appreciate Martin requesting Bernie's presence at every political event he attended. Every moment she spent at Martin's side was another moment she rejected a modeling job.

Over the past weeks, Alan spent much time golfing with Martin. He had become quite entranced by Martin's charm and his golf game. It was accurate to say that he was blinded by the front that Martin had put up. Alan's friendship and trust were easy to gain, which was why he relied on a prestigious group of lawyers to help him make decisions regarding his businesses. When it came to his personal life, however, he sometimes moved without thinking things through.

The weeks of quiet between his daughters were agonizing. A month had gone by. Finally, the day came when Alan decided enough was enough. He was tired of his girls not speaking and wanted to be in the same room as both of them at the same time. So, Alan decided to call each of them and ask them to meet him for dinner at the club. He didn't tell them that they both would be there.

Bernie was the first to arrive. She walked in with a smile on her face. She clearly wasn't expecting anything. Martin was already with her father because they had been out golfing. She had treated herself to a massage and a coffee at her favorite bistro. She was in an exceptional mood.

"Good evening, Bernadette. You look well-rested." Her father smiled.

"Yep, I had a fairly relaxing day. I got a massage and some coffee. It was nice. What did you two do today?"

Martin smiled back at Bernie. He was awfully quiet, but he looked pretty happy as well.

"We played eighteen holes and then came over here to play pool. I'd agree that it has been quite a relaxing day," replied Alan. "Why don't you have a seat? I have something to tell you." He looked at Martin and then back at Bernadette. "I have decided, since Martin's business is money, to appoint him as the executor of my estate as well as power of attorney in case anything happens to me, and I'm unable to make my own decisions. I didn't want to leave such big burdens on you girls, and we both know Alex would struggle if faced with such an emotional decision."

"Daddy, that's a major decision. I don't know what to say about that other than, are you sure it's what you want?" Bernadette was appalled but hoped it didn't show on her face. She couldn't believe that her father would do this. He usually had lawyers present when he made these types of decisions.

"Did you speak to your lawyers about your plans?" asked Bernie.

"No, sweetheart. This is a personal decision. You love Martin, and as I've gotten to know him over the passing months, I feel comfortable with this decision. I don't want to put you kids through any more fights or arguments regarding my estate or well-being. I figured that this would be a little easier on you all. Besides, I've seen Martin in action, and he's an amazing businessman. He'll know how to handle all of this."

"I feel that you should have a lawyer involved with this, even though we're all family."

"I've drafted the documents, and Martin has already signed them. We took care of everything this afternoon between golf and pool. I thought you'd be pleased with this decision."

"I'm not sure I understand, and I don't know that Bell or Alex will either."

"Why do you say that?" asked Alan.

"I don't know," Bernie replied. She was feeling a bit panicky. She wasn't even sure herself that Martin's intentions were pure. "Maybe it's fine. I need to use the powder room. Excuse me," she said. She wanted to scream.

This was completely unexpected. Bernie entered the ladies' room and stopped in front of the floor-length mirror. She looked fine, but she didn't feel it.

Turning from the mirror, she walked over to the vanity. Leaning over, she splashed some cold water on her face. "Great, I messed up my eyeliner." She sighed as she reached for a facial tissue.

"Having a rough day?" asked a familiar voice from behind her. Bernie jumped. She hadn't expected anyone to be there.

"What are you doing in here?" she asked. "This is the ladies' room, my friend." She let out a half-laugh.

"Sorry, I didn't mean to scare you, but I saw you leave the table," said Bradley. "I could tell you were upset."

"Very observant, aren't you. Still, this is the ladies' room. What if someone comes in?"

"Trust me. No one's going to come in. I put up the maintenance sign. Besides, no other women are in the club right now." He reached over and placed his hands on Bernie's shoulders. "You can trust me. You know that."

"Oh, Bradley," she said as she whipped around to face him. "I thought I had everything figured out, yet things have moved faster than I can handle. I married this seemingly perfect man. He has a presence, and he's handsome. People pay attention when he's in the room. He made me feel like I was his queen and special. Now that the wedding and honeymoon are over, I'm not sure what to think. He drags me to political event after political event. I'm no longer certain he's the white horse I thought I'd found. Random situations and conversations keep popping up that make me question my own sanity."

He nodded his concern and encouraged her to go on.

"Now Daddy's putting all of his trust into him, and Bell is taking all of her trust away from me. Daddy's usually a great judge of character when it comes to men, but then so is Bell. So, who's right? Obviously, they both can't be right in this instance. I feel like I'm losing my mind. One minute, Martin's hot; the next, he's cold. I don't know if we're on or off. My world feels like sheer madness. I haven't told anyone else this, but I'm not happier since entering into this marriage."

"Take a deep breath," he said calmly. "Bernadette, you're going to be fine. If you need help, though, you can always ask for it. You have many people willing to be there for you, and you know I'll do whatever I can for you. If things are as bad as you're making them sound, you know you can leave this marriage, right?"

"No, I don't think I can. I don't believe in divorce. I know I don't attend church on a regular basis, but I believe in sticking by my decisions, so I'm going to do everything I can to figure this out."

"Okay. I'm behind your decision, no matter what it is. As far as Bell goes, I have no idea what you are fighting about, but you know Bell. She'll eventually forgive and forget, and so will you. Regarding Martin and your father, what exactly is going on?"

"Daddy made Martin his power of attorney."

"Yikes. That is a little unexpected, huh? Usually, the old man has to know someone for years before he genuinely trusts them. Must be going soft in his old age."

"No, it's not that. He doesn't put trust in business partnerships as quickly because he has advisors to make sure he's making the right decisions. In his personal life, he wears his heart on his sleeve. If only he had advisors for his personal life." A look of helplessness washed over her face. "Anyway, I better get back before they wonder where I went," said Bernie.

"Okay. You head out, and I'll wait a bit so no one notices," Bradley said with a wink.

"Thank you, Bradley." She leaned in and kissed him on the cheek. "You're a wonderful man. Don't ever let anyone tell you differently."

At the table, Martin and Alan were still chatting about their plans and earlier game. Bernadette felt like a flat, third wheel. As she sat back down, Bell walked in. Bernie immediately went pale. She didn't know if she could handle any more drama that evening.

"Bernie, may I speak with you?" asked Bell.

"I don't have anything to say to you at this time," she replied.

"Bernadette, is that any way to treat your big sister?" asked their father. His look was disapproving, and Bernie could tell he wasn't going to let things be.

"No, I suppose not, but she deserves it, Daddy."

"She does now? What, pray tell, did she do to deserve such a cold shoulder from one of her biggest fans?"

"Daddy, you don't want to be a part of this," warned Bell. "Trust me. It's best to leave this between us."

"Why don't you two go back to the VIP room and hash this out while we order some appetizers and get this evening started? I expect you back shortly, so get to it," he ordered.

The girls just stood where they were and stared at their father. Martin sat back and quietly observed.

"So, help me, ladies, if you don't go back there and deal with this right now, I will cancel your trust funds."

Bernadette got up and turned to face her father and Martin. Bell grabbed Bernie by the wrist.

"We'll go and deal with this, but, just so you know, it's because we love you, and we don't want to hurt anyone else by our actions, and it is clear that this is hurting you."

"What she said," agreed Bell. We shall be back shortly." Giving Bernie's wrist a tug, she forced her along.

Once they were in the VIP suite, Bernie relaxed and let her guard down. She didn't really want to be angry at anyone, but this day was throwing daggers.

"Speak your mind," she said to Bell.

"Uh-huh. Talk about a friendly response." Bell let out a deep sigh. "I'm sorry for how I've been acting. I want to offer an ear to you if you need one."

"You haven't exactly been on my side as of late. Why would you want to listen now?"

"Because, regardless of what's happening, we are sisters and have always been best friends. I'm tired of this battle between us. We shouldn't be fighting. So please, tell me what's going on, and I'll do my best to listen and help however I can."

A floodgate opened. Bernie couldn't hold in her emotions any longer.

"Bell, I don't know what's going on anymore. Things have moved so fast between Martin and me. On our honeymoon, he informed me that he wants me to quit modeling, and tonight, Daddy, out of the blue, named him as the executor of his estate and his power of attorney.

"Everything feels so out of control, and I know a huge part of this is my fault. On top of it all, you and Daddy have different views of Martin, and you both have always been such great judges of character. Who's right? I'm overwhelmed by all the changes, and I don't know how to sort out everything that happened to me over the past month. I feel like I'm losing my mind." Tears began to roll down Bernie's face, and her body began to tremble.

Bell wrapped her in a hug. Quietly, she said, "Take a deep breath. Just breathe for a second. You're going to be okay. I was wrong to act the way I did at the mall. I really am sorry for that. As for the rest of this situation, I want you to know I want to be your ally, not your enemy. If you want me to stay out of it, I will, but just so you know, I don't trust him. I have no idea why Daddy does. I cannot believe he gave all of that power to Martin and not one of us."

"He would have given it to us, but he thinks that none of us are capable, including Alex, of making the necessary decisions if it came down to it. He thinks we would be too emotional."

"He might be right, but still. He could have spoken to us about it rather than naming someone else who isn't blood. He's practically a stranger."

"Practically a stranger. Is that who I married? They've been spending a lot of time together. Clearly, Martin has some finesse, and Daddy sees something trustworthy in him."

"I'm sorry, Bern, I didn't mean it like that. Though you have only known him in person for a short time. Daddy really hasn't known him long at all. Not long enough for the decision he made today."

"I think this is going to require some adjustment for all of us," she said.

"Maybe. Do you want to discuss anything else?"

"Not really. I'm not in a very talkative mood."

"How about we stay here a little longer and enjoy a glass of wine?" asked Bell.

"Sure, that seems better than going back to the table. You can buzz him over," she said. Bernie felt a little better now that she and Bell were speaking. She didn't think she could handle this situation if Bell were not on her side.

Bell hit the button on the wall to signal Bradley.

"Ladies," he said as he walked into the room. "What can I get for you?" He smiled at Bernie. Bernie felt weakened by his charm. She felt even more vulnerable in his presence.

"We would like a glass of the house Pinot Grigio please," she said.

"Coming right up," Bradley replied with a bow.

Once he was out of earshot, Bell turned to her sister. "Bernie, I know this is neither here nor there." She paused.

"What?" Bernie knew she didn't want to hear what Bell was about to say. She could sense where the conversation was going.

"Bradley only has eyes for you. You know that, right?"

"Whatever. Like you said, it's neither here nor there." Her response had been on the defensive side.

"Right, but in case you didn't realize it, that boy is genuinely taken with you. He has been for quite some time, and he thinks you neither care nor have you noticed."

"We've been friends for a long time. I never thought of him as anything else because he works here, and I didn't think it right to mix business with pleasure. I doubt he really cares like you say he does. We just like to joke around. There was a brief time when I admit I thought about him and what it would be like to go on a date, but again, he works for our family. It seemed morally wrong."

"Whatever you want to believe, chica. I wonder why he never approached you even before Martin came along."

"Probably because he knows we're just friends."

"Okay, this is getting nowhere." She laughed.

Bradley walked back into the room carrying the two glasses of wine. He handed the first to Bell, and then with a bow and a wink, the second was delicately handed to Bernie. She smiled and could feel herself blush.

"Thank you, my friend," she said pointedly.

"Any time, my beautiful flower." He walked out of the room, and Bell gawked at her.

"My butt he doesn't like you." She grinned. "You, *my friend*, are full of it as well if you say you don't feel anything when that boy smiles at you. You're beet red."

"Hush, you. I'm not discussing this any further." She was embarrassed that her body could have such a disobedient reaction to another man as a married woman.

"Fine, Bern, we won't say another word about it. Moving on, do you want to come with Alex and me to see Bon Jovi tonight? We have an extra ticket because Hector had to bow out at the last minute. Some show crisis."

"Bon Jovi? Seriously? Heck yeah, I want to go see Bon Jovi!" she squealed.

"Okay, it's a date then. Alex will pick us up at seven tonight. He's hoping we can acquire some backstage passes. I'm not holding my breath, but you never know."

"That would be sweet, but you're right. I wouldn't hold my breath."

"Are we okay now?" asked Bell.

"Yeah, we're okay."

"We better get back to Daddy and your man."

"Yeah, I suppose." She picked up her glass of wine and returned to the guys. Bell followed closely behind.

"Daddy, Martin," said Bell, "Bernie and I will be picked up in an hour by Alex. We're going to the Bon Jovi concert tonight."

"What, where are our tickets?" asked Alan.

"Sorry, Daddy, Hector bowed out, so we had one extra ticket, which I offered to Bernie since she and I haven't had much quality time together as of late."

"I understand," said Alan. "I'm glad you two seem to have worked out whatever your tiff was over."

"Me too," said Bell.

Bernie looked over at Martin and noticed a look of irritation. His face lightened the second he noticed her gaze. She wondered if he was really upset?

"Is that okay with you, Martin? May I go to the concert?" she asked.

"Yeah, don't let me stand in your way," he said coolly.

"Sweet!" said Bell. "I'm super excited!"

"Do you girls have clothing to wear tonight?" asked Alan.

"Oh, shoot," they looked at each other, "I guess we didn't think about that. We don't really have time to go back to the house at this point," said Bell.

"Okay, you know I keep a few things around just for these situations," said Alan.

"Bernie, go ask Bradley to give you the key to the wardrobe in the VIP room."

"Come on, Bell, we'd better do this quickly."

"Before you go, what would you like for dinner tonight?" asked Alan.

"Oh, I'll have a black and blue salad, with the steak medium rare, please," said Bernie.

"The same," replied Bell.

"All right, that was simple enough. Now go get changed," he said.

As the girls walked away, Alan couldn't help but muse over how wonderful his children were.

"So, Martin, where were we?" he asked.

Both girls were dressed and ready to attend the concert. They had chosen little black dresses for their night out. Bernie chose a pair of purple shoes to go with hers, whereas Bell chose a silver pair. They had matching bags, and they both looked stunning, as usual.

Alex showed up just as they were finishing their meals. He walked into the club as if he owned the place, which he technically did. Alan had written in his will that this place would belong to Bell, Bernie, and Alex if anything happened to him. Alex didn't want anything to happen to Alan, but knowing that this place was partially his was nice. It felt like home, and he treated it that way.

"Hello to my favorite family," he said. "How are you all doing this fine evening?"

"Great, Alex," said Alan. "Would you like a glass of wine before you go?"

"No, sir, I think it's best we get a move on. We don't want to be late. The show starts at eight."

"Okay, kids, you have a great evening. Martin and I are going to hang out here, chat it up some more, and play some pool. We'll see you later." He hugged each of the girls goodbye and shook Alex's hand.

Bernie walked over and kissed Martin. He barely reacted. "I'll see you later, love."

"Love you," he replied coldly. No one seemed to notice how Martin was acting except Bernie. *Where is this coming from?* She wondered. She turned and followed Alex and Bell out the door.

She didn't think another thought about Martin and his poor reaction until she got home that night.

The three had a blast at the concert. Alex had gotten them front-row seats. Bernadette had never seen Bon Jovi before, so this was a complete thrill. She sang at the top of her lungs to every song.

At the end of the show, Alex flashed three backstage meet-and-greet passes at Bernie and Bell.

"How did you get those?" asked Bell. "You were never out of our sight."

"I already had them," he said. "I wanted it to be a surprise."

"I think you pulled it off," said Bernie. "We're definitely surprised."

"And excited!" Bell said as she jumped up and down.

The trio was ushered backstage, where they shook hands, exchanged pleasantries, took a picture, and then left. There was no need to sit and drool. The Price family just wasn't like that, and neither was Alex unless the person he was drooling over was a potential lover.

The picture was their holy grail of sorts. Alex kept a collection of photos from different events the three of them had attended. His goal was always to meet a group or person and get a picture to add to his collection. Bernie and Bell were very happy to be a part of this hobby.

After exiting the concert hall, the party wasn't over yet. The siblings decided to go to the Happy Hatter on Main for a night cap, or in their case, a nice hot cup of tea or cider. Bell ordered a Dirty Tea Cup: green tea, honey, and a shot of vodka. Bernie ordered a Brandied Apple which was apple cider, honey, cinnamon, and brandy. Alex ordered the most interesting cup of all, a Tea Time Crime, which was black tea, honey, tequila, and Kahlua topped with a dash of grenadine and a dollop of whipped cream.

"How come we don't come here more often?" asked Bernie.

"We do," laughed Alex. "It just happens to be when you're not with us."

"Oh, sad," said Bernie.

"Sorry, Bern, we kind of frequent this place on nights when we're already in a happy nostalgic mood and want to wind down. These drinks are relaxing, and they aren't for downing. They make you feel warm and cozy."

"I can agree with that. Hopefully, you'll bring me with you next time." She smiled at them. She wondered what Martin was doing and what sort of mood he would be in when she got home. She brushed the thought aside. The night was going too well to worry about home.

The siblings chatted for another hour. Then they decided it was time to call it a night. Bell had an early morning, and it was well past her bedtime. Alex also had an early morning, but this was normal for him. Bernie didn't know what her morning would involve, but she was sure there would be things to do, such as moving her belongings into her new home, which she had procrastinated on for weeks.

Alex dropped Bernie off, and Bernie shuffled up the walkway to the door. She fumbled for her key and began to turn the lock when the door jerked open. Martin stood there with an angry look on his face. He grabbed Bernie by the upper arm and yanked her into the dark house.

Chapter Thirteen

Bernadette tripped as Martin pulled her inside. She landed hard on the floor and scuffed both her knees as he dragged her toward the living room.

"Where have you been?" he demanded. "It's two in the morning, and I have sat here waiting three hours for you to walk through that door. The concert was over at eleven. Answer me!" he bellowed.

Tears ran down Bernie's face. She tried to push Martin off, but his grasp was too firm. "The concert went longer than it was supposed to, and then we had meet and greet passes," she sobbed. "After the meet and greet, we went out for a night cap. Please let go, Martin, you're hurting me," she cried.

"Hurting you? You think this is hurting you?" he demanded. "If you'd like, I can show you what it means to hurt."

"No, please, I'm sorry," she said. "I didn't mean to upset you. I don't really understand what's going on or why you're so angry."

"You don't know why? Really? I'm upset, Bernadette, because my wife is out whoring it up with her sister and her good-for-nothing adopted brother. And she's not doing her wifely duties. Did you bother to invite me along? Did you call to let me know you'd be late? These are all reasons for which I'm upset," he screamed as he shoved her away. "Go get yourself cleaned up and come to bed. We will have a long discussion tomorrow morning about expectations and the proper way a married woman should act."

Martin walked over to the fridge and pulled out a glass. "Here, drink this orange juice," he said. "You probably need to replenish some vitamins."

She took the glass from his hand, and he turned and left the room. Bernie was dumbstruck. This was not the behavior she expected from someone who loved her. It made her want to pawn her diamond and run. If this was the real Martin, how much worse could it get? Or was this an isolated incident? Maybe she had done something wrong. He was right. She didn't call to tell him she'd be late. She should have done so, but even then, did it warrant this reaction?

She took off her heels and climbed up off the floor, glass in hand. She was shaking but managed to steady herself on one of the overstuffed chairs for a moment. Blood ran down one of her knees where the skin had been scraped raw by the rough stone floor of the entryway. She was supposed to be at a photo shoot on Tuesday.

This would not do. She hobbled over to the kitchen sink and stared out the window into the starless night as she drank the juice.

Daddy was wrong; Bell was right. *Shit*, she thought. *Son-of-a-bitch*. What would she do? Maybe this really was just a weird isolated incident, and he'd be fine tomorrow. She hoped that was the case. She finished her glass of water and headed upstairs. She'd take a nice long soak in the tub and debate what to do next. It was funny how her day began with this tub and would now end with it.

Walking through the bedroom toward the master bath, she noted that Martin was already face down, passed out, on the bed. He didn't look like the prince she'd thought he was. When she reached the bathroom, she forgot what she was doing. Feeling lightheaded and overwhelmed with sleepiness, she disrobed and headed for bed.

Bernie slept straight through the night. She never woke up to use the bathroom or get a drink of water, as she usually did. It was nearly eleven when she finally woke up to the smell of something tasty and Martin whistling a tune as he leaned over her with a tray. He'd brought her breakfast in bed: eggs, bacon, blueberry muffins, and an orange smoothie.

"Good morning," he said.

"Morning."

"I thought you might be hungry and in need of some real food after all of the drinks you had last night."

"All of the drinks I had?"

"Yeah, Bernie, you came home, you couldn't stand up, and you were falling all over yourself. I had to pick you up off the ground. You were so out of it."

"I kind of remember us fighting about something, but I don't recall coming to bed," she replied.

"Darling, you probably wouldn't. You were too intoxicated to remember anything properly. I got you inside, cleaned you up, and put you in bed."

"Really? How'd I get this bruise?" she pointed to her upper arm.

"That's from me trying to catch you as you were falling. I'm so sorry about that, love, I was trying to stop you from hitting the floor, but it happened too fast."

"That's embarrassing. I'm sorry, Martin. I don't know what happened, but I'll try not to do it again."

Bernie didn't know what to make of the situation. Maybe she had drunk more than she thought. The night felt hazy at best.

"Anyway, darling, after you're done eating breakfast, I need you to get all dolled up for this afternoon. Your father is throwing a large party for me at the club. I'm announcing my plan to run for Mayor."

"Mayor? I didn't know you wanted to be the mayor?" Bernie briefly recalled that there was a plan for a get-together the following day, but last she'd heard, it was a small group regarding the position of treasurer. She couldn't keep up with how quickly

Martin seemed to make decisions, and she wasn't pleased that he consistently kept her out of the loop.

"Oh yes, very much so. Wouldn't that be great, being the mayor's wife?"

"Sure," she said without enthusiasm. "I'd just love that." *Gag me*, she thought to herself. "What happened to treasurer?" she asked.

"Well, your father and I were talking last night, and we thought I could handle something bigger than treasurer with how well people seem to like me."

"Huh, okay, mayor it is." *Remind me to thank my father*, she thought. Bernie knew that no matter what she said, Martin had already made up his mind.

"Okay, let's do this." He tore Bernie's plate away before she was finished eating and pulled her out of bed. Then he patted her on the butt and shoved her toward her closet. "Please wear something befitting of the mayor's wife," he requested and wandered off.

"Okay, honey," she said as she managed to somehow keep herself from screaming.

Bernie began to rifle through her closet. Martin had moved all of her clothing over. *When did he do that?* she wondered. *Ah, here, a royal blue Chanel cocktail dress.* She would wear a little black jacket with it, which would be perfect. She dressed, twisted her hair on top of her head, dabbed on a little makeup, and slipped on her black stilettos. She was as ready as she would ever be for Martin's upgraded event.

"Hmm, maybe not," she said aloud. She had forgotten her deodorant and to brush her teeth. "How am I this forgetful?" She supposed Martin wouldn't appreciate her leaving the house without doing those things first. She took care of business and then went in search of her husband.

"Martin?" she called out. "Where are you? Aren't you getting ready?"

"I am ready," he called as he stepped out of the kitchen. He was wearing a black suit with a red tie and a red pocket square.

"Wow, didn't realize you had your clothes down there with you."

"Yeah, I thought I'd let you have some alone time to get ready."

"Thanks," said Bernie. "I feel a little off this morning, but I'm ready now."

"Let's go then," he said, holding his hand out to her. Bernadette let out an inaudible sigh and took his hand. She wasn't in the mood to be around Martin and wished she was in her own car, driving to some remote place where she could hide out for the rest of the millennia. She grabbed her phone from her purse and brought up Bell's text string.

"Bell, please tell me you're going to be at this party? Do you know about the party?'" she typed.

"Yes, Bern, I'll be there," she responded. *"You didn't know about the party?"*

"I briefly recall mention of a gathering, but not this larger soiree and announcement he seems to have recently planned."

"That's awful. You need to tell him you're not okay with his controlling demeanor."

"Oh good, I can't wait to have that discussion."

"Is something else going on?"

"Nothing, was just hoping you'd be there so I don't feel so out of place."

"Yeah, I'll see you soon."

"Who are you texting?" demanded Martin.

"My sister, why?"

"Why do you need to text when you'll be seeing her in twenty minutes?"

"Why is this an issue?" asked Bernadette.

"Because I don't like you chatting people up when I can't see what you're saying to them. You could be talking to another man for all I know."

"I thought you were more confident than that," said Bernie. "You seemed like such a strong and confident person when we were dating."

"I am confident that you don't need to be chatting with anyone else when you're in my presence," he stated.

"Wow, okay." She set her phone down. "Does that make you feel better?"

"Yes," said Martin as he patted her leg. "We're almost there. It's at your father's club."

At least that would be a fairly comfortable place for her to blend in. Maybe she and Bell could hide in the VIP suite for a while.

Upon arriving at the club, Bernie realized that the event was even larger than she'd anticipated. How had they put all of this together in such a short amount of time? The parking lot was packed. There were some very expensive vehicles that had to belong to some very prestigious and expensively dressed individuals. She wondered who she would find inside?

"Bernie!" yelled Bell from the doorway. "Get in here. I want you to meet Artemis Jasper! He's here with his niece, Eloise. He's actually in a great mood, so we should do this now!" Bernie was as excited about meeting Artemis as Bell was.

Artemis Jasper was one of the big wig designers from Hollywood who kept a home on the outskirts of town. He was born in Oklahoma and continued to keep the state as his main stomping ground. The girls had tried to catch up with him several times, but it had never worked out. Either Artemis was in a bad mood, too big of a hurry, or they just couldn't get near him.

Bernie raced through the door, leaving Martin to enter the building alone. She spotted Bell and Artemis immediately and casually walked over to them. Bernie noticed Eloise was drinking a dry martini alone in a booth behind them. The girls had met Eloise previously.

Bernie did not find Eloise to be all that exciting. She wore an oversized hat and large, gaudy jewelry. As she looked on, Eloise stood up. Her dress was skin-tight and left nothing to the imagination. Her body made up for what her personality lacked. She looked lonely and a bit sad, which made sense since Eloise was rarely alone. She almost always had more than one man fawning over her.

"Bernie, this is Artemis Jasper, and you already know his niece, the ever-lovely Eloise Jasper." Bernie knew Bell was completely overdoing it just to get in their good graces. It was amusing, to say the least.

"How do you do?" asked Bernie politely.

"Quite magnificently," replied Artemis. "It's nice to meet you two lovely ladies. I've heard only great things about you both. Perhaps you'll come out and work with me on a line one day?"

"Oh wow, you would want that?" asked Bell.

"My dear, have you seen yourselves? You two are gorgeous. Of course, I'd want that. Next Spring, we'll be shooting a new line of swimwear. I would encourage you to be a part of it. I'll send a formal invitation in January. I hope you'll honor us with your presence." He smiled genuinely at both of them.

Eloise had looked uninterested, but suddenly, her eyes perked up. Bernie looked to see what had made her come alive. Her heart began to sink. Bell looked from Eloise to Bradley and back around to Bernie. Bradley had smiled at Bernie, but Eloise had interpreted it as being meant for her.

"What's his name?" she demanded of Bell. "Never mind, I'll ask him myself." She slunk off toward the bar. She was not known for her patience.

Bell took another look at Eloise and then looked back at Bernie, who was now visibly hurt. Luckily Artemis hadn't noticed that, clearly, Bernadette held more than just a friendship flame for Bradley.

"It was wonderful to meet you, Artemis," said Bell. "We'll catch up with you later. We have some things to tend to momentarily." She grabbed Bernie by her bruised arm and dragged her toward the VIP suite. Bernie flinched, and Bell's eyes went directly to the bruise.

As they entered the suite, Bell shut and locked the door behind them. She motioned for Bernie to sit. She wasn't asking. Bernie complied. She could tell Bell would not negotiate.

"What on God's green Earth is going on?" she demanded. "That's a pretty nasty bruise on your arm, Bernadette."

"I guess I drank too much last night. I fell down in the doorway when I got home. Martin tried to catch me, but he wasn't fast enough, so I'm bruised."

"Drank too much? You only had three drinks last night, Bernie. There's no way you were that drunk that you couldn't stand up or remember what happened. Did he tell you that you were too drunk? Did he do this to you on purpose?"

"No, Bell. I'm pretty sure I drank a lot more than you think I did. I don't remember going to bed last night. I think I blacked out."

"Did you drink more when you got home?"

Bernie hung her head down. She couldn't look Bell in the eye. "Not that I recall."

"This isn't like you. If I find out he's hurting you, I swear— I'll tear his— I don't know what, but I'll tear something off!" Bell threw her arms into the air and tipped her head back as she let out a low growl.

Bernie flinched. "I'm fine," she said, although she really wasn't sure that was true.

Calming down, Bell walked over and hugged her sister. Pushing away, she tipped her chin up to look Bernie in the eyes. "Are you okay? I'm so worried about you." Bernie could hear the pain in her voice.

She shook her head. "I don't know."gasping.

"Here," said Bell. "Take this." She handed her a tissue.

"Thanks," replied Bernie.

"What about Bradley?"

"What about him?"

"You turned the deepest shade of red I have ever seen when Eloise started to move in on him."

"I just don't want Eloise touching a man as sweet as Bradley. Her reputation precedes her. She ruins men," said Bernie.

"Oh, is that all it is?" Bell laughed. She knew that was a load of hooey, but she would let it go. A loud knocking erupted at the door.

"Who is it?" asked Bell.

"It's Martin. Is my wife in there?"

"No, Martin, I haven't seen her," said Bell.

"Well, if you do, will you please send her my way?" he requested in a business-like manner.

"Bell–what have you done?" asked Bernie quietly. Now she was worried. Lying to Martin might create a whole other problem for her. She had no idea what he'd do.

"What? I got you some more free time."

"We should probably get back out there."

"Oh, fine. Be a side party pooper," said Bell.

Bernie got up and walked toward the door. She stopped and turned to her sister. "Let me handle my relationship how I see fit. You told me you would, so please back off a little."

"I hear you, but I have to check in occasionally."

"Don't worry about me," she said, leaving Bell to contemplate the seriousness of her words.

Outside, Bernie saw several other people she knew, including her mother.

"Hi, Mom. What brings you here?"

"You mean besides all the handsome young men prowling about?" asked Mariska.

"Mom, aren't you the one prowling?" asked Bernie.

"Well, that may be, but still, so many handsome young men," she mused. "I came out to show my support for you and Martin."

"Thanks, but how did you know about this event?"

"Martin called me last night. He also asked me to get the word out to any of my political contacts, so I did." Mariska continued to scan the room for her next piece of meat.

"Apparently, I underestimated how quickly this family is capable of throwing a large event together," said Bernie.

"Ah well, kiss, kiss," she said. "I'll see you later. I have some mingling to do."

"Bye, Mom, have a wonderful night," said Bernie.

"You too, sweetie."

Bernie was disgusted, but that was nothing new when it came to her mother. She spotted Bradley by the dance floor.

"No Eloise on your arm?" she asked sweetly.

"No Eloise on my arm. I'm not much fond of the Eloise arm ornament," he noted with sarcasm.

"Ha. I see. I thought every man was fond of the Eloise arm ornament. Is that not the case?"

"Not so. I prefer something pretty and red for my arm ornament."

"You are trouble," she said, brushing his arm as she walked away. She realized at that moment that Bell was right. Bradley did have a thing for her. If only she hadn't been so blind.

On the other side of the room, she could see Martin heading her way. While she didn't want to be near him, she thought she'd better get over there before things could get any worse.

"Ah, there you are, my little minx," he said. "You disappeared on me, and you know how I hate that." He put on a playful air for the surrounding guests, but Bernie saw the stripes more clearly. "Why don't you come over here and meet some of our guests? This is Ann Mackey and her husband, Mitch Mackey. As I'm sure you know, they're writers for our local press. We're discussing my plans for when I become mayor."

"Lovely to meet you both," she replied as coolly. She waved her hand at Bradley. He looked over at her, and she motioned that she would like something to drink. He nodded his understanding. He was by her side three minutes later, handing her a glass of bubbly. "Thank you," she said.

"My pleasure," he replied.

Martin glared after Bradley, then turned and gave Bernie an 'I'm warning you' look. She shrugged her shoulders as if she had no idea what was wrong. Martin scowled.

At three o'clock, music began to play. Bradley walked up to Bernie and asked her to dance after he, of course, asked Martin if he minded. Martin motioned for him to go ahead. Bernie was shocked.

"You obviously didn't think this was possible," said Bradley. "Is he controlling?"

"No. I admit you have balls, and I really didn't think Martin would ever agree to you dancing with me. He's completely jealous of you."

"That's quite funny, considering I'm just the bartender, and he's the one who's married to you."

"Yes, well, Martin doesn't like anyone touching his things, and you are not just the bartender. You're the bar host and our family's personal aid. We pay you way more than any bartender would make."

"Touché," he said. "So now you're a thing? Before Martin, you were a princess who ruled this kingdom. What happened?"

"Nothing happened. I'm married now. Things change. People change. Life changes and moves on." Even Bernie felt the bitterness seeping through.

"Again, you know you can leave him, right?"

"I could, but I chose this, didn't I? Doesn't that mean I should at least try to make it work? Try to figure him out?"

"That depends. Is it hurting you to stay in this situation?" he asked.

"It's confusing me more than anything. He's so moody. I never know what's going to upset him. I didn't really see this side when we were dating. Once we got married, it was like everything changed, and suddenly I was expected to act differently."

"Hang in there. I'm sure it'll get better," he said as the song ended, leaving her alone on the dance floor. This time, Bradley had a note of bitterness in his voice. For some reason, she felt he was walking out of her life.

"Are you quite finished making me look a fool?" asked Martin from behind her.

"My darling, I would never make you look foolish," said Bernie. "I love you. You're my husband."

"Then why on earth would you flaunt yourself dancing with another man in front of me and our guests?"

"I wasn't flaunting. Bradley's a gentleman. I told you I've known him for years. He's like family."

"I don't care what he is. He's nothing to you from now on."

"Martin, you're overreacting a little. Nothing's going on. I would have rather been dancing with you," she lied.

"Enough. We'll discuss this later. I'm about to make my announcement." He turned huffily and walked away, leaving Bernie looking flustered once again. She'd begun to feel concerned about what awaited her once she arrived home. She'd definitely rattled his cage.

She followed Martin to the table her father and sister were sitting at and carefully sat herself down. Heaven, forbid she make another wrong move. Once she was settled, Martin trotted up to the stage and grabbed the microphone.

"Ladies and gentlemen, I called you here tonight to make an announcement. I would like to formally let you all know that, yes, the rumors are true. I have indeed decided to run for mayor. I hope I can count on all of your votes. Please enjoy this party and have some champagne and canapes on me."

The crowd erupted into applause. Bernadette was amazed at the people who began filtering over to congratulate and voice their support. She never imagined that someone so new to town could create such a huge following, but then, her father and mother were very well known around town, and Martin was in with them.

By four-thirty, most of the guests had gone. Martin finished saying goodbye to the last few and came to collect Bernie.

"What a nice turnout. I think we can head home now. This day has been a success," he stated proudly to anyone in Bernie's family who was listening.

Alan walked up and slapped Martin on the back. "I'm proud of you, son. You did a great job," he said. "I cannot wait to start working on your campaign. It can be a family affair."

"That sounds great. Perhaps Tuesday we can get together and discuss things further?"

"How about Wednesday? We have a show on Tuesday. Bernie's modeling in it. I'm sure you'll want to be there for that," he said.

"For sure," said Martin. Bernie watched as he put on his best smile, which she now realized may very well be his best fake smile. "All right, gang. We're heading out," said Martin, "I think Bernie and I could use a nice, quiet, relaxing dinner alone."

"You all have a great night," said Bell. "Call me later, Bern."

Bernie hugged her father and Bell, then turned to follow Martin out the door.

The car ride home was too quiet. Martin didn't say a word. As the ride dragged on, Bernie began to feel increasingly uncomfortable. She hated silence. She was one of the biggest talkers she knew, so this was excruciating to her.

Martin pulled the car into the garage and turned off the engine. He sat there momentarily in silence, then turned toward Bernie.

"Get your butt in the house. I've never been so humiliated by a woman in my life," he growled.

"What? Martin, you're that angry that I danced with a friend? I told you it means nothing."

"Get in the house." He threw open the car door so fast that Bernie thought it might come off the hinges, then slammed it in her face. She didn't want to leave the safety of the car. She'd never seen such anger in anyone's eyes before. How could a man who supposedly loved her be this angry? She was genuinely terrified of him.

Bernie slowly climbed out of the car and closed the door as quietly as possible. She made her way to the house as if walking down murderer's row. She poked her head through the door. Martin was standing there with a ping-pong paddle in hand.

"Get in here," he said quietly. "We have some things to discuss."

"Why do you have that paddle?" she asked.

"It's a symbol of what's to come if you ever do anything like what you did this afternoon again. If you insist on acting like a schoolgirl, you shall be punished like one."

"Acting like a schoolgirl? Because I danced with a friend? That's ridiculous," she insisted. "Besides, he asked your permission, and you said yes."

"It was your job to say no,".Martin said, his voice raising an octave. "I will not stand for such disobedience."

Bernie took a step back.

"Get over here and sit down," he demanded, pointing to the couch.

Bernie's body shook and a bead of sweat materialized on her forehead. She didn't want to do as she was told but feared the outcome if she pressed him any further. So she walked over and plopped herself down on the couch.

"What do you expect to happen in order to fix this mess?" she asked.

"I fully expect you to do as you're told from now on, starting right now, sweetheart. That is all I'm asking. I want us to be happy, and I want you to be happy. But I need you to start acting like you're in this relationship and not some schoolgirl hippie gallivanting around the city without a care in the world." Martin seemed to be relaxing some. His voice no longer sounded as angry, but she now understood how volatile he could be.

"Okay," said Bernie. "What does success in this situation look like?"

"Tomorrow, I'll be taking you out shopping for a new wardrobe. Everything you already own is going in the garbage. You need to look like the mayor's wife. No more sexy and seductive outfits. Everything is going to be businesslike."

"You want me to get rid of all of my things? No way!" she protested. "What gives you the right to demand such a thing? That is absolutely insane. I won't do it!" she stated firmly.

"You will do it, or you'll find out what this paddle feels like," he said. The cruelty in his voice was so thick Bernie felt like she'd been sucker punched in the gut. How could he have turned from sweet to cruel so quickly?

"After we replace your wardrobe, you'll make an appearance at your father's house and explain to him that you no longer want to model. You will tell him that your husband needs you by his side and that you want to be as supportive as possible with the upcoming elections."

"Are you out of your mind?" she demanded. "Modeling is my dream and my one true passion. If you take that away from me, what do I have left?"

"You have me and our marriage, darling. You'll get over it. Most women would kill not to have to work for a living." Bernadette doubted that was true.

"I sure as heck am not most women," she muttered, glaring at him.

"Wipe that look off your face. You'll make these changes and be happy to do so. Now come over here and give me a kiss."

Bernie would sooner spit in his direction. She found his requests to be utterly revolting. What sick person would do this to their wife? A zebra would. She'd married the zebra, and now his true stripes were showing through. Was Bell completely right about everything? So far, he hadn't hit her with the paddle, so perhaps he was more talk. Bernie didn't really want to find out.

She slowly walked over to him. He bent toward her and kissed her mouth. She barely moved.

"That's not very loving," he shouted.

"I don't feel very loving," she said. She wasn't sure what loving felt like at this point, but it had been a couple of weeks since she'd felt it.

Martin threw back his arm and thudded her loudly on the bottom with the paddle. Bernie jumped and let out a screech of pain. "Maybe that will give you some encouragement for the future," he said as he stormed out of the room.

Tears flooded down Bernie's face as she turned and ran for the door. She threw it open with a loud bang. There was no way she could stay there that evening. Not after he'd hit her. She hoped Bell was home and alone. She needed her big sister, even though she didn't want to admit she had been right.

She put the pedal to the floor inside her car as she raced toward her old home.

She thudded her fist on the door. No one answered. She sat down on the front steps and began to sob. As she sat, her phone began to ring. It was Martin. She didn't pick up. Shortly after the phone stopped ringing, she received a very lengthy text message which read:

If you breathe a word of this to anyone in your family, including Alex, the consequences will be catastrophic. You seem incapable of behaving yourself, so I've hired someone to keep an eye on you. Don't push me. You chose to be my wife, and you will act as such. I'll give you this evening, but things will be different tomorrow. If you insist on testing me, you must learn to accept the consequences.

Bernie was shaking. She cried even harder. How would she get herself out of this if she couldn't even say anything to Bell? How bad would this get? Had he really killed those people that Bell and Matthew had been going on about? She was feeling more scared by the second.

As she sat there, she noticed a blue Lexus pulling into the driveway. Bell jumped out and rushed to her side.

"Bernie, are you okay? What's going on?"

Bernie sucked in her tears. "Martin and I got into a fight. I needed to get away."

"What happened? He didn't hurt you, did he?"

"No, nothing like that," she again lied. "It was all verbal. I'm sure it'll be fine tomorrow."

"I hope so. If you want to talk about it, I'm here," Bell said as she leaned over and hugged her. Bernie hugged her hard. "Are you sure you're okay?"

"I'll be fine, Bell. I just need to cool down and allow him the same."

"Okay then, what would you like to do tonight?"

"I haven't eaten much today."

"Yeah, I'll say. You took about two bites of lunch, then pushed it aside. From the sounds of it, you barely ate breakfast. What sounds good?"

"Sushi would be nice," she said.

"Sushi it is. Do you want to eat in or take out? What are you in the mood for?"

Bernie was glad Bell had moved on to food rather than her relationship. She wouldn't say anything to Bell until she could figure out how to deal with this. Her sister was very understanding, and she was thankful for that.

"I say we go get sushi from The Grand Sushi, bring it back here, and veg out. I might stay over if that's okay with you?" she said.

"Oh, honey, of course that's okay with me. You're my little sister and ex-roommate. I miss having you around."

The night was nice. They ate sushi and enjoyed each other's company. Bell challenged Bernie to a few games of cribbage which Bernie repeatedly whooped her butt at. Being back at her old home was nice. She felt safe and normal. That night she slept well. She didn't even think about what Martin would do when she finally arrived home.

"Bernie," Bell said quietly. She poked her in the arm. "Bernie, are you awake?"

"No, Bell, I'm not awake. Go away. Let me sleep," she grumbled.

Bell leaned in next to her sister's ear. "Bern, I can't let you sleep. He's here."

Bernie's eyes shot open. She knew Bell could see the panic, though it only lasted a second. Her sister's brow furrowed, and her mouth opened as if she wanted to say something, but no words came out.

Bell had been in an abusive relationship before, and knew what it looked like. Luckily, she'd gotten out before any major damage could be done. Bernie had married the man, making leaving much more difficult.

"You're lying to me, Bernie," she whispered. "I can see it in your eyes."

Bernie put on her best poker face. "No. I just can't believe he actually showed up to retrieve me. The nerve of him," she spat. He couldn't even let her come home when she was ready.

"You don't have to go. You can stay here as long as you want. If you need to get away, you're always safe with me. Besides, it's Labor Day, and we should be playing volleyball and partying it up with the employees from the club," said Bell.

"Don't worry, Bell. I'm safe," she said. Her statement was convincing, even to herself. He'd smacked her butt with a paddle once. Frats did that sort of thing all the time. "I'm sorry, Bell. It doesn't look like I'm going to be available to celebrate this one," she said, patting her sister's shoulder.

"You'd better get going. He'll wonder what's keeping you," replied Bell.

Bernie rolled out of bed. "Tell him I'm grabbing a shower. Oh, I need some clothes, Bell, please?"

"Yeah sure, what are sisters for?" she left the room to tell Martin Bernie's plan and to grab some clothing.

Bernie walked across the hall to the bathroom and turned the shower on as hot as she could stand. She wanted to burn the energy from last night off of her skin. She was still feeling bewildered. What was he going to be like today? A never-ending stream of questions washed over her with the shower spray. Shaking her head, she pushed the worry aside. She felt her muscles begin to relax. A knock sounded at the door, and Bernie's body tightened again.

"Hey, I actually found a set of your clothes in the laundry room. I'll set them on the vanity," said her sister.

"Thanks."

"Do you need anything else? Should I make you some coffee or tea to go?"

"Please. A coffee would be nice," Bernie replied.

"Sounds good. I'll have it ready for you," said Bell.

Bernie heard the door close, and then two seconds later, it reopened. Footsteps approached the shower. She sighed, trying to release some tension, but her heart rate had sped up, and she was moments away from a panic attack.

Bell threw open the shower curtain, and Bernie jumped, flailing. Bell reached out to steady her.

"Sorry," she whispered. Bernie was clutching her chest as she tried to slow her heartbeat. "Listen to me," said Bell. Her eyes were wide as she stared Bernie down. "If you need help, you have to ask for it. I'll find a way to get you out of this. I know something's wrong. I know this isn't you. You don't run away when a fight happens, so this must be pretty bad. I'm scared. No one can help you if you don't say the word. Call any one of us. Me, Alex, Matthew. Please don't get yourself killed because you think you have to make your marriage work."

Bernie looked at Bell and swallowed her emotion. "I promise that if I need you, I will call."

A tear ran down Bell's cheek. "Okay," she said. "I love you, Bern."

"I love you, too, Bell."

Bernie hurried through the rest of her morning routine. She worried that things would get worse if she kept Martin waiting too long. She piled her hair on top of her head and left the bathroom.

"I see you've decided to start the day," said Martin from behind his newspaper.

"I would have been out sooner, but I felt that I needed to get cleaned up to look my best today," she replied smugly.

Bell's jaw dropped. Bernie knew her sister had never heard her speak with such contempt.

Martin crushed his paper down onto the table. "Nice of you to do so, though I probably would have chosen some nicer clothes."

Bernie locked dead eyes on her sister. Bell continued to gape and said nothing.

"Come on, Bernie, we have some shopping to do," said Martin. He motioned toward the door.

Bernie turned toward Bell. "I'll be back later for my car." Her sister stared back at her, and then slowly, she nodded her understanding.

Inside the car, the air was thick.

Bernie turned to Martin and, looking him in the eyes, asked, "What's your plan?"

"Well, my dear, my plan is still as it was yesterday. We're going shopping. I've already disposed of all of your old things. You won't have to deal with that when we get home."

Bernie's stomach turned, but she didn't say a word.

"We're going to the Fitzgerald Mall. I've made an appointment with Jenna Max. She's a personal shopper who's already picked out an entire new wardrobe for you. We just need to get your sizes down."

"So, I don't even get a say in what I'm going to wear?"

"No, darling, you don't. You're the wife of someone important, and you'll look it. Jenna knows what a mayor's wife should wear."

"This is definitely not what I signed on for when I married you," she said defiantly.

"This is exactly what you signed on for when you married me. A wife's job is to do as her husband says. This is no longer a courtship. It's a dictatorship, and what I say goes because I know what's best for both of us. It's my job as the man to take care of this family."

Bernadette swallowed the lump that had formed in her throat. She was at a loss for words. Until that moment, she hadn't known Martin to be so revoltingly sexist. She would have never married him if she had. Bernadette believed in women's rights, and she definitely believed in equality.

They pulled up to the mall and walked silently from their car to the entrance. Jenna was waiting.

"Hi, you must be Bernadette," said Jenna. She smiled politely. "Martin has told me all about you."

"Let's get this over with," said Bernie.

"Oh, okay," said Jenna. She had a horrified look on her face. Martin led the way into the store and the ladies followed.

"It's not you," Bernie whispered," It's him," she said, pointing at Martin.

"Oh?" replied Jenna.

"He's informed me that while I was out, he threw away all of my belongings and that you're now going to dress me without any say. I'm very happy about this, as you can see," said Bernie.

Martin had apparently caught some of the exchange because he was now glaring at Bernie. She knew this would be dealt with later but couldn't hold the anger in any longer.

Jenna didn't respond. She stuck to the necessities for the remainder of the time spent with Bernie and Martin. However, Bernie did notice that Jenna glared at Martin whenever he wasn't looking.

When Jenna had finished measuring and sizing Bernie up, Bernie turned to Jenna and said, "Thank you."

"You're welcome," she said with sympathy. Bernie knew Martin would not be getting Jenna's vote and that Jenna would tell others of this incident. She was quite pleased with herself.

When they arrived back at their vehicle, Martin jerked Bernie's door open and said, "Get in the car. You're playing a dangerous game."

"No, you're playing a dangerous game," said Bernie.

"Oh, am I? Please, enlighten me."

"Maybe I'll leave you," she said. "You don't deserve me as your wife."

"I don't think you'll leave," he said through pursed lips.

"Try me. I refuse to be anyone's puppet. I'm a fully grown woman who is respected in society. I should not be treated this way. I cannot believe what a jerk you've turned out to be. How can you be so heartless?"

"Heartless? You think I'm heartless? I completely remade my home for you. I'm buying all of these beautiful expensive clothes for you. I spend time with your family and provide for you to the point that you don't even need to work. I'd say you're quite ungrateful."

"Ungrateful? Seriously? You threw away all of my belongings without giving me a choice or finding out what's important to me!" she screamed. "You've taken away all of my decisions. All of who I am! I actually want to work, and I don't want to be some politician's arm candy." Bernie could feel the tears threatening, but she sucked in some air and swallowed them back.

"Lower your voice. People might hear you."

"Good. I hope they do," she snapped.

Martin frowned back at her, saying nothing for several minutes. Finally, he reached out and squeezed her shoulder. "You aren't leaving me much choice," he said quietly. "Perhaps you need a little incentive."

Bernie shook her head. "I don't think there's anything you could give me that would make me fall in line and act like someone I'm not."

"How about the lives of your family members?" he asked. A glint of crazy flashed in his eyes. "You made a vow to me. You said you'd stand by my side in sickness and in health. Until death do us part. I don't think my requests are outlandish. If you refuse to hold up your end of the bargain, I may be forced to hurt one of your family members, or worse."

"You wouldn't touch them! You can't," she said. The wind was leaving her sails.

He gave her a murderous look. "Is that a chance you want to take?"

Bernadette lowered her head into her hands, and the tears let loose while she didn't make a sound. "Please don't hurt them," she squeaked.

"Then, you better march that nice firm butt of yours up to your father's door and tell him you're retiring from the modeling world, or he'll be the first person on my list," said Martin. "Now go, and you better come directly home after. I'm not negotiating with you today."

Bernie paled, and her stomach contorted into a knot. She exited the car and headed for her father's front door. As she rang the bell, she wondered if there was any way to let him know what was happening without making things worse?

Her father greeted her with a smile. "Bernadette, what brings you here?"

"Daddy, we need to talk," she said quietly.

"What's up?" he asked.

"Martin and I have been talking, and I've decided to give up modeling," she said quickly.

Her father's eyes narrowed. "You want to give up modeling? Why would you want to do that? You love modeling."

"Well, Daddy, Martin needs my support if he's going to be mayor. It's easier this way. I want to help him with his campaign," she lied.

"Why don't you think about it tonight, do the show tomorrow, and then let me know after. I don't want to see you quit."

"No, Daddy, I won't be at the show tomorrow. I can't do it." She lowered her eyes in shame and turned away.

"Bernadette," he called after her. "This show has been scheduled for months. I'm disappointed that you'd end things so abruptly. How will I find a replacement?"

"I'm sorry," she said, feeling defeated.

She walked down the drive toward Bell's house. She wanted badly to go inside and tell her everything, but she did as she was told. She got in her car and drove home. Her heart was broken in so many ways. She felt like she'd been physically beaten, and for all she knew, she may look it as well in a short time.

When she walked through the door, Martin was waiting for her as per the norm as of late. She was surprised to see him holding two glasses of wine, one of which he handed to her. She rolled her eyes and took the glass.

"Why don't we have a seat on the couch. We can civilly discuss things." Bernie took a sip of her wine and followed him over to the couch. They sat at opposite ends, with Bernie eyeing him suspiciously.

Feeling more relaxed, she blurted, "How can you be so cold?"

He shook his head. "I'm not cold. You should recall that from the first night we were together. Plus, I've sent you dozens of flowers over the past year. A cold person wouldn't bother with such tokens," he said.

Bernie's eyes bobbed momentarily, and then she said, "You hate women."

"If that were true, I wouldn't bother taking care of you. It hurts me to hear you speak like that," said Martin. "Look at this house. It's all for you."

"Just because you own a pet and give it things doesn't mean the pet's happy," she said with a yawn. Her body began to slump. She didn't know what was happening.

"Hey," he said, snapping his fingers. "Don't check out on me yet. We're not done talking."

"Go to hell," she murmured.

Martin's nostrils flared. He shoved himself off the couch and left the room. When he returned, he pushed her onto her side and forced her hands behind her back. Bernie had no idea what was happening when he clamped the handcuffs on her wrists. She had lost complete control of her mind and body.

"You're going to spend the evening in confined quarters to think about how you're acting." He gave the cuffs a firm tug. "This way," he said as he motioned toward the back of the house. Bernie couldn't move, so he dragged her down the stairs and into the den, where he threw her down on his brown leather cigar chair. She watched incoherently as he messed around with the thermostat on the wall. Bernie could have sworn she saw the bookcase open to reveal a large iron door. He pressed something else on the thermostat, and the massive door opened. *Is this a dream?* She was no longer sure.

"Pretty neat, huh? I had this installed when I remodeled the house. I figured it might come in handy one day though I hoped it wouldn't come down to it. The room is soundproof, and there's no way out from the inside unless you know the code." He walked over and hoisted her off the chair, moving her to the cot inside the cell. He threw her down and uncuffed her hands. "You can hang out in here until I get back later."

As he walked away, Bernie said, "Ha. I hope you die." She gave him a crooked smile.

"Yeah. That's not going to earn you any extra points. Apparently, I haven't made myself clear on my expectations of you." He walked back over to her, and she could see the glint of metal. "Give me your hand," he said. She held one wobbling hand out to him, and he clamped a cuff on her wrist, then he dragged her across the cell and jerked her wrist upward. "Now, give me the other hand," he demanded. She complied, and he clapped the second cuff on her other wrist. She was hooked to the wall. She could barely touch the ground. She stood there wobbling around on her tiptoes.

Martin left the room momentarily and returned with a small leather bench that was only about two square feet in diameter. "Kneel on this," he barked. Bernie was unable to comply. With one arm, he hoisted her onto the bench and pushed her legs apart so she wouldn't topple over. Then he lifted her dress so that her thong panties were visible.

"Brace yourself he said," with a little too much excitement. The next thing Bernie knew, the breath was knocked out of her as the hard wooden paddle made contact with her exposed flesh. She lurched forward and slammed her head into the wall. The exercise was repeated too many times. Tears flooded her face, and her butt felt like it had been lit on fire.

"That should be enough for tonight," Martin said as he removed the cuffs from her hands and pulled her off the stool. She was blacking out. This had to be a nightmare, or perhaps she had died at some point and ended up in Hell?

"Alrighty," he said, "I'll check back in later, and oh— you're no longer allowed to spend time with your family or friends unless it's at a political gathering where I'm present. When I come back, I hope you'll exhibit a better attitude."

Bernadette was lost in darkness. In the distance, she heard the slow rhythmic beating of her heart. She felt nauseous. As she lay there praying for the nausea to subside, she heard Bell's voice say, "Diamonds can be pawned, but zebras are forever."

Chapter Fourteen

The next morning Bernie awoke to find that she was in her own bed, and she felt as if she'd been hit by a truck. Her dreams had quickly gone from horrible to hellish. Some of them made sense, others not so much. She'd dreamt of happier times with her sister and horrifying times with monsters lurking around each corner. She had no idea what was real and what was make-believe. She couldn't figure out what had happened after she'd left her father's house.

"Good morning," said Martin, "I'd love for you to make me breakfast. I want eggs, toast with almond butter, and a grapefruit. Please," he said.

"Okay," she replied. She felt as if she was in slow motion. She was very stiff and sore.

"Here," he said. He handed her some painkillers. "Take these. They'll help with your hangover. You really should try not to drink so much. Maybe keep it under three glasses of wine next time."

Bernie popped the pills in her mouth and headed for the kitchen. She had nothing to say to him. She didn't recall drinking anything the night before. She felt as if she were outside her body. What had he done to her?

As she cooked Martin's food, she munched on some baby carrots and thought hard about her actions. She needed to get away from him, but how? Maybe she could go to Alex? No, Martin would probably expect that. What about Bradley? She knew it would get her in trouble, but she could run out the door while he ate breakfast and find Bradley. She would tell him everything.

"Hey, sugar, how's the food coming?" he purred into her ear.

"It's almost ready," she said with false sweetness.

"Good, I hope you made some for yourself. I'd like us to eat together this morning."

Bernie's heart sank. He intended to keep her in sight.

"Yeah, I decided not to have eggs, just some toast with peanut butter and jelly."

"Sounds good." Martin grabbed a couple of plates from the cupboard and handed them to her. "Here you go." Then he grabbed the juice from the fridge and poured a glass for each of them while Bernie plated the rest of the food. He seemed so normal. She'd never let that fool her again.

They carried their food to the dining room and took a seat. Bernie looked over at Martin. She would have to play his game for now. She smiled innocently.

"How was your night?"

He smiled back at her. "It was quiet."

"What did you do?"

"I watched a couple of movies on Netflix. I think you would have liked them both."

"Do you remember what they were?"

"Yeah, one was *Operation Dumbo Drop*, and the other was *Super Troopers. Super Troopers* was a bit more exhilarating," he said with a laugh.

"I love that movie," she replied. "I've seen it probably twenty times."

"Really? That was the first time I'd seen it, but it was definitely worthwhile. I laughed a lot."

"Yeah, I can quote most of that movie. It cracks me up, too."

Martin nodded and then changed the subject. "Today, we're going to watch videos relating to previous campaigns for mayor, and we're going to discuss my approach to winning this election. A fundraiser is coming up in a few days and a lot of important people will be there."

"Okay." Bernie was not thrilled. She really couldn't give a flying hoot about politics. She was horrible at following who was for or against what, and at this point, she would love to do whatever she could to sabotage Martin's campaign.

After brunch, Bernie was given permission to shower and change into something else. What that would be, she didn't know since all of her clothing had been replaced. She slowly made her way up the stairs to her closet.

When she opened the doors, she was shocked. There were many formal gowns, pantsuits, sweaters, scarves, hats, pearls, and practical shoes. The only word for the "everyday clothing" that she could think of was *frumpy*.

While perusing her closet, she found some expensive-looking, seemingly comfortable, velour jogging suits. She settled on a black one with lacy panties and a matching bra. They weren't so bad, but still, not something she would normally choose. Martin had clearly made a request in this department.

The shower helped bring her back to life, and it felt wonderful to be in some soft and somewhat comforting clothes. Bernie wanted to stay upstairs for the rest of the day but knew he would come looking for her eventually. She blew her long red hair dry, put on some makeup, and trudged back downstairs to the den.

Martin was sitting at the computer reviewing hundreds of emails from all kinds of people that Bernie couldn't care less about. Each one of them either wanted to help or wanted questions answered. The campaign was the last thing on her mind, but she would have to get into the game if she wanted to find a way to escape this hell hole.

"You look nice and comfy."

"Thanks, I feel somewhat comfy," she replied.

He walked over and sat down on the leather loveseat. "Come on over and join me," he said.

Bernie walked over and sat down. She grabbed a blanket from the back of the chair and wrapped it around herself. The house had become significantly cooler overnight. It felt like fall was coming, even though it was only the end of July.

The two sat in the den for hours, watching video after video. Martin would ask her opinion, and Bernie would tell him what she believed he wanted to hear. She kept under the radar and behaved herself in his eyes. She was acting like *Martin's wife* should behave.

At nine that evening, after they had devoured a pizza and had a glass of wine, Martin decided it was time to call it quits. "Why don't we go sit in the whirlpool?" he asked. "I know you enjoy a good soak. I'll throw some Epsom Salt in. Your body will feel much better tomorrow.

"Okay," said Bernie hesitantly. She wasn't sure she wanted to do that, but perhaps it would ease the stiffness she was feeling. She'd have to try to plan her outing for after he fell asleep.

They soaked in the whirlpool for a half-an-hour. The water burned her skin at first, but then she relaxed into it. They didn't speak. They sat quietly, listening to some soft music that Martin had turned on. Bernie thought she'd fall asleep with how comfortable the water made her feel, but she knew that would be a horrible mistake.

At ten o'clock, Martin finally decided to go to bed. He was snoring nearly as soon as his head hit the pillow. Bernie lay there for twenty minutes before she decided to make her escape. She'd left her clothes by the door to grab them and dress on her way out. Stealthily creeping through the house, no noise could be heard, even when she went out the front door.

Bernie was at the club in record time. She didn't look like herself and hoped her father wouldn't see her walk in. Perhaps he wouldn't be there. Bradley met her at the door, smiling, until he realized something wasn't right.

"I had a feeling you'd be walking in right now," he said.

"You did?"

"Yeah, I don't know what it is, but I feel connected to you. I just know when you're nearby."

"That's pretty awesome," she replied.

"What exactly are you wearing? That's not something the Bernadette I know would be caught wearing. Are you okay?"

"No, hence the reason I'm here. Well, not the whole reason. This is minor compared to the rest of the situation. Anyway, I came here, Bradley, looking for you specifically," she said.

"Okay?" he replied. "Let's go to the VIP suite. There's no one in there at the moment." He grabbed her hand and ushered her to the back of the club. He sat her down on the sofa and motioned that he would be back in a moment. He handed her a glass of her favorite Pinot Grigio when he returned. "Now tell me what's up," he said.

"Everything has basically fallen apart." Tears rolled down her face. "Martin is an absolute horror."

"Did he hit you?" asked Bradley, the fear and concern on his face.

"You have no idea. It's worse than that." She watched as his eyes widened. "He's basically taken my identity away. He got rid of all of my clothing and belongings and replaced them all with frumpy stuff that I would never wear, just so he could look better for his campaign. He made me quit modeling because I defied him. I had to lie to my father about my reason for quitting because he threatened my family's lives if I tell them anything. I'm pretty sure he's been drugging me. I don't remember anything about last night, but I have some sweet bruises on my butt and wrists. Bradley, I'm scared."

Bradley gaped at Bernie, and then he pulled himself together and hugged her tightly.

"I'm not going to let him hurt you. I'll help you get out of there."

"How will you do that? He knows a lot of people, and supposedly he even has someone following me. I fear what will happen if he finds out I left the house. I also worry that with how violent he can be, he might actually kill me or someone else."

"We'll figure this out. There has to be a way to get you out of there," he said, squeezing her hand.

"I can only think of one way to go about this, and it's not going to be easy," said Bernie as she mentally reviewed her plan. "You have to find Matthew and bring him back here. He'll know what to do. He's the private investigator trying to gather evidence against Martin. He tried to warn me, and I didn't listen. He said I could ask for his help at any time, but I can't afford to call him when I'm around Martin, and if Martin has someone following me, I can only assume he also checks my phone activity."

"How do I find him?" asked Bradley.

"Contact Alex. If he doesn't have the information, Bell will. This next part is very important. You cannot tell them what's going on. Martin has threatened my family's lives, and I don't want anything to pull them any deeper into this situation. They need to continue believing that I'm not in danger. Tell Alex you're trying to track down some long-lost family member. I know he'll gladly help you out. Family has always been important to him."

Bradley frowned at her and shook his head. "Oh, Bernie, how is this happening?"

"I don't know," she cried. "I thought I knew what I was doing. I thought I'd found real love. He acted like a gentleman for months. He seemed so genuine, but I was wrong. I was so wrong. Even my father was fooled by him. I kept telling myself that I had to deal with it and that, with time, things would improve. Time has only brought out the worst in Martin. I now realize that staying isn't an option."

"You did find real love. It just wasn't with him. I've loved you since the first day I met you. I think I'll always love you, no matter who you're with," he said softly. "I'll do anything to get you safely out of this mess."

Bernie reached up and grabbed his chin in her right hand. "Do you really mean that?" she asked, looking longingly into his eyes. "Are you sure you want to risk your own life? I'd understand if you said no. Your safety is important too."

"Yes, I really mean it. I'll gladly risk my life if it means helping you to safety. You make the world I live in so much brighter.

"Oh Bradley, Bell has occasionally mentioned that you felt this way, but I never allowed myself to believe it."

"I work for your father. Sometimes blindness in these situations helps us to avoid other difficulties. You just didn't think about it because of the boundary it would mean crossing. In this instance, however, I think your father would have approved. He and I have always had a certain understanding and closeness."

"I'm sorry," she said. "Help me get out of this, and I promise to open my eyes a little wider."

"I would have helped you either way." He winked. "Don't let him give you any more drinks. You pour them yourself, okay?"

"Okay," said Bernie. "I never thought I'd have to worry about being drugged by my own husband.

"With the storm that's brewing, I think I'd better get a move on. There's no telling what he might do next. I'll start by contacting Alex and go from there. What's Matthew's last name?"

"It's McKinney. Matthew McKinney. If Bell and Alex don't have his information, I don't know the next step. I'm afraid to go to the authorities because of Martin's threats against my family."

He leaned forward and pulled Bernie into a hug. "I won't let you down."

"Thank you. Remind me that I owe you big time after this."

Bradley looked down at her and, without hesitation, pressed his lips to hers.

"Stop," she whispered as she gently pushed him away. "Not like this. Not in the light of this awful situation. Just find Matthew and bring him back as quickly as possible. I have to go." She hoped she hadn't taken too long already. The last thing she needed was for Martin to find out she'd been gone, but then again, he could already know.

"I'll start working on this as soon as you're out the door. I know you'll be fine, you have to be, but I couldn't handle the thought of you walking away without kissing you goodbye," he replied sheepishly.

"Later, Cordine." She smiled. She knew he was scared that this could be the last time they ever saw one another. She felt a twinge of the same fear scurrying through her mind.

She turned away from him and began her journey toward home. *Lord, let him not be awake when I arrive home.*

The drive was not nearly long or quick enough for the different fears playing across her mind. Bernadette pulled into the driveway and cut the engine. There were no lights on in the house. As she quietly crept up to her and Martin's room, she noted that she could hear him snoring lightly. She tore off her clothes and put them aside.

Instead of getting into bed, Bernie headed for the bathroom. She decided that getting up to use the lavatory in the middle of the night would make for a more plausible story when she tried to crawl back into bed. Everything went as planned, and she was asleep beside Martin in no time. Her dreams didn't go as smoothly. It was as if she was playing out every scenario of how the night could have gone inside her vivid imagination.

She had only been asleep for half an hour when she was jolted awake by a loud thud against the wall.

"WAKE UP!" yelled Martin. He was standing over her, paddle in one hand, cuffs in the other, and Bernie could see a gun holstered at his hip. He'd thrown on all of the lights in the room, and the look on his face was one of absolute rage. "What did you do?" he demanded. "I told you to behave yourself. I thought we had an understanding. Now I find out you went to the barkeep for help? You did what? Asked him to save you from me?"

"Martin, please, I didn't do anything."

"Don't 'Martin please,' me. I know where you've been. I have eyes on you at all times, Bernadette. I know you're lying!"

"Can you blame me? You're crazy. I'm a human being who deserves to be treated as such," she responded flatly.

"GET UP!"

"No."

"GET UP or I'll MAKE YOU get up!"

"NO!"

If Bernie had thought Martin's rage could grow no more, she was dead wrong. He leapt toward her and grabbed her by the hair, yanking her from the bed.

"LET GO OF ME!" she cried.

He slammed her face-first down into the bed and wrenched her hands behind her back, handcuffing them in place.

"This time, you've gone too far. Someone's going to pay for your bad behavior. Someone you love," he snarled.

"No, please, Martin!"

"Please? Please, you say? You don't want to please me, so why should I please you?"

He hauled back the paddle and began beating her with it.

"Please, stop," she begged, but he kept on. Thirty paddles on the back end. Bernie couldn't even cry anymore when he was finished. He grabbed her by the arm and dragged her across the floor. Her body jerked and thudded with each step as Martin descended to the basement.

At the bottom of the stairs, he left her slumped over and sobbing. When he returned, he held a syringe. Shoving her to the side, he injected its contents into her glute.

"Why don't you sit in here and think about what you've done," he said quietly.

Bernie continued to cry. She'd never felt so helpless or scared in her life. Every synapsis in her body was firing on pain. She thought she would be sick, but then all consciousness subsided, and she was nothing more than a pile of beaten flesh lying on the cold hard floor.

Martin shook her lightly to see if she was awake. Realizing she was out, he carried her into the panic room and dropped her on the cot. Rolling her over, he removed the handcuffs and covered her with a blanket. "Sweet dreams," he said as he closed the door and locked it behind him.

Bernie dreamt of being lost in a horrible ice storm. Unconsciously, she pulled the covers closer around herself. There was a chill in the air that evening.

Chapter Fifteen

The following morning, Bernadette awoke to a pounding headache and the smell of coffee. She was lying on the loveseat in the den, her body contorted awkwardly. Looking around, she noted a steaming cup of coffee sitting on the end table. She shook her head slowly, remembering visiting Bradley and climbing back into bed. She also remembered Martin waking her up and beating her. Beyond that, things were cloudy. One thing was for certain. She had been drugged.

In the distance, she heard Martin whistling. His footsteps grew nearer.

"We have someplace to be this afternoon, and I need you to be on your best behavior, so head upstairs and shower, please." He tossed her an apple.

Bernie moved toward the door but stopped in front of him and looked him in the eye. "You drugged me," she said.

"Prove it," he replied with a smile. "Why do you make me go to such extreme measures?"

Bernie felt weak. It took everything she had to say, "I'm sorry. Will you forgive me?" She was scared. She'd never been so scared in her life. Not only for herself, but for her family.

Martin grabbed her around the waist and pulled her close. Leaning down, he kissed her on the forehead. "I love you so much, Bernadette. Don't make me punish you anymore." Bernie knew that whatever he felt for her, it was not love.

He spun her back around and slapped her on the butt. She winced and nearly fell over.

Four hours later, no one would have known Bernadette's previous state. She was clean, fed, and dressed to the frumpy nines. She still felt weak, but she was ready to go to Martin's event and act like the obedient robot. Martin told her exactly what was expected of her during the car ride. She was to smile and not speak. He didn't want her walking either, fearing someone would notice her injuries.

Bernie did as she was told. She wrapped her arm through Martin's and smiled a fake, tired, slightly sad smile. She stayed by his side all night and didn't move unless he moved. The one time she needed a bathroom, he escorted her there and back.

She kept herself busy thinking about her family and Bradley. Daydreaming about how she would spend her time if she got out of this mess. She had been stupid, and she now realized it. How could she have been so foolish? She wanted to cry thinking about it, so she diverted her mind back to the memory of the last vacation she had taken with Alex and Bell.

It was about a year ago, and they had gone to Hawaii. The trip was heavenly. Lots of sun and sand. They'd laughed a lot and eaten a lot of great food. She wished she could go back to that memory and live there.

While Martin and Bernie were perusing the party, Alex walked in. Bernie was happy to see him. If he was still out mingling around town, then her family must be safe for the time being. She smiled a little more honestly as she watched him walk toward her.

"Good evening. How are things going?" he asked with his usual Alex grin.

"We're well," replied Martin. "Making an appearance. You know, every bit helps when it comes to the upcoming campaign."

"Oh, indeed it does," said Alex. "Bernie, I haven't seen you in a while. What have you been doing?"

"She's been ill for a couple of days. She came down with food poisoning and has barely moved or eaten in the past 48 hours. As you can see, she's still a little under the weather," said Martin. He patted Bernie's hand.

"That's too bad. I guess Bradley, our concierge at the club, has been out sick for the past two days as well. Must be something going around."

Bernie's forehead began to perspire, and her eyes enlarged as she stared back at Alex, praying he'd understand that something was wrong. She shook her head ever so slightly.

"I'm glad you're feeling better, Bernie," said her brother.

Bernie didn't say anything. Martin continued to speak for her. She couldn't help but wonder what had really happened to Bradley. She also realized she'd been out of it for two full days. Her knees began to wobble. What had he done to her over those 48 hours? He had to have drugged her multiple times.

"We're glad as well," said Martin.

"Anyway, Bern, call me. We'll have to do lunch. I need to make the rounds, and then I'm off. Got a big day tomorrow, and I need to prepare."

"Okay, Alex. Wonderful to see you as always," said Martin.

Alex was smart. Surely, he noticed all the red flags. The biggest of which was her being sick and not calling or messaging him. She always reached out to Alex because he had a way of making everything better. He had a way of knowing what his sisters needed, whether it be his amazing chicken noodle soup, or other supplies.

Bernie felt like her legs would buckle as her mind switched over to Bradley. *Why did I drag him into this mess? What if Martin kills him?* She prayed he would be okay.

Outside the hall, Alex dialed Bell's number.

"Hello?"

"Bell, something awful is going on."

"What do you mean?" she asked. There was a quiver in her voice.

"I mean, I was just at the Ruseau Charity Event, and I saw Bernie. She looks like she hasn't slept in days. She barely spoke to me. Martin answered all the questions I directed at her. I know I saw fear in her eyes. She's scared. We have to do something. On top of that, Martin gave me some BS lie about Bernie being sick for the past two days. She never called me."

"Oh, God," said Bell. "I haven't spoken to her in days. I just assumed she was in her own little world. She asked me to stop checking in so much. She swore she'd be fine. What do you think's going on?"

"I don't know for certain, but I think he's abusing her. When have you ever known that girl to let someone else speak for her? She literally didn't say a single word. He held her to his side like she might disappear if he let go."

"Yeah, I've never. I'm going to track that son-of-a-b down and kick his butt!"

"Bell, let's not go overboard here. You don't want a share in whatever sick slice of pain he's serving her. We don't know for certain what's going on or how dangerous this situation could be. We need more information."

"I'm going over there. I don't care. I need to find out the truth."

"Oh, hold on. I see them!" said Alex.

"What? What do you mean you see them?"

"I mean, they just left the building, got into his car, and are driving away."

"I'm going to call Bernie right now and find out what's going on," said Bell.

"She won't be able to speak freely," said Alex.

"We have our own understanding. I'm sure I can get the information without Martin recognizing what we're talking about."

"If he lets her answer the phone. Good luck. If you get through, see if she'll talk to you, but don't do anything irrational. I know how you get when you're all worked up about something. I don't want anything to happen to either of you."

"We'll be in touch," Bell replied.

On the other side of town, Martin and Bernie had arrived home.

"Come downstairs with me," said Martin. "There's something I'd like to show you."

Bernie looked at him for a moment, then reluctantly followed him to the lower level and watched him stop at the thermostat. To her horror, the bookcase next to the thermostat opened to reveal a door. A chill ran down her spine. There was no doubt in her mind that she'd been in there before.

"Go inside," said Martin. Bernie didn't move. "I won't repeat myself." He pushed his coat aside to reveal the gun at his hip.

She walked into the room, taking it in as if for the first time. "How long do you intend to keep me in here?" she asked.

"A couple of hours. I have some errands to run, and I don't want you going anywhere."

"Is this what our marriage will be like from now on?"

"Not if you do your part," replied Martin. "I love you, Bernie," he said before closing the door.

Bernadette whipped him the bird, despite knowing he wouldn't see. She turned back to the cell. There was a cot with a pillow and a blanket on one side and a hook positioned above her head on the furthest wall. She saw another panel for controlling the door but no actual latches. The floor was tiled but had a black rug in the center. A jug of water sat on the floor by the cot. Beyond that, the room was empty.

She flopped down helplessly on the cot and prayed that someone would find her. She heard some quiet creaking above. She assumed it must be Martin moving around. She stared at the ceiling and wondered if Bradley had found Matthew or if Martin had gotten to him first?

Bernie listened patiently. She hadn't tried screaming, but what good would it do? Martin was the only person in the house. There was no sound except the occasional faint creak of the house from overhead.

After what felt like ten minutes, the creaking subsided. Bernie wondered if Martin had left the house or if he was sitting in the room right outside her door. She had no way of knowing. He could be up to anything, and that was what she feared most.

Bell called Bernie immediately, but there was no answer. She waited another twenty minutes, then tried again. No one answered. She decided a visit in person might be better, so she hopped into her car and drove to the house. No one responded to her persistent doorbell buzzing.

"Where could they be?" she asked out loud.

Bell decided to drive over to the club to see if Bernie and Martin had stopped on their way home. When she walked inside, she saw Martin talking to someone in one of the back corners, but Bernadette was nowhere to be seen. The other person had their back to Bell. They were dressed in black and had their hood up. She couldn't tell if she knew them.

She approached the pair cautiously, keeping out of sight. She positioned herself around the corner from them to listen to their conversation. She could hear Martin well, but she had to listen hard for the other voice because they spoke in a whisper. Realizing she was hearing something she shouldn't be, she took out her phone and began recording.

"I want them gone. She isn't obeying me, and it's time to show her how serious I am. I don't care how you do it. Build a bomb, wire it, pour gasoline on it. It doesn't matter. Once they're out of the way, money will be no problem. We can leave this place and disappear together."

"What do you want me to do with the bartender?"

"You've been dosing him with Rohypnol regularly, correct?"

"Yeah," they replied. "He has no idea where he is or what's going on."

"Dose him again and dump him off somewhere. I doubt he'll even know his name when he comes around. Most likely, if he tries to report anything, he'll come off sounding like a junkie."

Bell's jaw dropped. Poor Bradley! She couldn't believe the words coming out of Martin's mouth. She finally had proof. She stopped recording and walked toward the VIP room. Apparently, she hadn't been as sneaky as she'd thought, because she realized she was being followed. She ducked into the room and hid her phone inside the sofa. It took everything she could muster to hide the fear and adrenaline coursing through her veins. Martin burst through the door to find her sitting casually on the sofa.

"What are you doing? Spying on me?" he asked.

"No," said Bell. "I was looking for Bernie. Since I didn't see her, I came in here to decide what I want to do next. You know, I haven't seen her in a week. That isn't normal for us to go that long without getting together."

"She doesn't want to see you." He sneered. "She thinks you're damaging to our campaign."

"She does, or you do?" asked Bell. She managed to keep her voice level.

"She does."

"Where's my sister?" demanded Bell. "I want to hear this from her directly."

"She's at home, probably soaking in the whirlpool. She loves that thing," he said.

"I went to the house. She didn't answer. I rang several times. I also called her cell phone."

"Hello," he said as he tapped her on the head. "Whirlpool, and she doesn't want to talk to you like I said."

"Don't you dare touch me! I know the truth about you. Matthew was right. I know you're up to something."

"I don't know what you're talking about. Silly models think they know things but should stick to what they know best."

"Oh really? What might that be exactly?"

"Well, I would say arm candy, for starters. Do you get anything for yourself, or is everything handed to you by Alex? You're just a pretty face, and that won't last long, will it? Eventually, you won't be a model anymore, and then what?"

"Bernie's a model. How could you say such things?"

"Bernie is well educated and will do well as the mayor's wife. What do you have? You're nothing."

"Thanks for the enlightening conversation, jerk."

"Say whatever you want. You know it's true. Anyway, enough," Martin said. "You're not worth my time." She glared at the back of his head as he left the room.

Bell let fifteen minutes pass before she dug out her phone and attempted to leave. She didn't see Martin anywhere, so she made a dash for her car.

As she pulled off the highway and onto the county road leading to her house, she realized another vehicle was following her. The driver sped up until he was right on her tail. Bell gunned it, but the other driver overtook her.

As she looked over, she could see the outline of a man. He looked directly at her as he cranked the wheel over and slammed his car into hers. Her heart was pounding a dangerous rhythm, and she worried she might pass out. The clamminess of her hands caused them to slide on the steering wheel as she lost control of her car. The next thing she knew, she was rolling down a hilly embankment toward the river. Her car pummeled through overgrown bushes and stopped at the river's edge.

She was hanging upside down in her car, tears rolling down her face. She reached toward the dash and pressed the call button for Matthew.

"Hello?"

"Matthew, it's Bell," she whimpered, "I'm in some serious trouble."

"Where are you? What's happening?" he sputtered.

"Someone has run me off the road. I'm trapped in my car down by the river's edge. I think I can get my belt off, but the doors are crunched. I'm scared, Matt. I don't know what to do." Her voice shook. "There's smoke billowing out from under the hood. I don't know what to do!" she shrieked.

"Hang tight, Bell. I'll call for help and send them your way. It's going to take way too long for me to get there. I'm in Texas right now, but I'll head your way as soon as I hang up the phone."

Bell's mind raced. She didn't know what was going to happen, but she needed to give him as much information as possible. "Listen!" she yelled. "In case I don't make it out of this, someone has kidnapped Bradley. They've been drugging him and plan to dump him somewhere tonight. You have to find him! And Bernie's in trouble. Martin's planning something horrible, I overheard him, and I recorded the conversation on my phone. I don't know what's going on, but it's bad. The shit has hit the fan! Do you hear me? THE SHIT HAS HIT THE FAN!"

"Okay, okay, I hear you. I'm going to help."

"Hurry, Matt! Hurry!" she cried.

"Stay on the line with me. I'm calling for emergency backup from my computer."

"Matt!" Bell squealed, "Flames are shooting out of the hood! What do I do?"

"Hold on for me. Look around and see if there's anything that can break a window. Don't give up. You have to get out of the car. Do you think you can do that for me?"

Bell didn't answer. The line had gone dead.

Chapter Sixteen

The next morning, Bernie was still locked inside the panic room. Martin had lied about how long he'd be gone. He had to keep her on her toes, so he didn't bother to visit her. He had too many things to do and couldn't deal with her antics.

He called a meeting with both of Bernie's parents at Alan's house for two o'clock that afternoon. In the meantime, he planned to be seen somewhere else in town. He decided to go golfing with a couple of the guys from the country club. Ed and Joe had become fast friends. Despite their friendship, it was killing Martin to botch his game, but he needed to prolong it as much as possible.

At one-thirty, Martin was only three-quarters of the way through his eighteen holes with Ed and Joe.

"Excuse me, guys, I'm supposed to have a meeting this afternoon, but I misjudged how long this round would take. I'm going to make a quick call to let them know I'm running behind."

"No problem, bud, we can take a short break for that," said Joe.

"Yeah, that's fine," said Ed. "Gives me a little more time to bask in the glory of kicking your butt for once." He grinned.

"You wish, man. As soon as I get back, I'm bringing a bolder game with me." Martin said. He turned away from the guys and walked off the side of the green. He dialed Alan's number.

"Hello, you've reached Alan."

"Hey, it's Martin. Listen, I'm running a bit behind on my golf game today. I'll call you as soon as I'm on my way."

"Sounds good, Martin. Give 'em hell out there," Alan said.

"I will, sir."

Martin hung up and made another call.

"Hello?"

"Yeah, it's me. We're game on for two o'clock."

"Sounds good, love."

Martin snapped his fingers and hummed a tune as he walked back to join his buddies on the golf course.

"Where were we?" he asked.

"So, Mayor, what will you do to win this game?" asked Ed.

"Hmm, I'll just have to tighten up my game and get my hands a little dirty, but I think you'll find I'm great at bringing her home." He smiled. His eyes burned with intensity.

"Okay, well, let's see it then," said Ed.

The trio turned and headed for the fourteenth hole. Everything was grand in the world of Martin Day. Everything was going as expected.

At two, Martin called to tell Alan he'd arrive by two-thirty. Alan informed Martin that Mariska was already there with him and that they would see him soon. Martin turned back to his game and finished up the last hole. He had barely beaten the guys. They were both quite impressed that he was able to pull ahead in the end.

At two-forty-five, Martin began driving toward Alan's. As he approached, he noticed that something was very wrong. There were huge clouds of black smoke billowing up from his father-in-law's house. Martin immediately dialed the fire department.

"Hi, this is Martin Day. I've arrived at the Price house at 1268 New Bell Lane to find smoke billowing out of the place. I think it's on fire. I have no idea if anyone is inside. Please send help!"

"Yes, sir, I have dispatched fire and medical. They're coming your way. They should arrive in four minutes. Do not go up to the door. Stay back, and let the firefighters assess the situation."

"Yes, ma'am, I'll keep my distance until they give me further information."

"Okay, hang tight. They should be there soon."

Martin hung up and began the waiting game. The fire department was right on time. They arrived four minutes from the time that Martin had called. A police officer appeared at his side, asking questions regarding what he knew about the fire.

"I told you," said Martin. "I was golfing with friends at the club, and I had a meeting set up with Mr. Price and his ex-wife after. I was running behind. I came upon the house, and it was already on fire. You can check my timing with the club. They can vouch for my location."

"I understand that, sir. This is just standard procedure. We need to find out who was present and what they witnessed."

"Good, well, find out who did this," said Martin with a stern look on his face.

"Sir, I didn't say anyone did this. What makes you think someone did this? It could have been faulty wiring or a dryer that malfunctioned. It's hard to say."

"I don't know why I said that. It just seems odd that a fire has broken out like this in the middle of the day."

"Fires do not care what time of day it is. Let me take down your name and number. We may be chatting again later," said the officer.

Martin glared at him. "Here's my card. It has all the pertinent information on it."

"Thank you, Mr. Day," he replied. "I'm sure we'll be in contact."

Martin began to walk away, then paused. "Have they determined whether or not anyone's inside?"

"No, sir, they're still working on that."

Martin took a seat on the curb to wait. Two minutes had passed when he heard a loud commotion. Two people were being dragged out of the house. He jumped to his feet to try to get a better look. The paramedics were on the job. He decided to stay and watch for a while.

"You know these people well?" asked the officer standing near him.

"Yeah, they're my wife's parents."

"Oh, I'm sorry to hear that."

As they watched, it became clear that both victims were still alive, but barely. Paramedics were hurrying about and shouting orders at one another.

"Will they contact me when they have further news?" asked Martin.

"Yes, I'll make sure they call you and your wife," he replied. "Again, I'm sorry you're going through this."

"I don't know how I'm going to relay this to my wife," said Martin sadly.

"Yeah, things like this are never easy," said the officer.

"I'm going to head out. I need to find my family and let them know what's happening."

"Take care," said the officer.

Martin hurried off. He thought he'd done well considering the circumstances. He really had no intentions of relaying this message to any of the family. As he pulled away from the house, he recognized the limo pulling up. It looked as if he wouldn't have to tell them. Alex and his big mouth would take care of it for him.

Alex hopped out of the limo and ran toward the first officer he saw.

"What happened here?" His voice cracked.

"There's been a fire. Do you know the owner of the house?"

"Yes, I'm his son. Please tell me everything's okay?"

"We have no real information as of yet. They pulled two people out of the house. A man and a woman. They're being taken to the hospital as we speak.

"Has anyone been notified of this?"

"No, sir, I don't believe anyone but you and the gentleman, who just left here, knows anything of this tragedy."

"Tragedy? Has someone been pronounced dead?" he demanded.

"No, I apologize. That came out poorly. No one has died, but the people they pulled out were in pretty rough shape. As you arrived, I was notified over the radio that they believe it's a Mr. Price and a Ms. Fitz."

"No, way! I can't believe this is happening. Both of our parents were in there? What am I going to tell the girls—" He barely got the words out. His hands trembled as his mind raced through every possible scenario.

"I don't think you have to worry about that, the gentleman who called the fire in was planning to do so."

"What gentleman? Who was it?"

"He said his name was Martin, I believe," replied the officer.

"Oh great," said Alex. "I highly doubt Martin intends to relay this message to anyone. As a matter of fact, he probably started the fire. Please tell me you plan to look into him."

"Rest assured, we will look into every possibility regarding how the fire started. If it was foul play, the perpetrator will pay for their actions."

"I hope you're right."

"Why don't you give me your information? If I find anything else out or need anything from you, I'll call."

"Wonderful," said Alex. He handed the officer his card and got back into the limo.

"Andre," said Alex. "Take me to Bell's house. We have some unfortunate news to relay, and then we have to track down Bernie."

Andre punched the gas, and they were at Bell's front door a moment later.

Alex hopped out of the limo and ran up to the door. He rang the bell frantically, but there was no answer. Panic was beginning to kick in when the door slowly opened. He was shocked at who was standing inside.

"Matthew?" asked Alex. "Where's Bell?"

"Alex, you'd better come in and have a seat."

Alex didn't move. "What's going on?" he demanded.

"There's been an accident. Bell's car was found flipped over and on fire down by the river. There was nothing left of it. There was no sign of her. Authorities believe she was killed in the crash, but they have no body yet, which means no identification."

Alex turned white, and his knees buckled out from under him. "What? What are you telling me?" He quaked. "This cannot be happening. This cannot be happening!" Losing control, he started hyperventilating. "Please tell me this isn't true? Please, oh, God," he gasped.

Matthew bent over him, grabbing his shoulders. "You have to get a hold of yourself. This isn't helping anyone. I know you're in shock, and you're scared, but we need to get it together to plan our next move. You have to slow your breathing, or you'll pass out."

Alex took some short breaths and worked up to a long slow inhale and exhale. Then he asked, "Where's Bernie? Is she safe? Something's not right. Do you see all the smoke?" He pointed up the drive. "Alan's house is on fire. They pulled both of my parents out of there, and they're in rough shape. The medics couldn't tell me if they'll live, and now you tell me that Bell is already gone? This has to be Martin's doing. Why haven't you put him away yet?" he demanded, giving Matthew a shove. "You're a private investigator. Surely you must have enough evidence on him by now!" He stepped forward and gave Matt another shove. "This is your fault!"

"You better knock that off," Matthew replied sternly. "Get in here." Alex shook his head but followed Matthew to the living room. His legs were so wobbly he collapsed onto the couch.

"Listen, I'm trying. I know this is Martin's work, but I need to find a way to tie it all up into a neat package, or the bastard might walk. Do you want him to walk?"

Alex stared at him. Tears glistened at the corner of his eyes. "No. I want him to go to prison for the rest of his life."

"Good, then help me find the answers. I need you to stay strong. We need to locate Bernie. And just so you know, I'm completely invested in your family. I'm in love with Bell. I've been in love with her since our first meeting."

"You are? I knew something was going on, but I didn't know to what extent. She can be sort of private when it comes to her relationships. She doesn't like to jinx them, as she says."

"Yeah, I feel the same. While I was in town, we spent all of our free time together. We wanted to keep things quiet until we got Bernie to a safer place, but as you can see, the situation has blown up."

"What are we going to do? How will we catch Martin?"

"I've enlisted a few local investigators to look further into Bell's disappearance, and they're going over every detail of the crime scene. We're also working on a search warrant for Martin's house. Once I pull a few more things together, we should be able to arrest him on some fairly solid charges. Honestly, I'm hoping that some kind of evidence will be present at either the car site or the fire to connect it to Martin."

"My whole body is numb. I don't know if I can move," said Alex.

Matthew scribbled something on a piece of paper and handed it to Alex. He pressed his finger to his lips. Alex looked down at the paper, and his eyes widened as he took in Matthew's note. Then, with a nod, he headed for the door.

Across town, things were dark on Bernie's end. She was impatiently waiting in the dark for something to happen. Anything. As she sat, she could have sworn she felt the presence of someone outside her cell door, but the door didn't open. There was a small thud from overhead, but nothing else followed.

After several more hours passed, she heard the latch click. Martin appeared in the doorway.

"It's time for you to come out of there. We have things to attend to. Here's your phone," Martin said, handing it to her. Bernie thought it odd that he was handing the phone over. She glanced at it and realized she had several missed calls from Alex.

"I wonder what he wants," she thought aloud.

"That's why I gave it to you. He's been calling for at least an hour straight."

Bernie dialed her voicemail box and listened.

"Oh no," she gasped.

Martin gave her his best concerned look. "What's wrong?"

"My sister's missing, and my father's house has burnt down with him and my mother inside." Falling to her knees, she began to dry-heave. Why hadn't she listened to Bell? This was her own fault. She pulled herself onto the leather loveseat and sobbed uncontrollably. Alex had said in his message that Bell may not have made it. They were not certain. They hadn't found her remains, but her car had been on fire and there was nearly nothing left. She knew he hadn't wanted to leave this in a message, but he had been calling for two hours with no answer.

Martin knelt down and put his arms around her. "I'm so sorry, sweetie," he said. She didn't move, she accepted the hug, but she knew better than to trust or believe that anything loving was meant by it. She knew that Martin Day was the driving force behind this horror show.

Chapter Seventeen

An hour after Alex's message, Bernie's phone began to ring again. She hadn't moved from the den. The shock had anchored her to the loveseat. The ringing sounded so foreign that she jumped when she heard it.

"Hello?" Her tone was washed in sadness.

"Bernie, it's Alex. Thank goodness you picked up. Did you listen to my messages?"

"Yes," she squeaked.

"Matt's here. He's going to be working a lot, so he won't be coming to the hospital with me." Alex's words were cryptic and heavily annunciated. She had no idea if anyone was listening to her calls, but his discretion was appreciated.

"I also have further news. Are you sitting down, honey?" he asked.

"Yeah, I haven't moved since I received your messages," she choked.

"Bernadette, Mom didn't make it. She passed away during the ambulance ride to the hospital. I'm so sorry," his voice caught at the end. Bernie felt like she could die.

"Why is this happening?" she wailed.

"I know, honey, none of this is fair."

"Alex, I love you. Please, get me out of here." She hung up the phone. She was done waiting it out. It was time to make a plan and take action. Martin walked into the room as she sat there, trying to sort all her thoughts.

"What's going on?" he asked. His voice held no emotion.

"My mother's dead. She died in the ambulance before she arrived at the hospital."

"I'm so sorry to hear that," his fake condolences sounded so genuine, but Bernadette would never be fooled again. You could never trust a zebra. Her mom had pounded that into her head. Martin interrupted her thoughts, "Is there anything I can do?"

Yeah, you can go to hell, she thought. "No, not right now, though we should go visit Daddy and see how he's doing. I don't want to deal with this. I don't know how to deal with this. I don't want to plan funerals," she had begun to ramble through her bewilderment.

"Funerals?" asked Martin.

"Bell hasn't been found. She's presumed dead!" screamed Bernadette. Suddenly everything broke down on her. She fell to the floor and was overtaken by a torrent of hysterical sobs.

Martin again crouched down and wrapped his arms around her. "It's going to be okay, sweetie."

Nothing would ever be the same again. Bernie had brought this monster into her family, and she needed to be the one to get rid of him. After twenty minutes, she finally pulled herself together. She needed to call people to see if anyone had seen Bell. She was so tired, but this had to be done. She needed to stay hopeful.

After an hour of phone calls, she found no one had seen her sister. She even spoke to the police chief, and he had nothing good to say. They couldn't prove foul play had been involved in the fire, but he wanted to speak to her further, down at the station, in a day or two. Her mind was everywhere. How was there no evidence of foul play? It all seemed hopeless. She felt as if someone had ripped a piece of her heart out. How would she live without her big sister? A second wave of tears washed over her.

"Get up," said Martin. "We should head over to the hospital and see how your father is." Bernie could hear the ice in his voice. He reached down and grabbed her hand. He pulled her up a bit too abruptly. She really didn't want to go anywhere with him, but she needed to check in on her father. She followed him to the car and guardedly climbed in. She didn't think he would pull anything else that day, but she would be vigilant just in case.

Twenty minutes down the road, they pulled into the hospital parking lot. Bernie didn't want to get out of the car. She had no idea what to expect concerning her father and his condition. She saw a familiar face as she peeled herself away from the leather seat. Alex had just stepped out of his limo. He must have noticed Martin's car pulling in because he stood by the front door waiting for them. Silently, Bernie thanked him for waiting. She needed an ally right now, and she knew he'd provide that.

Alex looked wrecked. He grabbed hold of Bernie and hugged her tight. "This is just too horrible. How can such awful things happen to such innocent people?" he asked no one in particular.

She looked at him and gave a defeated head shake. She had no answers, and she could hardly make words come out. Alex linked his arm through hers. She felt the protectiveness emanating from him. He was taking on the role of consoling watchdog. She knew that he would do whatever he could in his power to take care of her. He was reliable, and she loved him for that.

Inside, her father was in the critical care unit. Bradley sat outside his room in the hall, wearing his hospital gown. Bernadette noticed that the look on Martin's face had turned to a mixture of anger and confusion. She looked at Bradley. He looked tired and as if he wasn't all there. She wanted to know what had happened to him, but she couldn't ask with Martin standing beside her.

"They wouldn't let me in," he said. "I'm not family."

"It's okay. We'll see what we can do for you," said Bernie. She walked over to the nurses' station. Luckily, Martin didn't follow her, and she felt she was at a safe enough distance that he wouldn't be able to hear. Maybe the nurse would be able to tell her about Bradley. "Hi, my name is Bernadette Price. Alan is my father. I have two questions for you. First, are you able to tell me what happened to Bradley Cordine? He's a good friend, and he works for my father. We're the closest thing he has to family."

"You and your father are actually listed as his emergency contacts. I'll give you what I know. That poor man was drugged with Rohypnol and dumped off on the side of the road last night. His doctor believes someone has been drugging him for days. He has no real memory of the past few days but seems to be coming out of it. He recognized your father immediately when he saw the news of the fire earlier today."

"Do they have any idea who did this to him? Have the police been involved?" asked Bernie.

"An officer was here earlier today, and I believe a private investigator, as well. They haven't said who was responsible as of yet. I believe further investigating is underway." Bernie hoped the private investigator was Matthew. She really needed him to be on his game right now.

"Thanks for the information. I do appreciate it. Do you have an update on my father?"

"Let me get his doctor," she replied with a sympathetic look.

It seemed like forever before her father's doctor arrived. In reality, it had only been ten minutes, but ten minutes was too long in such a situation. Time was everything. She had no idea where his life was balancing at this point. Was she soon to be an orphan, or was he strong and pulling through?

A young female doctor approached Bernie. She was thin with early graying hair. Her face held a frazzled, smileless expression. Bernie did not view this as a good thing.

"Are you, Mrs. Day?"

"Yes, but please, call me Bernie."

"Bernie, we have done everything we can for your father. He's not improving as quickly as we'd hoped. I believe preparing yourself for the worst and spending as much time as you can with him would be in your best interest. He's in rough shape. The smoke inhalation was extensive. He quit breathing, and we had to revive him. He was pinned beneath a section of the spiral staircase and lost quite a bit of blood from a large laceration in his stomach. We're keeping him comfortable and doing what we can, but the rest is up to him."

"Thank you for all you've done," she said. One tear ran down her face.

"Hang in there," said the doctor. She patted Bernie's arm and walked away.

Bernadette walked back to her father's room and grabbed Bradley's hand.

"Come on, you deserve to be in there, too. You've been a wonderful friend to him. He always spoke fondly of you."

"Are you sure, Bernie? I don't want to cause any problems," he said quietly so only she could hear.

"Trust me, I feel safer with you in there," she said." Martin had already gone into the room with Alex, so he was unlikely to hear them, but Bernie wasn't taking any more chances. They were both scared though they hid it well. "Do you remember anything from the past several days?" she asked.

"Bits and pieces. I was leaving the club, and a man and a woman jumped me and injected me with something. Everything went black, and I could only hear a word or two on and off. It's blotchy, like some big puzzle that I can't quite put together."

"Did you find Matthew?"

"I think he found me. I owe him my life. The last thing I recall is leaving him a voicemail."

"Thank you, Bradley. I'm sorry everything's such a mess."

"No, I'm sorry. I just wanted to help."

She nodded her understanding and turned away. Bradley followed her into the room. Alex was holding Alan's hand. Bernie walked up beside him.

"I love you, Daddy," she said. "I want you to know that Alex, Martin, Bradley, and I are all here. Please wake up. We need you. We've lost Mom, and the authorities believe we may have lost Bell too." She began to cry. "I can't do this without you. I don't want to plan any funerals, let alone three."

The four of them stayed by Alan's side for two hours. Alan didn't move. At eight o'clock they all decided it was time to get some food. Bernie and Martin parted from the group and headed for home. They stopped and grabbed burritos on the way.

Bernie wanted to get home and pack an overnight bag so she could get back to the hospital and settle in for the evening. Martin would stay until ten, but then he had to head home and get a good night's sleep. He had a political event to attend the following day. Bernie was glad he wouldn't be there. It was the only thing that made her smile. His narcissism stopped him from recognizing how poor he would look in his constituent's eyes when they realized he didn't stand by his family in their time of need.

As she rummaged through her closet, she heard a phone ring. It sounded like Bell's ringtone, but how would it have gotten into her closet? Following the sound, she located the phone. It was sitting on a shelf with her favorite stilettos. It continued to ring. She reached out a shaking hand and picked it up.

"Hello?" All she could hear was static, and then the line went dead. Bernie stared at the phone with confusion. Where had this come from? The phone chirped at her. A text message had come through. She flipped open the text screen.

Play the recorder when you're alone. - B

The number was unknown, which was odd. Suddenly another message came through.

Though I cannot be with you in person, I'm looking out for you and doing anything I can to help.- B

Bernadette dropped the phone. Was her sister alive? Or was Bell right, and ghosts did exist? How else would her phone get in here? Bell always joked that if she went first, she would haunt her just to prove her point. Bernie hoped Bell wasn't still holding onto that idea. It was one thing to know she was around but another to know she was there but could not be seen. She shuddered at the thought.

"Bell?" called Bernie quietly. "Are you here? Can you show me a sign?"

The phone buzzed again.

Bernie picked it up.

Don't look for me, Bernadette. I mean it. Leave things alone, and just know that I'm still here.

She jumped back and dropped the phone yet again.

"Well shoot," she said aloud. "You sure know how to freak a girl out." Bernie looked at the phone lying on the floor. What did she mean by '*play the recorder*?' She hadn't played the recorder since she was in third grade. As she sat pondering the message, she suddenly had an epiphany. She felt like an idiot when she realized Bell must have been talking about the voice recorder on her phone. She must have recorded something. She hoped whatever it was had been worth it, though she doubted the possibility very much.

Bernie picked up the phone and flipped it back on. She paged through Bell's apps until she found the voice recorder. She pressed play, and what she heard curdled her blood. Martin had asked someone to do away with her parents. The voice responding was quiet but sounded like a woman to Bernie.

Martin had planned the whole thing. He informed his partner that he would be golfing. He would call to tell her parents that he would be late, and in the meantime, the partner would go in and rig the house to look as though faulty wiring had been the culprit. The fire would be lit before Martin got there so it couldn't be pinned on him. To make matters worse, she also heard Martin tell his partner to drug Bradley and dump him in the middle of nowhere.

Her entire body shook with rage. Bell had sacrificed her life to protect her family. This recording was exactly what she needed to put Martin away for good. She had to make a plan to get it into the right person's hands. She turned off the ringer on the phone and stowed it back on the shelf behind her favorite stilettos. Best to leave it hidden in the house rather than on her person. She didn't want him to find it and ruin her only evidence against him.

She walked into the bedroom and grabbed a pillow and blanket from the cedar chest at the foot of the bed. She didn't care about clothing. She only wanted to be comfortable while she waited. The hospital was always cold.

Taking a deep breath, she stowed her emotion and walked downstairs to find Martin.

"I'm ready. Let's go!" She didn't know where he'd gone.

"Okay!" he yelled back. "Just give me a minute. I'm finishing up an email."

Probably to his partner about payment, she thought. Who knew what else Martin was planning? Her life had turned into one big dangerous game.

He walked out of the den and hooked his arm around her waist. Pulling her to him, he gave her a great big kiss. She cringed but didn't pull away for fear of how he'd react.

"What was that for?" she asked.

"Because you're such a beautiful sweet young thing." He smiled.

Bernie felt sick looking at him, but she kept a strong, emotionless face.

"Come on, let's go sit with your Daddy," he said. She could hear the inconvenience in his tone. Not only was he a zebra, but a sociopath too.

Chapter Eighteen

Back at the hospital, Martin and Bernie sat with Alan. Bernie had asked Alex to watch for Martin to leave before he came inside. She feared Martin might not let her stay if he knew Alex would be there, so she told Martin that Alex was not planning to return until the following morning.

Alan lay deathly still, which, considering the burns, may have been a good thing for his sake. Bernie shuddered to think what Martin would do if Alan were to survive. She would have to think of some way to protect him. Luckily, Bell had gotten her the phone, and their father's health situation hadn't reached a point where Martin needed to make any life-or-death decisions. Given a choice, she knew Martin would unplug Alan without another thought.

At ten, Martin didn't leave as foretold. Bernie ascertained that he was waiting to see if she'd been truthful about Alex. At eleven, having seen no other visitors, Martin finally decided it was time to go. He leaned over, kissed Bernie on the head, and walked out the door without a word. Alex appeared five minutes later.

"Girl, I've been hiding out in this hospital for over an hour waiting for him to leave," said Alex.

"I'm sorry, Alex. He's super paranoid. I think he stayed longer to be sure I'd told him the truth and that no one else was coming. He doesn't want me alone with you or Bell."

"That dude is freakin' crazy. I'm genuinely scared for you and myself at this point. You really married a psychopath," he said succinctly. Bernie could see the loathing on his face.

"Thanks, Alex. I needed to hear that right now."

"I'm sorry, honey. I shouldn't have said that." He looked at her with big round, puppy eyes. Alex reached out and brushed the hair away from her face. "You know I'm on your side, right? I love you. You're family, and this is a nightmare for both of us. We still don't have any confirmation on Bell." A tear rolled down his cheek.

At that moment, Alan began to move. His eyes blinked open, and a pained look washed over his face.

"Daddy! Daddy, are you awake?" asked Bernadette.

"Bernie—" He coughed. "So glad—" He swallowed. "So glad to see you."

"Daddy, I'm so sorry," cried Bernie. "This is all my fault." Alan looked at her with confusion.

"Do you know what happened to you?" asked Alex.

Slowly, Alan said, "I remember a fire. Your mom was there."

"Anything else?" asked Bernie. Alan didn't respond.

"Martin did this," said Alex. "I know he was behind this."

Bernie looked at Alex and shook her head yes. "I have proof."

"You do?" asked Alex.

"Yeah. There's a recording that captured his entire plan."

"Wow. This is pretty rough," said Alex. "We can talk about that more in a moment, but for now, I'll go get a nurse and let them know he's awake," he told Bernie as he headed for the door.

Bernie looked at her father as the tears began to fall again. "Mom didn't make it," she squeaked. "She didn't survive the fire!" Torrents of tears flooded her face once again. Her father had a horrified expression on his face. She chose not to mention Bell. If she did, she worried that would be the end of him. Alex walked back into the room and squeezed Bernie in a side hug.

"Oh, baby," said Alan roughly. "I love you. I'm so sorry this has happened. I should have been more vigilant." A tear glistened at the corner of his eye.

"Don't move. Just try to be calm. I don't want you getting more upset," said Bernie.

"We probably shouldn't have told him everything that's been going on," commented Alex.

"No. I needed to know," he rasped. "Time is short."

"No, I refuse to believe that!" howled Bernadette.

"Yes, I can feel it. Be strong, sweetheart. I know this hurts. I love you, Alex, and your sister, beyond words. I want you to know that I've set up accounts offshore in the UK. Call it a safety net. I set them up when your mother and I were divorcing. Visit my cousin Mitch. He has all of the details. "Martin doesn't know about the accounts. They're not documented in anything he has on record. If it comes down to it, you leave town, get to safety, and start over. I'd say there's three quarters of a billion between the accounts. I had Mitch designate them as the other half of your trust funds. I know I shouldn't have hidden money, but I wanted to be sure your future was secure."

"Daddy, that's a lot of money! You've already done so much for us," said Bernie. Alex had a look of shock on his face. They had no idea their father had that much money to set aside.

"Well, kids, this is one of those happy surprises, though I'd hoped it would be under better circumstances when I told you about them."

"What about the businesses?" asked Bernie.

"See Mitch," said Alan. "Promise me you'll get to safety. That you'll get out of this alive," he rasped.

"We will," she cried.

"Alex, I'm counting on you to keep an eye on my girls."

"Always, sir," said Alex.

"What a fool I've been. I let my family down. I should've seen through him. I should've questioned your choice more. I'm sorry, Bernadette. I fear I've failed you as a father."

"No, Daddy, it's my fault. I'm the one who brought him into this family. I'm the one who was blind. Even if you had forbidden me to marry him, I would've done it anyway. I loved him, and I thought this was real."

"Sweetheart," he lightly squeezed Bernie's hand. "It's not your fault."

"We should have done something much sooner," said Alex. "None of us did what we hoped we could have done to avoid this. We were too nice. We didn't take proper action on something we thought was wrong."

Alan's eyes began to bob open and closed.

"I love you, Daddy," whispered Bernie.

"I love you," he said quietly. His doctor marched into the room and began to examine him.

After the examination, Dr. Watts informed Bernie and Alex that Alan's vitals were getting worse and that they should stay close. In the end, the damage from the fire had been too much.

Twenty minutes later, all was silent. Alan had passed on. Doctors and nurses came bustling into the room to do what needed to be done but then left Bernie and Alex to pay their final respects. The two sat and mourned their losses together. Bernie had never seen Alex cry. She knew this was a huge blow to him as well. They only had each other left. The world felt as if it were one huge floodgate being ripped open all at once. The pain felt unbearable.

She turned and looked at her brother's face. "Alex, we have to deal with the recording. It's the proof we've been waiting for."

"How'd you get it?" he asked.

"I found a cell phone in my closet. I think Bell put it there."

"What do you mean she put it there. How? When?"

"After the accident. I have no idea. Maybe she's a ghost?"

"Seriously, Bernadette, you think she's a ghost? I have a hard time buying that."

"She called me, but the line was all static. It was from an unknown number. It freaked me out. Then all of a sudden, I got something like three text messages, all from that same number. She said she was watching over me and to play the recorder."

"Play the recorder?"

"Yeah. The voice recorder on her phone. So, I did, and it's a recording that she captured of Martin talking to his partner about killing Mom and Dad in the fire and drugging Bradley. They planned the whole thing."

Alex looked at Bernadette. His eyes were ablaze. "That son of a—"

"Listen, Alex, he doesn't know I have the recording, and if he knew Bell had it, that could be why he had someone run her off the road. He cannot find out, but we must get this to the police somehow. I think you're going to have to do it. Someone, possibly the woman on the recording, has also been watching me.

"Alex, he's done such horrible things to me. It took me a while to figure it out, but he was drugging me and beating me. He also has a panic room in the basement that he's been locking me in. I don't want to find out how far he's willing to go. I fear he may kill me if this goes on much longer. We have to put an end to it tonight."

"I won't let anything else happen to you. I will take the recording to Matthew, and we'll take it to the police. That way, we can get all the evidence turned in at once."

"Matthew's in town?"

"Yes. Bell called him when she was in the accident. He sent backup to find her and immediately headed our way. When he arrived, he found the burnt car and no Bell. The scene was still being processed. They didn't give much information. I'm still praying they find her."

"Me too," said Bernie. "I just want to wake up from this nightmare."

Alex nodded. Then looking at her, he asked, "Where's the phone right now?"

"It's at the house," she said apologetically. "I couldn't risk having it on me when Martin was around. I didn't want him to find it. He notices everything, it seems."

"Okay, so how will I get the phone?"

"You'll have to follow me home, I guess."

"Oh girl, talk about some *Mission Impossible* type shit. What do I do once I get to your house?"

"Park a little way off from the house, get out, and walk to the side of the house where our bedroom is. I'll toss the phone out that bathroom window since it doesn't have a screen. You run, do not walk, to your car as soon as you have it. Make sure no one sees you. Anyone could be watching the house."

"You better wrap it in something. We don't want it getting damaged in the drop."

"Good call. I'll wrap it in something brightly colored so you can find it. I think this is our only option."

"It's almost one in the morning. We should probably get a move on," said Alex.

Bernie sighed. "I suppose so." She didn't want to leave her father. She walked over and kissed Alan on the cheek. "I love you, Daddy. We won't let you down. Martin will be held accountable." She walked out the door with Alex trailing behind. "You can have them come up and get the body now. We have said our goodbyes."

The nurse nodded at Bernie. "Okay, sugar. I'm so sorry for your loss."

"Me too," she whispered as she walked away.

Outside in the parking lot, Bernie turned to say goodbye to Alex.

"Wait," he said. He disappeared into his car for a moment. She could see he was digging for something. "Here," he said as he emerged.

"What?"

"Come here," he said.

She walked up to him and he shoved something cold and heavy into her hand.

"What?" She looked at her hand. "This is a gun," she whispered. "Alex, where'd you get a gun?"

"It's my driver's. He's licensed to carry it. I think in this case you need it. I know you don't have a permit, but I'll be damned if I'm going to send you back into that house unprotected. I have the safety on. You remember how to remove it, right? It's been a while since the gun range, but I know you can do this if push comes to shove. Treat it with respect. Now go. We need to get this plan rolling."

"Thanks, Alex." She hugged him and put the gun in her bag.

Chapter Nineteen

It was one-thirty in the morning, and Bernie was slinking around like a burglar in her own home. She crept into her closet to grab the phone. Martin was downstairs in the den working on some campaign ideas. As she picked up the phone, it began to buzz, again making Bernie jump. "Dang it all, I don't need a heart attack on top of everything."

She flipped open the phone. Bernie could see that the same number from earlier had sent another message.

Bernadette, you must make your getaway tonight. There's no time to waste. This situation has become much too dangerous.

Where are you? she typed, but no answer came. She removed the gun from her purse and looked at it. "I guess this is it."

She placed the gun by her favorite stilettos, then moved toward the bathroom with the phone. She'd barely wrenched the window open when she heard Martin moving up the stairs. She panicked briefly. She'd forgotten to wrap the phone in something to protect it during the drop.

On the back of the door hung a bright yellow bra. She plunged the phone into the bra and tied the straps tightly around the cups to hold them shut. She flung the phone out the window moments before Martin walked into the bedroom.

"Sweetie, what are you doing? When did you get home? Is everything okay?" he called lovingly. She slowly slid the window shut.

"I got home a few minutes ago. I'm getting cleaned up for bed," she said sadly.

"How's your father?" he asked.

"Oh Martin, Daddy's gone," she cried.

"I'm so sorry, kitten. Do you need me to come hold you?" Martin asked. She heard him grab the door handle.

"No, I just want to take a bath and then go to bed." She sighed.

"What time did he pass?"

"I think it was about eleven."

"Eleven? Why are you getting home so late?" he asked sharply over the sound of running water.

"I was paying my respects."

"For two hours? What the hell, Bernadette. Why didn't you call me? I could have been there with you."

"I was in too much shock, Martin!" she shrieked.

"I don't care what state you were in. I'm your husband. When someone dies, you call. You don't wait two hours and then tell me!" he boomed.

"It's my father, Martin. You don't care about him or anyone else in this family."

He grabbed the door handle again and tried to open it. The knob didn't turn.

"You open this door right now, dammit!"

"Over my dead body!" she screamed.

"We could probably arrange that." His voice ran cold. "You get twenty minutes, then you get your butt out here. This conversation isn't finished."

Bernadette climbed into the tub and sank down into the hot water. She'd filled the tub with Epsom salt and lavender. She needed to buy herself some time. Surely, Alex and Matthew would have the police knocking on the door within the hour.

Outside, the wind picked up. Lightning flashed in the distance. The weather forecast had predicted storms around two that morning. From the sound of it, the weatherman had gotten the prediction right.

As Bernie lay in the oversized tub, she thought about her situation.

I must be crazy, she said to herself. *Why the heck was I so delusional as to believe my siblings were wrong? The two people who have always been there and had my back.* She knew the saying about love being blind. She now understood it more than ever.

She felt as though her world had crashed in on her in one day, but she knew it had taken months for her to get here. Martin had been playing this role for years. She just happened to be another one of his pathetic victims. No more. No one else was going to be a victim of Martin Day, or whoever he really was. She'd put an end to that tonight.

As Bernie continued soaking in the tub, she quietly sang Lorrie Morgan's version of "It's a Heartache." The tears ran down her face, and she felt the toxicity built up over the past year drain from her body. She'd take back her life tonight. She'd stand up and fight for herself like her parents had always taught her.

Outside, the thunder rolled a distance away, but Bernie knew a storm was coming. She hoped Alex would get to someone before the storm kicked in. The bath water was growing cool, and her alone time was ending. It was time to put on a thick skin and face her demon.

She grabbed the oversized Egyptian cotton towel and patted herself dry. Quietly, she opened the bathroom door. Not seeing Martin, she walked over to her closet to find some clothes. She threw on an ugly brown workout tank and some matching sweat-pants. She wasn't going to be in any beauty pageant tonight. At this point, the clothing didn't matter. Before she left the room, she grabbed the gun from behind the stilettos and stuck it in the back of her waistband.

When she emerged from the closet, he was sitting on the bed, staring at her. She stopped in her tracks. "You startled me," she said.

"Oh. I'm so sorry. Did that bring you back to reality?" He glared at her.

"It amazes me how coldly you can look at your wife when she just lost a big part of her family," said Bernadette. "But then I hear that's how you've always been." Her words had frozen over..

"What's that supposed to mean?" he asked sharply. He played dumb so well.

"I think you know what that means. Matthew told me about your past. I was stupid and didn't believe him. Tell me, Martin, did you ever love or even care about me at all?"

His eyes grew darker. "You're my wife, Bernadette. Of course, I love you. How could you question that?"

"Cut the crap, Martin. Stop selling me this load of lies. I'm not buying it!" she yelled. "Answer my question!"

"Sweetheart, I'm not sure where this is coming from. You've been through something awful. You're not thinking right. Why don't you come over here and sit down?"

"Why, so you can slap some handcuffs on me? So, you can paddle me and lock me in the panic room? So, you can torment and humiliate me and hurt the people I love some more?" she reached behind herself and grabbed the gun from her waistband. Martin's jaw dropped as she pointed it at him.

"I told you. I'm done with your lies. I want answers." She hoped it wouldn't come down to using the weapon. She wasn't that type of person, but it definitely made her feel safer.

"You probably don't even know how to use that. Silly little models who think they—" Bernie fired a warning shot. It whizzed past Martin's head and embedded in the painting hanging above him. His face paled as he glared at her. Stepping forward, she removed Martin's gun from its holster and put it in the back of her waistband where Andre's had previously been. *So much for not using it,* she thought.

Calmly, Martin asked, "What would you like to know?"

"Did you ever love or even care about me? I want the truth." She waved the gun.

"Not at first. Well, actually, I didn't love or care about you until right before we got married. I found myself falling for you, which wasn't in the plan. I thought maybe this whole thing could be real. Maybe there was a possibility to have everything I wanted."

"What did you want?"

"Everything," he said. "I wanted power, money, a wife that others were jealous of. I wanted to be the envy of the town."

"Why me? How did you pick me?"

"When I lost my grandfather, I realized I needed money in order to keep the lifestyle I was used to. So, I studied women like you and

341

found that I had a niche for working my way into their lives and gaining their trust. I studied you for months.

"You were perfect. You were a model. You came from a family with money. You owned property and businesses. You were respected and loved by everyone. Men wanted to be with you, and women wanted to be you. I knew that if I had you and your father on my side, I could achieve anything I wanted. There was no ceiling to stop me. It was only going to go up from there."

"What the hell, Martin? Why'd you kill my family? That seems a little counterproductive, don't you think?"

"I didn't count on you being so rebellious. I knew I could get your father to accept me. It was easy getting him to make me the executor of his estate, but I didn't know you were going to be so difficult. I asked you to do as I said. Most models are good at that. They listen. They do what they're told. You didn't do what I asked. It must be the lawyer in you. If you'd only done as I'd requested, none of this would have happened!"

"This is entirely your fault, Bernadette. I didn't want to kill anyone, but when a man's wife doesn't listen, he has to take extreme measures. It's maddening how disobedient you can be! I had to redress you to make you look presentable. I made it clear what I expected and needed from you. You chose to ignore my requests and, in turn, smeared my love in the dirt."

"NO! This is not my fault! Don't put this on me. This is not love. Its madness! You're absolutely insane, Martin!"

"Insane? Really?"

"Yes, really! You tortured me. You had my sister killed. You had my parents killed. How could that not be insane?"

"Well, I guess when you put it that way, it does sound a little insane. But I was just a man trying to protect what was his, and you happened to be part of that.

"This is over! You don't deserve any of this! What have you ever worked for in your life? You take what you want and destroy what doesn't fit into your plan! You even stole Matthew's girlfriend when you were in college together. Was that the beginning for you, or did it start sooner?" she demanded.

"I don't know what you're talking about," he said haphazardly. "I didn't take anything from Matt."

"What about the other families. Did you tamper with that plane that crashed?"

"I couldn't have them leaving with my money now, could I? I loved her, but her family wanted to take her away from me. There was no way around it."

"You really are cracked, aren't you?"

"Ha. No, I'm a man who has wants and needs. Sometimes you have to go out and get what you want," he said.

Bernadette realized there was no talking to him. Maybe she should sing a song, and he'd get it? No, he'd never get it.

"Understand me when I say, I'm leaving you!"

"Over my dead body," he said quietly. He got to his feet and started for the door.

"Where are you going?" she demanded.

"I'm taking care of this whole mess, Bernadette. You want it fixed? You've got it. You can be with your family!" he screamed. He tore out of the room and down the stairs. Bernie ran after him, still holding the gun. He disappeared into another room. She couldn't bring herself to shoot at him as he ran away.

"I created this house for you, Bernadette! I put this together because you wanted something more sophisticated. The bachelor pad wasn't good enough. I never told you this, but I acquired this home suddenly because the owner went missing, and the bank was putting it up for auction. None of that stuff was mine, but you didn't bother to ask questions or hear me out, did you?"

"The owner had been missing? Where'd he go?" she demanded. "Did you kill him, too? You psychopath!"

"Don't call me that, dammit! I'm not a psychopath. I'm brilliant!"

"Sure, brilliant as a baseball bat. You suffocated me and ruined my life. You're pure evil. I was addicted to you! I loved you! You could have had it all through love and kindness, but you chose destruction instead

Martin reappeared in the doorway from the den. Bernie noticed he was holding a large gas can. He ran from the room, dumping gas as he went. Bernie remained calm.

"You're crazy."

"I'm crazy for you, baby!" He laughed.

She walked down the stairs and into the kitchen. Martin was still pouring gasoline.

"I'm gonna light your fire!" he yelled maniacally.

Bernie slowly pulled open the utility drawer by the kitchen sink. Her eyes honed in on what she was looking for. She pulled out the shiny green lighter and closed the drawer. No need to fire more bullets than necessary anymore. She slipped the lighter into her pocket.

"Hey, Martin!" she yelled. He was once again upstairs but appeared on the balcony overlooking the kitchen.

"Yes, dear?"

"You can have these! I'm done being your perfectly made-up servant!" She peeled off all of her clothing and threw it on the floor. The lighter popped out of her pants pocket as they hit the ground. She dropped Martin's gun on top of the pile but held fast to Andre's.

"Bernadette, you're gorgeous but not so bright," said Martin.

"Really?" she asked. "Then I guess you aren't expecting this." She picked up the lighter and held it out for him to see.

Realizing he'd underestimated her yet again, he came flying down the stairs and lunged at Bernie, knocking her to the floor. Andre's gun flew out of her hand. She landed on the pile of clothing. He grabbed her around the neck. Luckily, her arms were still free, and she was able to pull Martin's gun out from under herself. She pressed it to his neck, and he pushed himself away from her. Getting to her feet, she flicked her thumb on the lighter and lit it. Then she tossed it as far as she could behind Martin. He made a mad dash for the door to the garage.

"This is me divorcing you!" she yelled, running for the front door. The inside already looked like an inferno as she jaunted down the pathway to the front of the garage. The garage door began to open. She knew she had mere moments before Martin would be out and after her again.

In the driveway sat the only belonging that Bernadette had left. Her beautiful blue Mustang. She made a dash for the car. Thank the heavens she'd left the keys inside. The top was down, and she was able to easily hop in. She tore out of the driveway. The lightning struck much closer now.

As she rounded the block, Bernie heard sirens in the distance. She knew where they were going, and she'd be long gone before they arrived. She only hoped Martin would still be there and he'd finally be forced to pay for his crimes.

Chapter Twenty

Bernadette tested the constructs of gravity as she rounded the curves heading out of town. She watched the set of lights approaching. Common sense set in, and she realized she had to pull over. She also realized that she had nothing to cover up with. Talk about a hard-to-explain situation. What was she going to tell this cop? She felt as if she'd just escaped prison. What if he thought the same?

She watched the officer step out of his vehicle. Her mind was racing. She realized he wasn't dressed like a normal officer as he walked toward her. He was in civilian clothing. Then as he got closer, her heart relaxed, and she had to stifle an excited scream. She jumped up out of her car and ran naked down the shoulder.

"Whoa!" said Bradley. He ripped off his t-shirt. "Bernie, you're naked! Here, let's put this on." Her arms flew every which way as she tried to hug him. He stopped trying to put her in the shirt and hugged her back. "You're safe. It's okay," he whispered. She melted against him, and the tears rolled down her cheeks. "I've got you, Bern."

Once she'd calmed down, he tugged the shirt over her head and helped her pull her arms through the sleeves. She grabbed his face and pulled it to hers. She kissed him passionately, and he kissed her back.

She came up for air and said, "I'm so glad to see you."

"I can tell. You were in great need of my shirt." He laughed.

"Yeah, thank goodness you weren't an actual officer. That was going to be very awkward to explain. How'd you find me anyway?"

"Alex arrived at your house with the police. Martin was trying to leave, but the cops managed to block him in. When they asked where you were, he was honest and told them you'd taken off moments before. Alex called me and asked if I'd try to track you down. I was at my father's house at the time. He's an officer here in town. I had a fifty-fifty chance of choosing the right road, so I went with my gut."

"Your father? I thought you didn't know your father?"

"It's a long story. Anyway, I didn't ask him, so hopefully I don't go to jail for this, but I took his cruiser while he was in the bathroom.

"Ha! Aren't you the badass," said Bernie. She grinned back at him.

Bradley wrinkled his brow at her. "What I really want to know is why you have no clothing on?"

"That's easy," she said. "Martin took away all of my belongings and wanted to change everything about me. I gave him the ultimate farewell. I threw all my clothes on the floor and lit that mother up. I walked out the door with the only things that belonged to me. My car and my skin."

"Wow. I'd say you definitely made a statement."

"Ha, ya think so?" for the first time in weeks, Bernie felt genuinely relieved and safe. She could tell Bradley was nothing like Martin. He was a real white horse, but then somewhere deep inside, she'd always known. "How are you doing? Are you okay"

"I still can't remember everything, but as the hours pass, I feel more myself."

"Thank goodness. I was so scared for you," said Bernie.

He smiled and wrapped his arms around her. "Everything's going to be okay now."

"I know, but some of the damage is irreversible. Nothing is going to bring my parents back."

"True, but time heals. You have to forgive yourself and move forward. Anyway, I have something to show you." He smiled. "Come over to the car with me."

"I don't know what it is, but I don't think I deserve anything," she replied sadly.

Bradley went to reach for the back door of his car. He'd barely unlatched it and it swung open, when a pair of feet came flying out.

"Oh, thank, God, Bell!"

"Bernie! Oh, Bern, I was so scared for you. Thank goodness you're okay!"

"Thank goodness I'm okay? You were the one everyone thought was dead! I thought I'd lost you too. Where've you been?"

"The night you went to the benefit, Alex called me and told me something was wrong. I suspected that Martin had hurt you. I told Alex I was going to track you down. I couldn't find you, though. Instead, I found Martin, and as you know, I was able to record a decent amount of the conversation, but Martin heard me as I walked away.

"We had an argument in the VIP suite, and then he left. When I finally left the club, I was followed, and that person ran me off the road. I managed to call Matthew. He called the police after he reached out to a local detective friend who was nearby. He came and got me out before the police arrived. He then helped the fire along."

"What? Why?"

"It was Matthew's idea. He felt that since Martin was trying to kill me, we should make it look like he had succeeded and that I should hide until we knew it was safe again. The problem is, we thought we had more time. The fire was the very next afternoon, and we were too late to save Mom and Dad." A tear ran down Bell's face. "I didn't even get to say goodbye to Dad."

Bernie pulled her into a hug. "Dad said he loves us all more than words can express."

"I'm sorry I wasn't able to be there, Bern."

"It's okay. I understand. I'm thankful you're here, and I wasn't being told what to do by a ghost in a phone." She let out an uncomfortable laugh.

"You thought I was a ghost?"

"How else do you explain how the phone got into the closet?"

"Matthew put it there," she replied. "He waited for you and Martin to leave, then he used your garage door opener to get into the house. He said it was the easiest break-in ever."

"Is that a normal thing for him?"

"No," Bell laughed. "This was an unusual circumstance. We wanted you to know what Martin was up to and that you had to get out since we had no idea the extent of what he was doing to you or if you'd open up to us yet. We both figured the cold hard proof would be best."

"Unfortunately, when I found the phone, nothing would have surprised me. Martin had shown his true colors. I was scared to talk to anyone because he threatened your lives."

"I'm so sorry," said Bell.

"All we can do is move forward," said Bernie.

"Hey, ladies, Alex is going to meet us a couple of miles up at exit 54. He's bringing Matthew. Why don't we head that way," said Bradley.

"Okay, we'll take my car, and you can lead the way," said Bernie as she and Bell walked toward the Mustang.

A few minutes later, they reached exit 54. Alex and Matthew sat waiting patiently. Both were excited to see Bernie and Bell drive up.

"Oh, Belinda Price, thank goodness you're okay. I mean, I knew you were, but man, that's a horrible secret to keep," said Alex.

"You knew?" asked Bernie.

Alex had a sorry look on his face. "Well, yeah. It was necessary not to tell you too much. We didn't know what sort of things Martin was capable of, and we wanted to keep you and Bell both as safe as possible."

"The police have heard the recording and taken Martin into custody," said Matt. "The past two days, I've had a couple of detectives following him, as well as you, Bernie. The man Martin had following you was not the same person that lit the fire, but a witness saw someone leave your parents' house just before the fire department was called. We couldn't track them down, but at least we have someone who will testify that another person had been there. The recording was enough evidence to arrest Martin."

"Matthew, I owe you an apology. I can't thank you enough for all you've done. It could have gotten much worse. I'm beyond sorry that I didn't listen to you. I feel like this is entirely my fault." Bernie's face was again covered in tears.

"Stop," said Bradley as he reached up to dry her face. "Most people wouldn't have believed it. There was no evidence at the time, and things didn't get bad until after the wedding. You couldn't have known what was coming."

"Honestly," said Matt, "most of the victims in these situations don't come to grips with the truth until it's too late. Martin was a tricky and conniving kind of guy. He knew how to fly under the radar when he needed to."

"I'll say," commented Alex. "It's taken way too long for his actions to catch up with him."

With a sullen look, Matthew reached out and rested his hand on Bell's shoulder. "I need to get you all to the station to give your statements. It's time to put this tragedy to rest."

In that moment, Bernie smiled briefly as she realized that this was the man Bell had been hiding from her. She was completely okay with it.

"I'm so lucky to call you family," she told Bell and Alex. "You're family, too," she said to Bradley. "We need to stick together."

Bell reached over and hugged her sister. Tears fell down her face. Bernie found her sister's sadness contagious, as the tears began to flow from her eyes as well. The realization was finally sinking in. Their parents were gone. The three siblings would have to give statements of everything that had happened. They would have to deal with planning two funerals and sorting through two house-holds, and knowing where to begin would be challenging. The pain was unbearable to Bernie, but she knew they would somehow make it through as a family.

"Let's go take care of business," said Bell in a half-whisper.

Both girls still had tears streaming down their faces. Alex looked like he was going to lose it at any moment.

"Can I just say something?" he asked, his eyes filling. "Does anyone else realize Bernie has no pants on?"

Bell snorted. "She really isn't wearing any pants. Thank good-ness for that oversized shirt," she said through her laughter.

Alex wrapped an arm around each of his sisters and led them to his limo. Bradley and Matthew followed closely behind.

As they drove back toward town, there was no laughter. The tears fell silently, and the three siblings held hands. Bernie knew that in time, some of the worst days of their lives would be far behind them, but for now, it was okay to let the tears flow.

About the Author

T.K. Ambers lives in Wisconsin with her husband and two cats, Bellatrix and Kit. Her perfect day would be spent lakeside, where she would swim, play games, and then wind down with a bonfire, s'mores, and stories told by family and friends.

www.facebook.com/HappilyWriting
https://tkambers.wixsite.com/author
www.instagram.com/tk_loves_books

Always remember, the best gift you can give an author is a review on Amazon.com.

Acknowledgements

Thank you to my family for all their support. Especially my husband, Neal, who puts up with my craziness. ;o)

Thank you to my aunt Paula, who is no longer with us. She read and edited the first manuscript many years ago. I still have the pens you gifted me with when I received my first publishing contract for Runway Dreams. I love them and think of you with each use.

Thank you to all my beta readers. Especially my stepdaughter, Ms. Darian, who took time to highlight areas of change in the first edition of this story, as well as the present edition. I'm forever learning from you.

Thank you to my 7th/8th grade English teacher, Ms. Bollinger. Without your encouragement, I may have never pushed myself to publish my work.

Thank you to my editor, Kate Seger, who answered all of my questions and helped me put this story in order. You've taught me a ton.